Restless Spirit

by

M. Kate Quinn

The Ronan's Harbor Series,
Book Two

Restless Spirit

Cover Art by *Kim Mendoza*

The Wild Rose Press, Inc.
PO Box 708
Adams Basin, NY 14410-0708
Visit us at www.thewildrosepress.com

Publishing History
First Fantasy Rose Edition, 2015
Print ISBN 978-1-5092-0208-9
Digital ISBN 978-1-5092-0209-6

The Ronan's Harbor Series, Book Two
Published in the United States of America

"When I initially asked you to bring a memento to the séance I didn't realize we would be sitting amongst so many. It's fine. Please, have a seat."

A triple-wick candle with its zealous flames had been placed in the center of the table. It cast a dancing glow over the purple covering Joanie had found downtown at Franklin's today.

"At this time we will place our hands on the table and stretch our fingers out wide." Ira's tone was authoritative. His words' substantive quality only served to rattle Aubrey more. Her knees shook under the table.

"Touch your pinky fingers to the person's beside you," Ira continued. "We are making an unbroken ring. We do this to protect against negativity."

Aubrey placed her hands on the table, watching out the corner of her eye at Asa beside her. His big masculine hands were outstretched. His right pinky sought and found her left. A kind of vibration extended from their connected digits, and she was tempted to pull away. She knew better than to meet his gaze she felt on her, wooing her to turn her head.

On her other side, Joanie also placed her hands into position and pressed the tip of her smallest finger against Aubrey's right one. One by one, they all formed an unbroken ring of their hands.

"Let us begin," Ira said, the cadence of his voice clergy-like. "We close our eyes and still our minds."

Aubrey squeezed her eyes shut, trying to keep her thoughts still as Ira had asked. But there was a big man, with a teasing dimple, sitting beside her, his electric finger pressing onto hers. She shook her head and tried to dismiss the sensation that quivered through her veins.

Praise for M. Kate Quinn

"A heart-warming, sexy must-read that will keep you turning the pages…Quinn has done it again with *RESTLESS SPIRIT*. This author is a master at building a world I want to crawl in and never leave."

~Shari Nichols, author of Witch Hunter

~*~

"Playful, funny, and romantic. *RESTLESS SPIRIT* will hook the reader on the first page and have them begging for more. A treat to read."

~Stacey Wilk, Author and Public Speaker

~*~

"*LETTERS & LACE* is an excellent romance with excitement, tension, and most of all undying love."

~C. Braswell, Preliminary Reader

~*~

"A mother's love, an uncle's fortune, a tangled web of deception—all lead to love in *BROOKSIDE DAISY* [a Gold Leaf Award finalist]. Scrumptious!"

~Shirley Hailstock, award-winning author and past president of Romance Writers of America

~*~

"*MOONLIGHT AND VIOLET* [winner of the coveted Golden Leaf Award for Best Contemporary Novel 2011] has strong character development, an appealing storyline and amusing dialogue. A rare treat!"

~Long and Short Reviews, Top 500 Reviews

~*~

"*SUMMER IRIS* [a Golden Quill Award finalist for Best First Book]…a remarkable talent for creating realistic characters. M. Kate Quinn is definitely an author to keep your eye on."

~Huntress Reviews

Dedication

For the cherished memories of four friends,
and for you, Judy.

Chapter One

It was 3:11 a.m. Again. In the darkness of the chilly November wee-hour, Aubrey Donner sat upright in her bed, her mind in a spin from having bolted awake. Her legs, in a war with the tangled bed clothes, bicycled free from the damp sheets. Panting, she gulped mouthfuls of air so cold she wondered if the furnace had crapped out on her. Again.

Shivering and covered in gooseflesh, Aubrey wrapped the quilt over her shoulders and spat a loud expletive into the darkness. *Seven nights.*

The same eerie dream had invaded her sleep each night for a week straight. And she always awoke at exactly the same time, 3:11. The foggy, gray, indiscernible intruder to her slumber, clung now to her memory like a cobweb awaiting its prey. She tried to pull the details into focus, but it was as if they were behind a veil of gauze.

Aubrey forced herself to get up. Her naked feet, cold like bricks, shoved themselves into her fuzzy slippers. There was no use in attempting to fall back asleep now. She poked her fingers into her hair and gave the brown mess a good shake.

Today, of all days, Aubrey needed her game on. The appointment with her boss was at seven thirty, and Dean Manning had intimated this meeting was about a host spot on Mid Shore Live's Sunday lineup. Finally.

No damned nightmare was going to zap her one big chance at possibly anchoring a broadcast on WMSL. Sundays on local television's Channel 31 were earmarked for political guest forums or in-depth interviews with local notables. Aubrey was game for either or both. Her heart zinged inside her tired, chilled body.

She had to hand it to her boss. Dean had told her to hang in there, that she wouldn't be an ad copy editor forever. Her gut told her this was it, and she needed to be right. So did her bank account and her finicky furnace, leaky roof, and clanging pipes.

She zombie-walked to the bathroom and cranked the shower full force. The steaming water cascaded over her skin while the plumbing serenaded her with its percussion. She willed her body and brain to snap fully awake. But, toweling dry, the lack-of-sleep headache still throbbed.

In no time, Aubrey found herself smoothing her hands down the fabric of her black pencil skirt and realizing she hadn't worn it since the funeral. *Was it really a year since Mom died?* Was it just eighteen months ago that she'd been called home from her life in the city to care for her sole parent?

She shook her head. There was no time to think about how, at thirty-three, she was living back in her childhood home in Ronan's Harbor, New Jersey. The apartment in Hoboken and the job at the *Ledger* were ancient history.

Downstairs, waiting for the coffee pod to run its course through the machine she'd brought with her from Hoboken, she sighed aloud into the emptiness of Mom's kitchen, everything original, nothing new.

A quick glance at her reflection in the stainless steel toaster told her the tortoise shell comb still had its grip on her russet mass of unruliness. She couldn't remember the last time she'd been to a salon. She could see her leopard-print bra through the flimsy fabric of her white blouse, a poor choice. With no energy to rectify it she made a mental note to keep her suit jacket on during the meeting.

Throwing back a swig of the black coffee, the bitterness stung its way down her throat. The brick-toned smear along the mug's rim indicated her mouth could use another dab of Sinful Cinnamon. But that would have to wait.

She grabbed her credential-loaded leather sheaf, slung her purse strap over her shoulder, and headed to the front door. Hand on the knob, she stopped.

A sudden waft of smoke caught her nose. *Burning vanilla?* She sniffed the air. *Wood smoke?* She tugged open the heavy door and stepped out onto the front stoop. Craning her neck, she eyed the neighboring roof tops. There was no smoky plume billowing from anyone's chimney. *Crap.* She charged back into the house. Maybe the damned furnace was blowing up.

Aubrey sped through the rooms of the cottage, sniffing like a bloodhound. The scent grew stronger, the odor cloyingly sweet. She tugged open the basement door, snapped on the light switch and clomped down the wooden stairs in her nearly new, bought-for-the-funeral black kitten heels. They pinched like hell.

The big metal monstrosity of a furnace loomed in the corner. It made some weird banging noise that sounded like a pathetic cough followed by a couple of tinny pings. But there was no odor of smoke coming from it. She told it to "shut up," then went back upstairs.

The scent was chokingly strong as she entered the living room. She hurried across to the front window and shoved it open using both hands to dislodge it from its many coats of paint. A rush of crisp autumn air flooded the space, ballooning Mom's sheer organdy curtains like sails in a breeze coming in off the bay. Hopefully, when she returned from her meeting, the sickening aroma would be gone.

Aubrey locked up and climbed into her too-old hatchback with the balding tires and noisy exhaust that wouldn't pass inspection when it was due come spring. She needed this meeting with Dean to be about something big. Really big.

She drove along Fisherman's Road, stealing glances at the smokeless chimneys. What the hell had caused that acrid smell in her house? And whatever it was, would it cost her money she didn't have? Yet. She turned at the end of the block and headed toward the TV station.

Chapter Two

Asa Kavanaugh gripped the arms of the guest chair in his captain's office and fixed his gaze onto his superior officer, Michael Keithly.

"Why me, Mike?" Asa's voice was more clipped than he'd intended. The abruptness had caused his K-9 teammate to turn his big German shepherd head, black eyes fixed on his master. Asa reached down to where Scout lay obediently at his feet and scratched behind the dog's alert ear. Scout knew the gesture's purpose and let his head rest back on his mighty paws.

"Of course, you, Asa." Mike stood from his seat. "You're the best we've got. And you're our only bachelor. Bad enough the guys with families have to be on call so much of the time." Mike shrugged one shoulder. "This is going to strain your schedule, to say the least. Besides, rumor has it you're a hottie."

"A hottie?" Asa laughed. Now, he knew this had to be a joke. "Says who?"

"Says Melanie Robertson, the lady I talked to from the TV station when I was in that meeting. You'll be meeting her when you head over there later. Don't be late. Noon."

Asa shook his head. "How many sessions of this series on the K-9 unit will they be doing?"

The captain shook his head. "I think that's going to be discussed at the meeting."

Asa stood from the chair, his six-foot-six frame towering over the stocky captain. "You owe me, Michael." He reached out to shake the man's hand. They shared a grin as though each knew Asa's declaration involved not much more than Mike paying for beers down at Clooney's Pub some night after work.

"Don't forget, tomorrow's that Pet Day event at the elementary school. You're scheduled to demo there at noon, at the end of the program."

"Quit while I'm still my agreeable self," Asa quipped. He tapped the side of his knee. "C'mon, boy."

Scout stood, shook out his sleepy bones, and meandered to Asa's side. Asa patted the dog's head. Why couldn't everybody be as amenable?

Mike coughed a laugh. "Yeah. That's what you are, all right. Agreeable."

Asa knew the guys in the department thought of him as kind of gruff. Aside from his congenial working relationship with Mike and his one buddy, Dylan Grant, he hadn't cozied up to other fellow officers in friendship. He was better off that way. Stayed out of trouble.

"I'll let you know how the meeting goes," Asa said, as he headed toward the office door.

"You do that, hottie."

****

It was teeming, Aubrey's squeaky windshield wipers slapping at full tilt. Her kingdom for an umbrella. She prayed to the parking lot gods for a close spot near the entrance to WMSL's offices.

Two rows back was the best she could do. She gathered her purse and leather bag, and shot from the car. The keys slipped from her hands and plopped right into a mud puddle. *Crap and more crap.* She gingerly lifted them up from their murky bath and trotted through the parked vehicles toward the front entrance.

One strap of her leather sheaf looped off her shoulder and lassoed a side mirror of a hulking Buick. Her running feet stopped short, her body jerking backwards against the wet vehicle, saturating her black suit jacket. She yanked herself free from the saboteur hunk of metal and sprinted to the door.

The warm blast of heat in the lobby was welcoming to her chilled, wet bones. She didn't need a mirror to know she was a wreck, but what she did need was a stack of paper towels and a chance to assess the damage. She made a beeline to the ladies' room down the hall.

If mirrors could laugh, the one projecting Aubrey's image would have guffawed. Her hair, darker brown in its water-logged state, was wiggly, an unruly rag mop. She'd lost her hairclip in the harrowing sprint through the parking lot, but even that wouldn't have been able to tame this mess.

The black jacket was soaked and across the side where she'd braced against the Buick was a swath of salty grime, probably left over from the road crew's remedy for last week's iced roadways. She slipped out of the jacket and viewed herself from all angles. The leopard bra glared through the damp white blouse, the dark dots of the print a blazing reminder that it had been a poor choice. She folded the jacket and draped it over her high-positioned arm. If she kept it there, like a shield, through the meeting she and her sexpot bra might not look like *Victoria* had blown her *secret.*

She checked her watch. Time had run out. She did

her best with the hair, which wasn't much help at all, then pushed open the ladies' room door.

The heavy metal door swung wide, and a giant of a guy, in faded jeans and a brown plaid flannel shirt who was intent on texting, got clocked hard on his butt. He startled, sidestepped away from the door, and collided with Aubrey in a body slam.

"Whoa," he said. His big hands grasped her upper arms, the strength in them keeping her steady. He was handsome, in a cowboy kind of way. His eyes, dark brown like semi-sweet chocolate, surveyed her, holding her transfixed.

She shifted her gaze, with her eyes landing on his tan, pointy where's-the-rodeo boots. The hand-tooled leather was dry as a bone and, fleetingly, Aubrey guessed the guy had thought to bring an umbrella.

"Sorry," she said. "So sorry."

The chocolaty eyes remained fixed on her, his countenance awash with curiosity. His scrunched brow pinched the flesh between his eyes.

Before she had the chance to process her mind's question, *what's he looking at,* Aubrey remembered the woman in the mirror. *Oh yeah*, she thought. She laughed, pulling her arms free of his grasp. A prick of heat climbed up her cheeks. "I, uh, got caught in the downpour."

"Uh huh," he said.

Didn't it just figure? she thought. When a guy like this—with all the physical attributes that she usually went for—showed up, he was either married or gay or, in this case, she had scared him speechless by her drowned-rat appearance and probably by the Bride of Frankenstein hair, as well.

"I'm, uh, late for a meeting." She lifted her chin to meet his gaze again.

"Maybe you'd better do something about those spots first," he said flicking his gaze to her torso.

She looked down. Two pearl buttons of her white blouse had popped open and gaping, for all to see, was her leopard bra with the tiny black satin bow strategically adorned dead center between her thirty-four C's.

"Oh crap," she said and clutched at the fabric. "Oh, jeez."

Amusement danced in the guy's semi-sweet chocolate eyes and a sudden urge to poke them, Stooges-style, twitched in her fingers. Instead, she charged away from him, waiting until she rounded the corner of the corridor before she paused to button back up.

****

Dean Manning sat at his cherry veneer desk, his laptop open in front of him.

"Hi," Aubrey said, as she breezed in. "Am I late?"

Without looking up from the computer screen, he said, "Nah, Melanie should be here any minute. Sit, Blitzen."

Dean was famous for his nicknames. He doled them like a flower girl tossed her petals. The moment the man had learned Aubrey's last name was Donner he had saddled her with the name "Blitzen." She figured it was better than Prancer or Dancer or, God help her and her bra, Vixen.

Her boss looked up. "What's with the hair, Blitz?"

Aubrey plopped into one of the guest chairs. "I got caught in the rain."

Dean stared at her. "You could use a hedge clipper, kid." He pointed to her head. "Can't you calm that down, or something?"

She touched a hand to the hair that had a mind of its own, particularly when it met with the elements. "Is it that bad, Dean?"

Dean tilted his head as he studied her. She held his gaze, almost seeing the switching gears of his thoughts as he produced a reassuring grin. "You know, it's kind of funky, bohemian maybe. Come to think of it, it works."

"Thanks, but that's not the look I was going for." She patted her hair again.

Dean pointed to his own cheek. "And, uh, you're oozing eyeliner or whatever that's called."

Aubrey pulled a tissue from her purse and swiped it across her cheek. "Of all days. Can you give me a heads up on this meeting, Dean? I'm full of questions."

With that, Melanie Robertson entered the room. She was dressed smartly in a red boiled wool cropped jacket and hounds-tooth woolen skirt. Her hair, jet black and shiny, was cut short, styled modern and choppy. Her appearance fit her role as Program Manager well. She reached out a hand, a chunky black onyx ring on her index finger. "Aubrey," she said. "At last we meet."

Aubrey switched the wadded tissue into her left hand before taking Melanie's hand. She felt something hard in the tissue but decided to wait until the meeting was over before fishing through it.

Aubrey'd had occasion to be in the fiftyish woman's company on several occasions, all of which apparently hadn't registered in the lady's brain. But by the way Melanie stared at her now, Aubrey guessed she might henceforth remember the *bohemian* in the room.

"Hi," Aubrey said and laughed a little. "You'll have to pardon my appearance. Caught in the torrent."

"Ah," she said. That was all, just "ah."

Aubrey wondered what that meant. "Ah" like in commiserative? Her gaze flitted over the expertly detailed woman. Nope. More like "ah" as in who goes out in this without an umbrella?

Melanie gave Dean a nod, a manufactured grin tight on her shiny red lips. "Morning, Dean."

"M.R., you need coffee or anything?"

Shaking her head, Melanie settled into a vinyl-covered chair and braced a black leather notebook on her lap. She opened it and shuffled through some paperwork.

"Shall I begin, Dean, or would you like to get the ball rolling?" she said.

"Floor's yours." He folded his hands on his desk.

"Good." Melanie took a breath, and turned to Aubrey. "I apologize that we haven't spoken sooner. I understand you've been copy editing with the station for over a year." She consulted the top paper on her stack. "And Dean tells us that you've been anxious to try your hand at on-camera work."

"Yes," Aubrey said. "Absolutely." Her insides hurt from twisting and untwisting, her guts a snag of braided ropes. *Breathe, Aubrey. Breathe.*

"Do you know Hank McAllister?"

"I know who he is," Aubrey said. "He does that animal program on Sunday mornings, right?"

"*Pet Parade.* That's him," Melanie said. "Hank is retiring." An effusive grin broke out over her heavily lipsticked mouth. "We'll miss him, certainly. But we are taking this opportunity to revamp the *Pet Parade* program, give it more life, more oomph."

Aubrey pulled her eyes over to Dean. Could he read in them the horror that zapped her like a lightning bolt? She was the furthest thing from a pet person that there was. Her mind reeled. She was allergic to cats, skittish around anything with wings, scales made her scream, and worst of all, dogs tended to use her as a chew toy.

Unless the dog was small enough to fit into a purse like her Aunt Molly's little terrier, she wouldn't get near one without a big stick in her hand. Dogs hated her. She had the scar on her thigh to prove it, too.

Dean's eyes tried to calm her. She knew the look, could read it like copy. *You can do this,* his gray-blue eyes said to her. *Simmer down.*

"We're considering you, Aubrey," Melanie tilted her head, awaiting a reaction.

"Wow" was all Aubrey could manage. She furnished a smile that hurt her cheeks, like one of those metal gadgets the dentist used to keep your mouth open. And similar to when that hardware was in place, she couldn't speak.

"What are your thoughts on that?" Melanie asked. Her head still cocked to the side, assessing. "How do you feel about pets?"

"Oh she'll be great," Dean spoke up. "Aubrey's a people person. Pet owners are going to respond well to her."

Melanie leaned in toward Aubrey conspiratorially. "You've got quite a fan in Mr. Manning."

A genuine grin replaced the painful one stretching

her lips. "It's a mutual admiration society." Aubrey swallowed hard. Dean had been a constant support to her since giving her the job in the copy department. She couldn't let him down.

She breathed in a lungful of air, and let it expel. So this was it. If she wanted the chance, wanted the much-needed extra money that came with that chance, then she had to step up. Now.

"I'd love the opportunity…" she began, like testing the recitation of a new language in a foreign land. "When do we begin?" She thought she sounded pretty damned believable. She pressed firm hands onto the leather sheaf in her lap to steady her knocking knees. There'd be plenty of time to freak out later, when she got home.

"What'd I tell you?" Dean slapped his desk. "This kid's going to bring in the younger demographic. And, the older folks will love her exuberance. The camera loves her, too." He lowered his tone. "Her hair doesn't always look like that, by the way."

Melanie chuckled a sound that couldn't possibly have been natural. It sounded like scraping metal. "I'm sure," she said. "We'd like to begin with a trial episode."

Aubrey took out her tablet and fired it up. She tabbed around with a shaky finger. "Okay, ready."

"Friday is the Annual Pet Day at Ronan's Harbor Elementary School, nine to noon. You know, that's where the kids, joined by their parents of course, bring their pets to school. It's a wonderful program. We'll send a camera with you, and you'll cover the event for Sunday's spot. Just go with your gut. Editing will cut it down to the allotted eleven minutes for the show. This will test you and test the response of our viewers to you. How's that sound?"

"Terrific. I believe Nora Randall is the principal there. I'll give her a call today, to touch base."

"What'd I tell you," Dean said, pride breaking out on his craggy pushing-sixty face.

"That's wonderful. Also, after you film the spot, before you leave, I'd like you to introduce yourself to Asa Kavanaugh. He's a K-9 officer with the regional unit. He'll be giving a talk to the children in the auditorium at noon. We're planning a series on the K-9 program in Monmouth County. If all goes well, you and he will be working together on the series."

"I'm sure I'll find him."

"You can't miss him," Melanie said, her mouth curved in what appeared to be her first genuine smile. "He'll be the one with the big German shepherd." She emitted that grating chuckle again. "That dog's head is the size of a cinder block."

Aubrey's heart fell to the bottom of her belly and lay there like a brick of cement.

Chapter Three

After Melanie left, Dean came around to the front of his desk and leaned against it. Arms crossed, he tilted his head. "Okay, Blitzen. What's going on?"

"What do you mean going on?" Aubrey tossed the tissue she held into Dean's empty mesh trash basket and heard a muffled ping. She leaned closer and peered into the vessel. The tissue had unfolded and in the center was a shiny copper penny. She reached in and withdrew the coin. "Can't afford to throw money away," she quipped, holding the coin out for Dean's view.

"Aubrey." Dean rarely used her real name and she snapped to attention. "I would have thought you'd be jumping for joy. You do want this, don't you?"

"Yes, of course." She met his gaze. "But…"

"But? Come on, Blitz, talk to me. It's just you and me here. What you say stays with us. But what?"

"There's a small problem."

"How small?"

"Miniscule."

"Okay, like what?"

"I'm not good with animals."

Dean took off his glasses and rubbed his eyes. He lifted his head and squinted at her. "That could be an issue then, huh?"

"I was bitten by a Great Dane when I was a little

kid. Ever since then I've been kind of, you know, scared shitless around the beasts. There's no faking my way around that."

"Oh boy."

"Cats give me hives. Big welts. The whites of my eyes all but bleed."

Dean didn't respond.

"I broke up with a guy in college when he told me he had an iguana. I mean, who has iguanas? They've got this ugly dangly thing under their jaw." She clutched her stomach. She was making herself ill.

She was starting to hyperventilate, something she hadn't done in years. The trauma of the dog attack had been long gone, but here it was again clutching at her lungs, surrounding her rib cage like a tourniquet.

"Blitzen, look," Dean said. He leaned over and touched her hand where it sat in her lap. "Dig deep. You want this. You need this."

It was all true. She wanted a real post at the station.

The memory of her last moment with her mom sprang to mind as though it were a frozen frame of a movie. She had leaned over the frail form swallowed in the hospital bed's blankets, the sound of hissing equipment in their midst. Clinging to her mother's parchment-paper hand, she held the gaze of rheumy eyes as they fluttered between worlds.

Mom's words were a rasp, but so clear they embroidered themselves onto Aubrey's heart. *Keep our home, sweet girl. Promise me. We worked so hard.*

Aubrey squeezed her eyes. Mom's double shifts at the Stop and Shop, her own babysitting gigs of her young teen summers, followed by a string of high school and college jobs reeled in her thoughts.

Her mind flashed, like a camera, with pictures of the mounds of other people's ironing piled in plastic baskets along the kitchen floor waiting for Mom's tired arms to make smooth what was wrinkled. Unwanted tears fought to escape her eye. In truth, Mom's embodiment had been to smooth the unsmoothed.

She was reminded of the morning's frigid air that had encroached in her bedroom. A new furnace was inevitable. And, no matter how she chipped away at the large-enough-to-fill-a-basket stack of medical bills, it still daunted like the words tooled on her heart.

Aubrey gathered her belongings. "Dean, I'll get my game on. I promise." She fixed her gaze on his. "I keep my promises. I appreciate your going to bat for me with Melanie."

"That's my girl," he said. "Make me proud."

A sudden tear pinched the corner of one eye. Dean Manning had a way of sounding like a parent, and it just made her more aware that she had none.

As she was about to leave, Aubrey turned to him. "Did you get the chance to meet this Asa Kavanaugh guy?"

"I did."

"Well?"

"I'm thinking his bark will be worse than anything his pooch will utter. He's probably a nice guy, but he's all business. Brought a clipboard to the meeting and checked things off as we talked, okay? You know me; I've been referring to him as Ace Ventura in my head all morning."

She laughed. "All righty then."

****

As soon as Aubrey opened her front door she took

a deep whiff of air. The acrid smell was gone. It was cold in the house, and when she expelled a breath, it formed a vapor that ushered her in. Remembering she'd opened the front window, she went into the living room.

The air was briny, filled with scents of the sea. She loved the smell, chock with childhood memories of days just she and her mom went crabbing at the pier and times sitting bayside watching sailboats slice across the water.

She closed the window, and Mom's curtains fell in solemnity, abandoned by their salty-aired dance partner.

Aubrey went into the kitchen to make a pot of tea before settling in at the kitchen's old maple table where her laptop awaited. She needed to finish the copy edits for the station and then begin work on preparing for Pet Day at Ronan's Harbor Elementary.

It gave her the willies. If her mom were alive now, she'd laugh, that pre-illness lyrical sound she'd had, at the idea that her cynophobe daughter would be talking to the animals.

A persistent sound pulled her from the search screen. At first she thought she'd imagined it. Aubrey strained to listen. The creaking was rhythmic, a steady, squeaky beat like a rusty heart coming alive. Her own heart stammered. *She knew this sound.*

How many times in her mom's final days had Aubrey come home to find her, frail and withered, folded into the old bentwood rocker that had been in the family for generations? No one had sat in the relic since Caroline Donner had died.

A sensation swept over her, chilled her skin. Gooseflesh rose on her arms. The creaking increased, pounded in her brain, reverberated in her chest. She was frozen.

A loud crash snapped her to action. She darted from the kitchen, through the dining room, to the living room. Mom's bentwood rocker had toppled over and had taken the delicate side table with it.

Aubrey was breathing heavily, as if her lungs were too stunned to function. Air suffered to enter despite her efforts to pull it in. Nothing else was out of place, not the floral arrangement on the coffee table, not a crumb of the potpourri displayed in a cut glass bowl. Her gaze found the now-closed window.

She righted the chair, and set the petite piecrust table on its tripod legs. She gave the rocker a gentle shove, watched it move to and fro, heard the creakiness. She swallowed hard.

Although the window had been closed, the house had always been drafty. She gazed again at the antique bowl filled with fragrant dried petals. Any draft so mighty as to upend a chair and a table would certainly have sent that potpourri sailing like confetti.

Nerves pulled taut, Aubrey assessed the space around her. The odd sensation that had claimed her moments earlier, the presence, whatever it had been, had vanished. She was alone in the room now, but something, she didn't know what, had been with her. Of this she was sure.

Mom had been on her mind a lot today, more than usual, this being the one year anniversary of her passing. Were the smoky scent and the upended rocker linked to this? What, if anything, did it have to do with her week-long restlessness in the middle of the night, the foggy dream?

Her gaze panned the room with its pretty décor, magnanimously coined by Aunt Molly as *shabby chic*, that had always been a source of Aubrey's comfort. But not now.

The stillness around her gave no ease to Aubrey's rattled nerves. In an instant the space had become a stranger.

Chapter Four

Asa finished work for the day and headed home. His little ranch on the inlet suited him, and every time he pulled his truck into the driveway he instantly relaxed.

"Come on, Scout." He opened the backseat's cage and let the dog jump down from the vehicle and amble free. Scout immediately darted to his favorite tree, a Japanese maple, and gave it a sniff.

The glint of the canal lapping at the bulkhead behind his house called Asa. He walked along the flagstone path to the back yard, Scout trotting alongside.

Although it was cold, he sat on a cushion-less lounge and let the view do its magic. The dwindling sunlight on his face was still warm. He took in a deep breath of the brackish air. In the four years since his life had taken a one-eighty, his solace had been this.

A memory of today's meeting at WMSL invaded his peace. He hated the PR portion of his job. He respected the meat of his work, owned it, lived it, but this prospective television series was going to be a pain in his butt. He knew that going in. Work was best when it was just he and Scout.

Scout had wandered to the edge of the dock and surveyed the water, his head tilted, eyes intent. He was a good dog. Obedient. Hard working. Asa wondered if

Scout knew he was appreciated. Did the dog get enough reassurance, enough praise? Asa just didn't have it in him to get all emotional with his dog.

It was a fine line the handler walked with his K-9 partner. The dog needed to know that he was cared for, respected, safe. But overly demonstrative love from his human could be confusing. Asa had never found it difficult before to hold back deep connectedness, but he'd lost the ability when Cheryl died.

He was glad for Scout and his dedication, that much was very true. "Come here, boy," he said. The dog immediately came to his side. He ruffled the tail-wagger's ears, and the dog's eyes closed to slits, in a kind of bliss.

They went inside, and Asa filled his companion's stainless bowl with fresh water. He set it on the tile floor, and Scout immediately began to lap at it. He had just placed a mixture of wet and dry food in another bowl on the floor when the phone rang.

"Asa, you ready?"

"Ready?" Asa felt his lips curve against the mouthpiece. "Ready for what, Mike?"

"You said I owe you, man. Come on, it's Friday. Half price wings at Clooney's. Dylan and I are here at the bar waiting. I'm buying."

Asa smiled against the receiver. "You bet you're buying."

He hung up the phone and made his way to his room to shower and change.

****

Clooney's was packed, the din a welcome buzz of energy. Asa meandered through the throng of weekend gatherers and found Dylan at the far end of the bar.

Mike stood in front of the bar talking to the bartender, Denny.

Dylan motioned his crew-cut head to the empty wooden stool beside him. "Hey, buddy."

"What're you drinking," Mike called over the noise.

"Something dark," Asa said. "To match my mood."

Dylan laughed. "Sounds like a personal problem."

"Okay, so how'd the meeting at the station go?" Dylan asked, taking a sip of his own draft. "I assume that's the source of your dark mood. But with you, it's hard to tell."

"It was fine, I guess. I'm just not looking forward to doing a series, of all things. They're saying they might want as many as five different tapings. I mean, come on. How am I ever going to get any real work done?"

Asa's beer arrived, and he drew a deep pull. Mike sidled up beside them and lifted his beer mug in salute. "To your impending stardom."

"The things you get me into." Asa tapped his glass against Mike's, then Dylan's, and took another sip.

The wings arrived. Asa grabbed a stalk of celery and slathered it with blue cheese dressing. He chomped a bite.

Mike's cell phone must have sounded, although Asa hadn't heard it over the racket. The captain put his beer down and fished the device from his cargo pocket. One finger in his ear, he shouted for whoever it was to "Hold on, I can't hear you."

Mike uttered a "Be right back" and exited the bar going outside the entry doors.

"So," Dylan said with a smirk, "how'd you like

that lady that thinks you're hot stuff?"

"I see captain filled you in on some of the provocative details."

"Well?"

Asa made a face, chomped another hunk of celery.

"Not your type, huh?" Dylan cracked his wise-guy grin.

He shook his head. "Wound too tight I think."

"You're nuts. Was she like giving you *the look*?"

"Didn't notice."

"Jesus. You could have played that card, man. *You didn't notice?* What the hell do you notice?"

The mortified woman with the crazy hair and the leopard print bra, advertised through the gap in her shirt, popped into his head. A smile claimed his mouth. He really was rusty if that was what drew his attention about a woman.

"What's that look for?"

Asa startled. "Huh? Nothing."

"You did notice that woman. I knew it."

"No, I really didn't. It was this other woman."

"Now you're talking."

"She had hair like out to here," Asa said extending his hands exaggeratedly wide next to his head. "She was a crazy-eyed mess after getting caught in the rain. Eye makeup drooling onto her cheek like she'd been crying tar."

Asa laughed. "Oh, and her blouse was soaked through and she was wearing an animal print bra, leopard, that you could see from a mile away."

"And that's what you notice?" Dylan shook his head. "Not the hot-to-trot chick that already likes you. Nope. Not you, Kavanaugh. You're never going to take the plunge. And, in case you haven't noticed, you're not getting any younger, my friend."

"Look who's talking," Asa said. "I'm two years away from the big four-oh, and rumor has it you've already done a hit and run on that number."

"Hey, I've got two kids to my name, pal. Sucks that the marriage went kaput, but, hey, dem's da breaks."

Asa was reminded of his buddy's son and daughter, little Stevie with his toothless grin and the precocious Shana who apparently spent all her time singing. Asa had watched umpteen videos of Shana singing nursery rhymes on Dylan's cell phone.

"You've got some great kids, Dylan." It was almost never that Asa got a pang of longing. But beer did that to him. Lowered his guard.

"Thanks, man."

Dylan was well aware of what his friend had gone through after Cheryl's accident, and Asa could read it on his face that he was reminded of the tragedy. Dylan brightened, and lifted his glass. "So, here's to beer and wings."

The captain came back into the bar and slid his beer over toward Dylan. "Enjoy the night, boys." He fished a couple of bigger bills from his pocket and tossed them on the bar. He got the bartender's attention. "Beers and wings on me for these two clowns. Okay, Denny?"

"You're leaving so soon?" Asa asked. "You haven't given me time yet to *thank you* for roping me into this TV gig. And, P.S., this guy here's a bachelor, too. Why didn't you choose Dylan? He's a born actor."

"The lady wanted you." Mike cracked a grin, and

wiggled his thick graying eyebrows.

"Seriously, you're off?"

Mike nodded. "Judy's in a panic. She just got home from work and found that the neighbors erected a shed in their backyard. According to my outraged wife, they knocked down her cement garden bench and, worse, blocked the sun from her plantings. She's convinced nothing will come back in the spring."

"Ah," Dylan said. "And you're off to give the miscreants a trouncing?"

"No, I'm off to calm Judy down and take her to dinner. A glass of white wine is what my wife needs."

Asa felt the pang again. He hated it. He'd put all that relationship stuff behind him. He stared at his nearly-empty beer glass. Was he getting soft? Usually he'd need to tie one on, which he almost never did, to start remembering what could have been. He pushed the glass away and grabbed another chicken wing.

After Mike left, Denny delivered another round to Asa and Dylan. "Not sure I should have a second," Asa said.

"For God's sake, man, you're a giant. You can handle two beers." Dylan was always razzing him about his height, but in reality Asa knew the guy was irked by his own five-six stature.

"So, get this," Asa said. "The TV station manager said the woman that's going to be interviewing me is new and he asked me to *go easy on her.*" Asa shook his head. "What'd he expect?"

"Kavanaugh, come on. You've got that don't-mess-with-me look that might make some people, particularly women, run in the opposite direction."

Again, the frenzied lady in the corridor popped into

his head. "My specialty," Asa said, and bit into a wing.

"Be on your best behavior. The unit's counting on you. So, give the lady a break."

"Aubrey Donner."

"How's that?"

"That's her name," Asa said wiping his mouth with a paper napkin. "I'll be a pussycat, okay?"

Dylan laughed. "Yeah, okay."

****

Aubrey breezed into the pub's front door, a twirl of dried leaves caught in a vortex ushering in with her. The hostess checked the open reservation register propped on a stand and informed Aubrey that Molly, her surrogate aunt, was already seated at their table.

"Auntie, hello!" Aubrey put her arms around the septuagenarian. Affection filled her heart. This woman was the closest thing she had to a bona fide relative, someone who shared her past, and most of all, the one person whose pain on this one year anniversary matched her own.

"How are you, my love?" Molly clutched a freckled hand on Aubrey's arm. "You're skinny."

Aubrey took her seat opposite Molly.

Molly made her smile. She'd had her hair done, the streaked gray coif starched into a fancy do. Baubles on chains dangled from her earlobes. The woman had been her mom's best friend since childhood, but the two could not have been more unalike.

Where Caroline Donner had been happy in a pair of faded jeans and a flannel shirt, her typical flower garden ensemble, Molly sat here with her sweeping fringed scarf swathed across her chest, cinched by an intricate brooch. She was more interested in salsa lessons than she was gardening.

Molly reached across the tabletop and covered Aubrey's hand. Molly's eyes glistened. "One year, my love."

Aubrey nodded. "A year."

They ordered martinis and toasted Caroline. Aubrey wanted to share her troubled dreams of the last week and the goings-on at her house. But how would Molly react to hearing about strange smoky smells, a tipped rocker, and most of all, the indefinable presence that had invaded her dear friend's home?

"Aubrey, you look tired"—Molly fingered the brooch pinned on her chest—"and pale."

Aubrey took a large sip of her potent beverage. "Auntie, do you believe in ghosts?"

"Well, of course," Molly waved her hand. "Who doesn't?"

"I think I may have one."

Molly leaned closer. "Do you? Tell me everything."

The waitress took their dinner order. As soon as she stepped away, Aubrey began. During the entire time she reiterated the details of the strange occurrences, Molly was silent taking intermittent baby sips of her martini. Her eyes never left Aubrey's face.

A little voice in the back of her mind asked Aubrey if Molly would later call the guys in the white coats to come take her away. When she had finished speaking, Aubrey waited.

Molly appeared to be mulling the story as she nibbled her fat green olive poked on a toothpick. "It's a sign." Molly pointed the now-empty toothpick at her.

Aubrey's stomach rose, then fell. "What do you

mean?"

"It can't be a coincidence," Molly said. "It is the one year anniversary of Caroline's passing."

"But why? I mean, what do you think it's a sign of?"

Molly clapped her hands. "That's what we have to find out, and I know just what you need."

Aubrey braced herself. She loved Molly, but the woman had a tendency to pull out the crazy when stress entered the room.

She was reminded of the time Molly had thought the way to remedy Mom's issue of post-treatment hair loss had been for the three of them to don Cher-like wigs. Molly had bought them at the party store, and hers had been glittery fuchsia.

"You're coming with me to the Cornelia Inn tomorrow night," Molly announced.

"And that's going to help this situation how?"

"It's a cocktail party hosted by the Elks Club."

"Molly, focus please. Why do you want me to go with you to the Elks' party?"

"So I can introduce you to my new fella. Ira. You'll love him."

God bless her, Molly McFadden always had what she referred to as a *fella*. Never married, the woman had trotted around on the arm of some new dreamboat for as long as Aubrey could remember. The old gal didn't just play the field, she played the planet.

"Ira's my first Elk."

"And how is my meeting him going to fix this ghost stuff?"

"Ira happens to be a medium."

"A medium-sized elk, say, as opposed to a large

one?"

Molly laughed. "Heavens no, my dearest. Ira's a *clairvoyant*."

"A clairvoyant? You mean like he's got an *in* with dead people?"

"Direct line! Aubrey, we're going to plan a séance. You've indeed got a ghost on your hands, and we can discuss that at the Cornelia Inn."

How long had it been since Aubrey had been to a cocktail party on a Saturday night, or anywhere other than in front of her television or her computer screen? Long gone were the days of partying with her best friend in Hoboken, the carefree nights meeting Joanie for dinner, the dates with guys she never liked enough to have them stick around.

She'd spent six months working part-time and caring for her mother. Then, after Mom died, all Aubrey did was work.

Their dinners arrived, grilled salmon on salads. While they sampled, Molly looked up and poked her fork at Aubrey.

"This cocktail party can serve two purposes."

Aubrey chewed as she waited for Molly to continue.

"We'll line you up with Ira's expertise, and maybe you'll meet a man. We'll scour the attendees."

Aubrey swallowed. "Auntie, please. I have enough to worry about."

"Why does having a man around have to be something to *worry* about? That's your problem. You think of men as a negative. Flip that thinking around, doll, and you'll be surprised at what turns up."

Aubrey was reminded of her longest relationship—

her college boyfriend Charles Alexander, or *Chaz* as he'd preferred. She should have recognized from day one that he was a bully. Chaz had ordered her first dinner for her as if she'd been some imbecile unable to choose her own entrée.

It had gotten worse over time. His deciding who she should be friends with and what she should wear. That right there would have been clue enough for practically anyone. But he was big and blond and had that twinkly shine in his eyes.

She shook her head. A sucker for things that shine, Aubrey had practiced remembering that often inside an attractive package lurked a disappointment. With Chaz, time had revealed a tyrant.

And Aubrey knew of tyrants. Her mom's father, Grandfather Montgomery Donner the Second, as if he needed a number to identify his pomposity, had been the quintessential dictator. He'd made Caroline's life miserable.

Aubrey didn't know him, of course. He'd disowned his only child, a mere teenager, scared and pregnant, when she'd refused to give up her baby. Hey, it was tough to be hated from conception, but the impact of Mom's tough life because of Aubrey's very existence was what coated her heart in resentment. And, her experience with Charles Alexander-the-not-so-great had just sealed the deal.

"What are you thinking about?" Molly asked. "Your forehead's all folded in on itself. Stop that. You don't want wrinkles."

"Sorry, my mind's all over the place."

"What you need is a nice member of the male species to take your mind off things."

She'd heard this a ton of times from both Molly and her friend, Joanie. She didn't have a boyfriend, or a "fella," because she didn't want one. Period.

She liked men, a lot, but found it easier to enjoy them either from afar or in brief doses. "Be right back."

She skirted the dining room tables and exited through the bar area where the ladies' room was located at the far end.

The bar was packed, no stool empty. It was noisy, bordering raucous. Males and females in small groups huddled around the row of backless stools, everyone drinking, chatting, laughing, spending time. She missed it, but she knew she wouldn't fit into that scene any more.

It wasn't that she was too old, hell no. Thirty-three was far from old. *Cripes,* she thought, *look at Aunt Molly.* She'd socialized circles around Aubrey for years. But this scene? It might as well be an open hatch of a plane, and she wasn't jumping.

On her way back from the restroom, she bumped into a tall man with a nice, broad back and solid-looking arms. Her rusty heart did a dance despite its armor.

But then a realization gave an open-handed slap to her senses. The man didn't even have to turn around for her to know he was the same one she'd slammed into at the station that morning, the really cute guy with the cell phone and scowl. The one who had ungraciously commented on her bra.

I'm a frigging magnet. She darted away.

"Hey."

She closed her eyes and fought the urge to turn around but lost.

The cowboy-looking man stood there with a frosted beer mug in his paw. Beside him, a shorter man with a buzz cut appeared a bit pie-eyed. He turned to face her, beady eyes glued.

The big guy's mouth was a grimace, his face contorted in aggravation. His friend handed him a stack of cocktail napkins and tried to help him mop up what apparently was a beer spillage.

Oh boy. She had no choice now but to approach. "I'm sorry. Did I do that?"

Recognition registered in his deep brown eyes. "You again?" he said. "Jeez, you need a horn or something, so people can hear you coming."

"I, uh, I'm sorry." Her insides were clenching, twisting like wrung rags.

Without looking up from his sopping, he muttered, "Almost didn't recognize you without the hair."

"I beg your pardon?"

He placed his mug on the bar. His chocolate-toned orbs now shone with amusement. "You know"—he motioned with his hands like something really big was on his head—"the hair."

"She's the one with the hair?" the shorter guy asked.

The tall one flashed his cohort a look to shut the hell up.

"I hear inside you're a real tigress, I mean, leopard," the shorter one said, and laughed at his own joke.

The tall guy's face looked stricken. He took his friend's beer mug out of his hand, plopped it onto the bar with a thud, and said, "You're done, buddy."

Aubrey felt the flush rise on her cheeks, a heat

similar to the one charging through her veins. *Had this buffoon actually talked about my hair? And my bra?*

"You're kidding me, right?" She dug into her purse and, squeezing her hand between two seated people, slapped a ten dollar bill on the bar. The bartender acknowledged her with a lift of his chin.

"Buy this idiot a beer, on me." She motioned her head in his direction.

"Wait, no. You don't have to do that. We're done," he said.

"Then use the money to put in the collection plate when you go to church, to pray for manners," she said, her voice clipped, full of venom.

He, with his rugged good looks and his obviously sour demeanor, was the cure for her longing. Jerks like him had a tendency to remind her that she wasn't missing much without a man in her life. She stomped away.

Back at the table, Molly eyed her. "Something wrong?"

"Oh it's nothing," Aubrey said. "Just some guy."

"Really?"

"Not like that, Auntie." Aubrey took a sip of her martini. "Not like that at all."

"What you need, my dear, is an Elk."

Aubrey finished her martini in two big swallows.

Chapter Five

Later that evening, snuggled in her faded flannel pajamas, Aubrey brought a mug of chamomile tea up to her room. She was determined to get a full night's sleep, ghost be damned.

Restless with the whirlwind of the day's activities circling in her head, she was wired and unable to close her eyes. Despite her sleep deprivation, her mind zoomed with the prospective new job and the involved animals, big and small. She groaned.

She just knew that behind closed lids her eyes would see either one of two unwanted scenes—the ghostly figure in her recent turbulent dreams, or the vision of herself on her way home from school as a twelve-year-old being chased by a massive dog. Either way she was screwed, and her nerves would pay the price.

She grabbed the remote from the nightstand and turned on the TV. Channel surfing, she heard something downstairs. She switched off the television and in the darkness, in the silence, Aubrey strained to listen. Her heart drummed in her chest. What would be worse, she wondered, a flesh-and-blood intruder or the return of whatever strangeness was going on? A loud crash sounded, zapping the breath from her lungs.

The aroma of burning vanilla crept into the room. Curling up in the air, smoke-like, it had sneaked in from under the door.

Dazed, Aubrey pulled the coverlet over herself, holding the fabric, clenched in her fists, to her chin. A claustrophobic grit trapped in her lungs.

She eyed the window. She could slip out through it, but then what? How would she get down off the roof? And even if she did, her car keys were downstairs in the kitchen. Her cell phone was there, too, charging on the counter.

Another crash sounded louder than the first. Adrenaline spiked in her veins. She threw off the covers and bolted from bed. She shoved her feet into her sneakers in case she needed to flee after she got downstairs. Looking around, she grabbed her flat iron, the only thing that remotely resembled a weapon.

The steps squeaked as she treaded slowly down, one by one. Shaking, she held a hand to the wall as she descended. Her mind raced. *Get the car keys, grab the phone, then get the hell out of here.* Maybe she'd go back to Hoboken and never look back.

At the base of the stairs she stood still. The house was silent, yet the air was charged, alive. The only sound was the thump of her own heartbeats banging in her chest, pounding in her ears. The vanilla smell was heavier in the air around her in the entryway. It was chokingly sweet, the acridity burning her nostrils, forcing tears to her eyes.

That eeriness, the same feeling she'd had each morning for a week, and today when her mother's rocker had overturned, surrounded her like arms of apprehension. Flat iron in hand she crept from the entryway toward the living room through the dining room.

Shards of crystal glinted in the moonlight coming in through the dining room windows. Reflexively Aubrey switched on the chandelier.

Mom's candlesticks lay in bits and pieces across the wide-planked floor. Aubrey bent to retrieve the base of one of the sticks, the largest piece that had survived. Her eyes scanned the room. The shelf above the sideboard, where wooden blocks spelled *welcome,* caught her eye. The wooden cubes were completely turned around, their country-red painted letters facing the wall, their blond backs outward. It felt like a message from the ghost—she was *not* welcome. Gooseflesh riddled her skin.

She surveyed the remains of the treasured antiques strewn across the floor. What, she wondered, could have caused the precious pieces to break in such a way? It was as if they'd been smashed with a baseball bat.

She backed out of the room, too freaked to do anything about the mess at this late hour. Her legs were filled with jelly.

Going from room to room, Aubrey turned on all the lights, bringing artificial daytime to her home.

Nothing was out of place in the living room. Her mother's chair still sat in the corner, upright and peaceful.

In the kitchen, everything was as it had been. Aubrey checked the doors' locks, grabbed her phone, her purse, and car keys and then went back upstairs leaving every light on in the house.

****

The phone rang, startling her from deep sleep. Up most of the night, Aubrey guessed she'd finally succumbed to slumber around five. Her eyes blinked

37

before finding the bedside clock, its illuminated face telling her it was after ten. *Crap.*

The dream had returned and this time the shadowy figure had spoken words. Had she really heard someone speak? It had seemed real, as if someone had been dangerously close, lips to her ear, breath on her face. *Confuse not friend or foe.*

The call connected, and she listened to the message being recited into her answering machine by Aunt Molly.

Aubrey quickly reached for the handset before Molly hung up. "Auntie?" she breathed. "You still there?"

"Aubrey, yes, goodness, I thought you weren't home."

Aubrey stilled her breath, or tried to. "No, I'm here."

"You sound flustered, doll. Did you have the dream again last night?"

"Yes," Aubrey said. "And, there was, um, a kind of freak thing that happened here, too."

"Oh, dear. This confirms we need Ira."

"Auntie, I just don't know about that. It's just, I don't know, so out there."

"Well, you meet him tonight and decide for yourself."

"About tonight."

"You're coming, and I'll have no argument."

When the conversation had ended, Aubrey still hadn't officially agreed to attend the cocktail party at the Cornelia Inn, nor had she said one way or the other that she would consent to Molly's latest "fella" performing some hocus pocus in her house, Mom's house.

God, she thought, *what would Mom think about all this? Mom, is it you trying to tell me something?* Her tired brain didn't know. She flopped back onto her pillow and willed herself to get another few minutes of sleep.

It felt like only minutes later when her doorbell rang. Any sound these days rattled her to the core. She pulled on sweats and padded downstairs.

She crept to the door and peeked out the rectangular window alongside it. Aunt Molly stood on her stoop, an oversized quilted satchel over her shoulder. Her dog Roscoe's scraggly head poked out of the top.

Although Roscoe, a tiny-sized terrier, was not much bigger than a meatloaf, he made Aubrey skittish. He was jumpy, and that made her jumpy, especially these days.

"Auntie," she greeted through the opened door. The dog yipped. "Hi, Roscoe."

Just hearing his own name set the dog to wriggling within the confines of the bag. Molly tried to settle him with soothing words as she stepped in through the open doorway.

Roscoe continued to fidget and finally sprang free leaping from the tote like a rocket. He sprinted past Aubrey into the house.

Molly clapped her hands. "Roscoe, come here," she called. She gazed up from her diminutive stature to meet Aubrey's eyes. "You okay, kid?"

"I'm fine, Molly, really." Aubrey managed a wide smile that felt tight on her face.

A guttural growl, too ferocious sounding for Aunt

Molly's little Roscoe, screeched from the living room. Aubrey and Molly momentarily froze, then they rushed to him.

The tiny terrier stood rigid in front of the bentwood rocker, his mouth pulled back, teeth bared.

Aubrey's hands began to shake.

The dog uttered a continuous string of low harsh barks. Suddenly he lunged at the chair and sank his teeth into the upholstery.

"Roscoe, no!" Molly called. "Bad boy. No. No."

The dog's head thrashed from side to side as he tugged the fabric. It tore into shreds. He clamped his jaw on the cushion and pulled out a chunk of foam padding.

A vision of herself at twelve—splayed under someone's car in their driveway, screaming "help" while a Great Dane barked with similar ferocity, his aim her leg, not a chair cushion—provoked Aubrey. Her entire body began to shake. It was as if the scar on her thigh, where twenty-seven stitches had bound her back together, was pulling taut and cutting her circulation.

Snapping out of her reverie, she watched Molly pull her dog into her grasp. The little guy fought to free himself from her arms. He continued to bark at the chair, intent to attack it further. Aubrey could see it in his black eyes, glazed with determination. She'd seen that look for years in her dreams.

"I don't know what's gotten into him," Molly said. "Roscoe, boy, it's okay." Molly's voice broke, her gaze on the wounded chair. "Oh, lord, Caroline's rocker. Look what he's done to your mother's chair!"

It was back, the eeriness she'd felt earlier. The

heavy presence poured over Aubrey's body like a bucket of paint, suffocating her.

Ears spiked upright, neck craned, mouth pressed into a stern line, there was no doubt Roscoe felt it, too.

Molly pressed her pet to her body, soothed a hand over his straggly fur. She cooed. "Baby boy," she said. She cradled him close. "It's okay."

But it wasn't. Aubrey's gut told her that. This was absolutely not okay. Molly's eyes, stormy gray and overcast with worry, implored for an explanation neither of them could furnish.

"Auntie, it's all right. See? He's fine now." Roscoe had stopped fighting Molly's arms and instead relaxed in their comfort.

"But Caroline's chair," she whispered.

Both women stared at the damaged antique. Aubrey's heart fell at the memory of her mom's reverence for the rocker bequeathed to her from her own mother. It was one of the very few things that Grandfather Montgomery had allowed mom to take with her when she and her baby had been banished from his life.

Aubrey had never met Grandmother Edith, either, she having died right after Aubrey had been born. Mom had spoken of Edith over the years, especially in her waning days when nostalgia had been her dearest elixir.

Too timid to defy her husband, Edith had stayed away from Caroline and her baby. And because of that, Mom believed her mother had died of a broken heart.

Just the thought of her grandfather's oppression gave her a stab in the gut akin to the one she got whenever around a barking dog.

A cool breeze rushed past her, and Aubrey pulled

in a breath at the suddenness of the surge. The eerie presence slipped away like fog chased by the wind. It feathered past them tauntingly like a silken scarf's touch on the skin. And then, like a movie screen gone black, there was stillness.

"It left, didn't it?" Molly whispered. "I feel like it just vanished."

"Yes, me too."

"They say animals are attuned to supernatural things," Molly said, giving Roscoe a squeeze. "What do you think?"

"I don't know," she lied.

Roscoe whimpered, his dark eyes glued on Molly. He offered an anemic bark.

"He's sorry," Molly said holding him to her face. "Aren't you, lovey?"

Aubrey wondered how anyone could hold a dog up to their face, even one the size of a lunch box.

"He's not c-r-a-z-y." Molly spelled the word conspiratorially, as though the dog were fluent in the English language but had yet to learn to spell. "But this place is. This is a spook house, and we've got to do something about it."

Molly's odd affection for her pet worked like a pair of expert hands massaging the tension in Aubrey's body. She felt her muscles loosen their grip at the pet's docility. Her brain emerged from its own kind of fog.

"I know, Auntie," Aubrey said. "Enough is enough."

Molly leaned forward to recite the word succinctly. "Ira."

Aubrey pulled her eyes to Mom's heirloom, the chair with its seat now ripped open, guts exposed.

She remembered when her mom, in her weakness at the end, had given Aubrey a rambling list of directives. She'd been passing a baton to the new keeper of their home and the life they'd shared in it.

A copy of my will is in my jewelry drawer. The cemetery plot deed is in the nightstand. The bank book is in the shoebox on the top shelf in my closet.

Mom had gone on like that intermittently for days as though needing to get it all out before the end claimed her. *Replace the shingles by the back door. Don't forget to get the furnace checked.*

Mama's rocker—that was how Caroline had referred to the old chair. Her raspy voice had not been more than a sob-clogged whisper. *"Mama's last request of me was to replace that old faded upholstery."* So many things had made Caroline cry at the end. *"We never got around to it, did we? You do that for me, Aubrey. Will you?"*

Aubrey cast her gaze around the room, at all the things that reminded her of her mother's toil, her determination to make the best life for Aubrey. And, damn it, no ghost was going to wreak havoc on her mementos.

"Okay," Aubrey said, blowing the air from her pent lungs. "Saturday. I'm in for the Elk event at the Cornelia."

"Halleluiah!" Molly said, looking up to the ceiling. Then she met Aubrey's gaze. "Oh, and I'll pay to have the rocker refurbished."

"Don't be silly, Auntie. It's my job to do. I promised Mom."

Chapter Six

There was a drug investigation underway in the nearby town of Neptune Junction, and Asa's department was scheduled to get involved. It was the work he lived for, the real crux of what he and Scout both had been trained to perform. It was what kept his mind from going backwards.

But today, on this bright Friday morning, he was heading over to the elementary school to perform a dog-and-pony show as part of their Pet Day, per instructions from the top.

Asa parked his truck and took one last pull from his travel coffee mug. He watched a young mom and her little boy scurrying to the building. A mutt on a leash pulling the child caused him to trot on his little legs.

How old could that kid be? Five, six? Asa wondered what their child would have been like at that age, if Cheryl hadn't died in the wreck. Just the thought of his fiancée brought the nightmarish memory to the forefront of his mind. He hadn't even known she was pregnant. No one should hear such news from an ME.

He hopped out and opened the back door. Scout, ever obedient, did not fidget as he kept his gaze attached to Asa's hand unlatching his crate. The door swung open, and still the intent shepherd waited for the cue.

Asa uttered a low whistle. "C'mon, Scout."

Scout jumped from the confines of the crate and hopped down out of the vehicle. Asa latched the leash to the dog's leather collar. They made their way to the front entrance of the school through crunching dried leaves scattered across the sidewalk.

They had an appointment with the principal in ten minutes.

****

Aubrey was buzzed into the building, along with the cameraman from WMSL. A muscular guy, Joe appeared totally unburdened by the heavy-looking equipment hoisted on his large shoulder.

With just one foot inside the door, the cacophony of barks coming from down a long corridor was enough to make her itch to run back to her car.

"Whew," Joe said. "Sounds like a kennel in here."

Her heart did a flip, and she did her best to ignore the niggle of apprehension brewing in her belly. They checked in at the office, showed their press credentials, and were handed a schematic of the classrooms. Each class had an essay contest-winning student that had won the privilege of bringing their pet to school. It was Aubrey's job to interview the kids and their furry, feathered, or scaly friends.

She and Joe walked down the echoing hallway. "Hell of a first gig, huh?" Joe said, with a laugh.

"Yeah." She laughed back, although not one cell in her body held any humor at the situation. "Shouldn't be too bad, though."

Joe's cell phone sounded. He was quick to fish it from his shirt pocket and silence the device. "I'll put this on vibrate, but I can't turn it off. My wife's pregnant, very pregnant, and any day could be *the day.*"

Aubrey couldn't help notice the pride in Joe's face as he spoke. The obvious happiness in him managed to soothe her nerves as they entered the first classroom.

Inside the kindergarten classroom, with many sets of little people's eyes on her, thoughts reeled. *Maybe copyediting isn't so bad. It's a good and noble job, even if the pay isn't great. Sure, I want to host a spot on WMSL, but this? Can I really do this for a living?*

Why not ask her to bungee jump into an alligator pit? Hell, who knew? Did folks have pet alligators?

Kindergartener Mara and her pet Yorkshire terrier were adorable, both with long silky hair. But Mara was so nervous to be interviewed that she peed her panties. Her pup, Pepper, followed suit by taking a whiz on the story-time carpet. The roomful of five-year-olds erupted in squeals.

This only made Mara cry harder and caused Pepper to run around in circles knocking down a giant tower of foam blocks. These had apparently been assembled with painstaking care just that morning. More crying, more squealing, more spastic Pepper.

Grade by grade, they listened to students read their winning essays aloud, and Aubrey met their pets. Aubrey sneezed her way through the interview with third grade Cecilia, accompanied by her border collie. Foster's flyaway fur floated in the air like the autumn leaves outside the window. Somehow each tuft of fluff found its way to Aubrey's nostrils taunting her allergies alive, filling her eyes with itchy tears.

Aubrey's other encounters included a calico cat named Melba, with one blue eye and one brown eye, and a parakeet named Elvis that rocked his body when his owner, Robby, serenaded him with "Hunk-a-Hunk-a-Burning Love."

A boy named Richie had a toy poodle that was afraid of zucchini. He told the tale of when Fluffy had been a puppy and a whopping zuke, from their family garden, had rolled off the kitchen counter with such a loud thud it had spooked the dog for life. Idly, Aubrey wondered if Molly's friend Ira exorcised vegetables.

Near noon, Aubrey and Joe made their way to the auditorium and stood along the side wall while teachers ushered their pupils into the rows of seats.

A police officer was about to give his presentation on the K-9 program of Monmouth County. This man was going to be the subject of the series that could cement her position with the station.

She was anxious to get a look at the officer and his K-9 companion, yet dreaded it too, as her eyes fixated on the empty stage. Aubrey just knew that a K-9 dog wouldn't be a toy poodle, and it sure as hell wouldn't be afraid of things like produce or wary reporters.

"Do you know the officer?" she asked Joe.

"I saw him the day he came in to talk with management. Big guy, the kind you wouldn't want to mess with."

"Did you happen to see his dog?"

Joe nodded. "Handsome beast."

There was something about the word *beast* that compelled every nerve ending to stand at attention. She smiled at Joe as though in appreciation of his assessment of the dog.

Aubrey wished she were as calm internally as she willed herself to be on the outside. She had to pass herself off as a non-neurotic professional, if she wanted to convince the station she was the ideal candidate for this job.

It wasn't the part of the program where the officer talked on the stage that bothered her. Joe would film that and she'd add the voice-over later. That would be easy. It was the post-presentation one-on-one that she was dreading.

The principal walked across the stage, while teachers shushed their restless charges. After a brief preamble, Nora Randall asked everyone to welcome Asa Kavanaugh and his dog, Scout.

Aubrey's heart buzzed around her chest cavity like a yellow jacket caught between two windowpanes, her heart careening rib to rib as if looking for a way to fly free.

He strode across the stage like a soldier, even-paced as though in a march. Under the lights the officer's blond hair shone platinum. Aubrey gulped.

It was *him*—the man in the rain, the oaf in the bar—the handsome blond with all the looks, and none of the charm. *Handsome beast, indeed.*

Asa Kavanaugh, tall and steely, stood center stage and he was alone. No dog. *Perhaps,* she thought, *he was dog enough.*

He began to speak, his words bouncing off her eardrums. Aubrey hoped Joe was recording all that he was saying because she couldn't still her mind enough to absorb any of it.

Her brain zoomed like a rewinding video. The way she'd looked that day at the station when she'd collided into this guy. His gawkish observance of her leopard bra. She hated that bra now.

And the night at Clooney's. He and his buddy, all

smug and obnoxious. His leer, his smirk, his dimple.

Good dimple, very good, but still. He was an ass. Yup. That was him—Ass Kavanaugh. And she was here to chat the ass up.

The appearance of a large German shepherd trotting across the stage caused her brain to hit pause. The animal was huge, paws the size of fists.

There was a loud reaction among the seated students. Was it appreciation? Wariness? She didn't know, couldn't decipher it over the thrum in her chest and in her ears.

Despite the rising voices, the dog did not waver his gaze from his master. Seemingly well-trained, there was every chance the pony-sized K-9 wouldn't leap from the stage and find somebody to munch on. Still Aubrey pressed her back against the cool cinderblock walls of the auditorium.

The dog sat at Kavanaugh's feet, big head tilted up, eyes on the man. "This is Scout," the ass said, with authority in his tone—his voice deep, commanding, male.

She glanced over to Joe, camera on his shoulder, eye to the viewfinder. His lens was directed at the man and the dog. She looked back over to the live scene. She bet Ass Kavanaugh looked good on film. The uniform, cargo-pocketed khakis, black boots, and the black crew-neck shirt that advertised the cuts of his muscles, the expanse of his shoulders, and how they compared to the cinch of his waist.

Her mind registered the obvious. This Kavanaugh man was hot. Smoking. But they always were. When it came to the ass brigade, Aubrey could see them coming a mile away.

The super-sized Scout performed exercises at Asa's commands, tricks like jumping over a pile of crates, searching for a stuffed rabbit hidden in a stack of boxes. Rounds of applause rolled like thunder across a plain. Scout and his trainer were a hit.

After the presentation, she and Joe walked along the sidewalk to wait in front of the flagpole as prearranged. Joe fiddled with his equipment while Aubrey fiddled with her earring, a nervous habit that had on more than one occasion managed to loosen a latch and render her lobe bauble-less.

She had a drawer in her jewelry box reserved for earrings missing their mates. She forced her fingers away from the tempting gold wire loop attached to her left ear.

A couple of minutes later Asa Kavanaugh and Scout, imposing like Bunyan and Babe, strode across the sidewalk. With each step toward her, Aubrey's heart slammed like a gavel. Her insides zoomed out of order. Scout was not tethered.

Stoicism blanketed Officer Kavanaugh, the expert construction of his face intense. He stood with purpose, Scout halting at his side. His eyes, dark brown disks, focused on hers.

It was a slow morph, his eyes finally registering recognition like a flash across a midnight sky. His somber mouth crooked up on one side giving life to the dimple that cut deep into his cheek.

"You're Aubrey Donner?" The incredulity was so apparent it was as if he'd caught her trying to pass herself off as the Queen of England.

"That would be me," she said. One eye was still on Scout who was studying her with curious black eyes.

One pointy ear twitched.

"Well," Asa said. He laughed and shook his head, hands on his hips. "Well."

"Yeah." Her fingers twirled the fastener of her earring.

"Okay, Aubrey Donner," he said, with a shake of his head. "Let's take care of this, okay? I've only got a few minutes."

She bristled at the dismissive tone. If it weren't for the dog, that looked hungry for a chew toy, she'd have thrown the microphone at him.

After a few questions answered with a curt economy of words by Asa, a question beckoned from the back of her mind. *How the hell am I going to get enough personality out of this cinderblock to produce a decent series for WMSL?* Her future as a show host depended on this. She eyed G.I. Joe and his wolf-like companion. This was going to be like getting someone with their jaw wired to sing the national anthem.

"I'll contact you over the next couple of days to coordinate a schedule," she said, handing him her business card. "We'll need to arrange a time to go over the station's plans for the series and put some dates on the calendar for us to come out and do some location footage."

Asa slipped the card into his pocket before latching Scout to his leash and patting the dog on the head. He then looked up at her. "Just so you know, this wasn't my idea."

"Duly noted," she said, fiddling with the gold hoop in her ear.

"I'll expect your call, then." He nodded to Joe, who was zipping his camera into its canvas casing. Offering a plastic smile to Aubrey, he said, "Have a good day."

Parents and children were leaving the school building in droves—a short day schedule, apparently. People scurried across the sidewalks and darted over the leaf strewn lawn to get to their cars.

While Aubrey waited for Joe to pack his gear, she spotted a man in a suit dashing quickly along the walkway struggling to light a cigarette with a hand cupped around a lit match.

He discarded the match with a snap of his wrist while he trotted over the curb and disappeared in the crowd of people gathering in the parking lot.

A thread-like stream of gray smoke began to form in a mound of dried leaves on the fringe of the sidewalk.

"Oh God," she said. "Joe, hold up." She darted over to the smoldering leaves.

As she approached, Asa Kavanaugh came up alongside her. The mound was now consumed with licking flames, the once-brown foliage changing into gray ash before her eyes.

Asa's big-booted foot slammed down onto the burning bundle. He extinguished the fire with his heavy stomps.

"That's crazy," Aubrey said under her breath.

"What's that?"

"How quickly it caught flame."

"Dried leaves have no chance in the company of a lit match." Asa eyed the parking lot, then turned his gaze back to Aubrey. "Did you see who tossed it?"

"Yeah, but I couldn't identify the guy, or anything. Just a guy in a suit, with a cigarette." He continued to stare at her. "Sorry."

Asa's mouth twisted sideways, a dismissive kind of twist that managed to ignite his dimple. Then he walked away.

A few moments later, Aubrey, back in her car, pulled down the visor to get a glimpse in the mirror. Aunt Molly would scold her good at the way she was scrunching her forehead into a nice crease. Maybe it was true that she'd get wrinkles quicker than she ought to if she continued to scowl like that.

She took a breath, forcing her face to loosen its tension. That's when she noticed she'd lost another earring. Great. A few minutes with Asa Kavanaugh, and now she looked like a cranky pirate.

Chapter Seven

Asa settled on the sofa and switched on the television. The beer was cold and felt good going down his throat. Scout lounged on the rug in front of the fireplace, his eyes nearly closed. A good nap was about to overtake him.

There was nothing on, and Asa wasn't in the mood to scan through his recordings. He had no head to concentrate on one of his favorite thrillers or crime shows. Not with that damned Aubrey Donner in his head. She hated him.

If it weren't for the fact that his orders were to participate in that stupid TV show, he'd almost enjoy her wrath. *Mad as a wet hen,* was what his mother would say. Considering the first time he'd laid eyes on Aubrey, that's just what she had looked like—-a drenched bird—it was pretty apt.

The rest of the beer didn't do the job he'd hoped. He wanted Dylan's observations from the other night to erase themselves from his head. He had no business noticing and thinking about this woman, good thoughts or bad—but especially not good.

He had a couple of hours before he had to be ready for the next K-9 promotional stop, this one hopefully more pleasant than the first. At least going to a cocktail party with the local chapter of the Elks Lodge had the potential of being enjoyable, and the Cornelia Inn always did a nice catering job.

Scout, as though reading Asa's thoughts, lifted his head to look at Asa. His ears were quirked, muscles rustling under his fur.

"Settle down, buddy. Tonight's event is solo."

Scout repositioned himself onto the rug, his body relaxing into nap stance.

****

After a shower Aubrey felt better, although all the water in the Atlantic Ocean wouldn't wash away the muddied concern of how she could get that *robo-cop* to play nice enough for her to effectively convince WMSL she could handle a recurring show.

She blew her hair dry and commenced the tedious task of the flat ironing. With each slide of the instrument that sizzled her hair into tameness she remembered Asa's mocking hands in demonstrating how big her hair looked after the rain.

She bet that hot stick in her hand would work wonders on his scoffing grin. She groaned. If she could muster on-camera cordiality with that guy, then she might be in the wrong branch of show business. She'd have to change her name to Ms. Houdini.

Her go-to black dress was still in the dry cleaner's bag, another post-funeral lay away. She pulled it from its sheer covering, slipped it over her head, and zipped herself up. She slipped her fingers into the slash pockets at her hips, and pulled out a single penny from each.

Staring at both her palms cradling copper disks, she couldn't fathom why they were there or, better yet, how they'd survived the rigors of dry-cleaning. She put the pennies onto the dresser as she reached for her good earrings.

She fastened Mom's diamond and pearl droplets to her lobes, while scolding herself for losing one of her gold hoops today. She silently vowed to keep her damned paws off the ears tonight.

The lipstick gave her mouth some color, the designer brand her one indulgence from the fancy make-up counter at the mall. She and her Sinful Cinnamon lips were ready to meet Ira the clairvoyant Elk.

Molly arrived to pick her up promptly at seven. Aubrey suppressed the smile spurred by the woman's getup, though she had to admit, for seventy-something Molly McFadden not only had great legs, but she knew how to flaunt them.

The little black skirt looked great on her, but it was the silver ankle bracelet with the rhinestone martini glass charm that begged Aubrey's mouth to grin.

The Cornelia was a Ronan's Harbor landmark, an old Victorian inn. Tonight, when they pulled up in front, the place was ablaze with golden lamplight pouring from every window.

A couple of college-aged boys served as valets. Molly graciously handed a spiky-haired boy her key ring from which hung a purple-haired plastic troll doll.

Inside there were Elks everywhere. At least Aubrey assumed they were Elks, but how could she know? It wasn't like they had antlers. Women, wives or dates she assumed, milled about the Tea Room as well.

"Auntie," Aubrey whispered. "How do you know who's an Elk and who isn't?"

"Taste test." Molly said. She then giggled at what Aubrey assumed was her face's reaction. She could almost feel the blanching of her pallor.

"Loosen up, ducky. Come on. Enjoy yourself for a change."

Aubrey shut her gaping mouth. "I ask this at risk, mind you. Are Elk men's wives part of an auxiliary organization like the Elk-ettes, or something?"

"My Elk doesn't have a wife, if he knows what's good for him. What do you call female elks anyway?"

"Cows."

"Oh that would never do. How about *felks?*"

Aubrey laughed. She was in a room full of Elks and felks, and one crazy lady who expected her to relax and have a good time. Really?

Aubrey pulled her thoughts back to the moment, to the sight of the Tea Room, Cornelia Inn's latest addition. It was pretty, but not frilly, a tasteful blend of lushness and stateliness.

The Victorian décor was accented by just the right amount of antiquity to keep it from appearing stuffy. Old hurricane lamps filled with ruby-tinted oil were clustered on a filigreed shelf.

A needlepoint settee was nestled in the bow of a grand window. It made Aubrey think of her mom's chair all ravaged by Auntie's possessed little pooch. She couldn't blame the mutt, however. Her uninvited house guest was the culprit, and her motive tonight was to find the Elk that could chase it away.

The innkeeper, Sarah, a woman who had been a friend of Aubrey's mother's through the Garden Club, spotted her and Molly in the foyer and rushed to greet them.

"Molly, girl, look at you," Sarah said. She turned to smile at Aubrey. "Aubrey, how good to see you. How are you?"

"I'm well, thank you, Sarah. And you?"

"Couldn't be better." She smiled.

"Where's that hunky new husband of yours?" Molly asked, with a coquettish tilt of her head.

"Benny's inside serving wine. Go say hi."

There was a group of people near the free-standing bar manned by Sarah's newly-wedded husband, Benny Benedetto.

Aubrey and Molly made their way through the attendees, Molly pausing to offer hellos to people along the way. Aubrey nodded to anyone who looked remotely familiar, doing her best to banish feeling awkward as Miss Congeniality's sidekick. Her fingers twitched to fondle an earring.

Big, affable Benny greeted them and poured each a glass of white wine.

"Hello, you big hunk of gorgeous," Molly chirped.

Benny laughed, his face awash with a combination of embarrassment and humor. "Molly, did you start the party before you got here?"

"Drunk on your handsome face is all," she said, over a lifted shoulder. Aubrey wanted to dig a hole to escape her aunt's bawdiness. Or maybe she should ask to borrow the woman's how-to guide. Instead she took a sip of chardonnay.

"You'd better keep a close watch over this one," Benny said, with a twinkly gaze.

"No easy task," Aubrey replied, to which Molly waved a dismissive hand.

A man wearing a black velour sports jacket with a white rose affixed to the lapel appeared beside them.

"Molly, my love," he chimed, like a stage actor.

Ira Tobias had a close-cropped, neatly maintained

steely gray beard in direct contrast to the flyaway, overgrown cottony hair on his head.

Molly and Ira embraced loosely, she whispering something into his ear that caused him to smile.

"Ira, this is my niece, Aubrey Donner. Remember I told you about Aubrey?"

"Yes, of course." Ira pulled Aubrey's hand into his grasp, sandwiching it between both hands and giving it a squeeze. "It's wonderful to meet you. Molly talks about you all the time."

"Nice to meet you, too, Ira."

"Aubrey's in a bit of a tizzy," Molly announced.

"Molly…" Aubrey said, looking around. It appeared no one had heard, or at least had cared, about her alleged tizzy.

"She needs you, Ira." Molly lowered her voice and clutched his arm. "*We* need you."

Benny stopped filling a wine glass mid-pour and tilted his head, as if he thought he was hearing things.

Aubrey wondered who else might be listening. "Ira," she said, with a little laugh, "I'm afraid Molly's being a bit dramatic."

Molly put up a hand. "Nonsense. How are you going to get to the bottom of things if you don't put this in the hands of a professional?"

Ira's tone took on a physician's soothe. "Why don't you tell me what's going on, Aubrey? I could be the cure for what ails you."

Suddenly feeling silly, she regretted coming to the Elk's party, and just wanted to go home. "Um, Ira, can we discuss this at another time?"

"I can contact you tomorrow. We'll discuss my performing a séance.Ira said, looking to Molly.

"Yes," Molly answered for Aubrey. "And when you decide the time is right, I'll come with you to Aubrey's. I'll bring the pizza. Ira you bring the Ouija board."

"Splendid!" His voice was so full of glee, Aubrey thought he might spontaneously combust. "Of course! Aubrey, dear, let me ask you one question. Is there someone special who's passed that you'd like to communicate with?"

"Um…" She thought of the sleepless nights, the scent that invaded the air of her home, the crashed candlesticks, and Mom's poor old chair. "My mother. I think my mother might be trying to tell me something, although what's been happening doesn't seem like her, if that makes any sense."

"Artifacts."

"I'm sorry?"

"The way to uncover a message is to have the right tools in hand. Do you have a piece of your mother's clothing, a piece of jewelry perhaps?"

She touched her earring, her fingers enjoying the feel of the teardrop shape. "Jewelry, yes."

"Are those beauties you're wearing pieces of your mother's jewelry?"

Aubrey nodded.

"They're lovely, stunning," Ira said. "Any clothing at all? A hat perhaps, or a scarf?"

Aubrey looked to Molly who shrugged. "We gave it all to charity."

"Hmmm." Ira stroked his steely beard. "Have you checked the basement or the attic? The garage maybe?"

"The basement's almost all dirt, so there's nothing of Mom's there. The garage, no. Nothing there. Maybe the attic. I haven't been up there in a long time."

Ira snapped his fingers. "Scour the attic. See what you find. At least we have jewelry to use. Select a piece you know she loved, enjoyed. Good?"

"I can do that," Aubrey said. A part of her did not believe she was having this conversation. But her gut told her this was just what she needed to do. When she got home, she was going to the attic.

Ira grabbed her hand again, sandwiched it like before. "We'll learn what message is coming to you."

"Told you." Molly beamed, her gaze fixed on Aubrey.

"A month ago I would have told you I didn't believe in ghosts," Aubrey said. "Go figure."

"She's got a ghost, all right," Molly said. "And it's a feisty one."

"My specialty." Ira's tone pinged with confidence "You've come to the absolute right man."

And like a divination gone awry, the absolute wrong man appeared out of nowhere. Asa Kavanaugh, distinguished in a dark sports jacket, crisp white shirt, but no tie, had sidled up to the bar.

He hadn't noticed her, but Aubrey's entire body noticed him. Her eyes feasted. The breadth of his shoulders, his towering height, his sun-kissed hair. She drank in his clean scent. The tip of her tongue ran over her parched Sinful Cinnamon lips.

Maybe ghosts weren't all she needed to banish from her life. Stupid, useless attractions to the worst kind of guys needed their own exorcism.

"Auntie, I think I'm going to head home."

"Don't be silly. Why?"

"I have a lot of work to do."

"But we came together, Aubrey. You can't leave me."

"Oh. Right."

"Stay, enjoy yourself. Have another glass of wine. Benny-boy," Molly cooed, "pour my Aubrey another white, would you, darling?"

Asa, with his back to them, turned at the comment. His chocolate eyes zeroed right in on Aubrey's, holding them captive, rendering her unable to slap herself silly, like she wanted to.

"Aubrey?" he asked. His tone was less-robotic, nice almost, kind of…warm. Oh, she hated that, and herself more for noticing.

"Asa," she managed. "We meet again."

A waft of freshly-showered man met her nose. He had a glass of red wine in one hand and a glass of white in the other. He took a step closer and handed her the chardonnay. "I believe this is for you," he said.

"Thank you." She shifted her gaze to Benny, who acknowledged her thank you nod with one of his own.

Asa gave her a crooked smile, his dimple glad to see her. "I didn't recognize you."

What was that roundness in his voice? The sweep of his eyes stirred her blood, forced its current, heating her skin.

What does one say to such a thing? Thank you for not recognizing me? Did the fact that his eyes gleamed with appreciation mean he was glad she didn't look like her normal self? Whatever, she couldn't respond, nor breathe, because every inhalation was full of him.

"How did you think Pet Day went?" Her question was lame but at least it was better than the you-smell-good that sat on her tongue.

Aubrey couldn't help watching his lush lips close over the rim of his goblet as he took a pull of his red wine. She considered poking her eyes out, but she needed them too much.

"We do what we have to do," he said.

"You didn't enjoy the program?" *This will never do,* she thought. This guy needed to act like he wanted to talk about his job, or her interviews would be a disaster.

Too bad he couldn't just stand there. Female viewers might be satisfied just to look at him. Her hand floated to her earring, manipulating the pearl between two fingers.

"It was fine," he said. He shrugged. "I guess I'm just not the type that enjoys talking to people."

It was too bad they were only offering wine at this event. Right now she wanted a shot of tequila.

She uttered what she hoped sounded like a little laugh, as though his words were a joke. "We've got a series to put together for WMSL. You're on board for that, aren't you?"

"I have to be. Not my choice, mind you, but yes, I'm 'on board.'"

"Well, at least it won't be a big crowd you'll be talking to."

"Just you?" His eyes flashed with something she couldn't define. Though whatever it had been, disappeared as quickly. "We're meeting tomorrow at eleven, I believe. That correct?"

His eyes held hers and once again she had no response that would do her any good. The "yay" buzzing around in her head was out of the question.

"Yes," she said. "And, uh, sorry that I couldn't

help you with any details on the man that tossed that match into the leaves."

Asa shook his head. "Some people just don't use their heads."

Molly's elbow jabbed Aubrey in her rib. "Aubrey, love, introduce me to your friend."

Oh brother, she thought. Not only did she have to keep her body from singing in reaction to the man, but now Mae West had noticed him.

She introduced Molly and Ira to Asa.

"Greetings!" Ira bellowed. He offered a hand, which Asa promptly clasped.

"My, you're a tall one, aren't you?" Molly held her head at its coy tilt.

"Yes, ma'am." Asa grinned.

"And how did you two kids meet?" Molly's grin had to hurt.

"Molly," Aubrey said, locking her gaze to her aunt's. "Mr. Kavanaugh is the K-9 officer that I'll be interviewing for Mid Shore Live."

"Oh." Molly clutched her chest. "Of course. Aubrey told me all about you."

A heated flush rose up from her neck to her cheeks. She didn't dare look his way.

"Aubrey Donner. How the heck are you, kiddo?"

She turned to the voice and saw another of her mother's Garden Club friends, Virginia Allen, known to everyone as "Gigi."

Aubrey knew, as did everyone in Ronan's Harbor, that Gigi was Sarah's, the Cornelia's owner, best friend.

"Gigi!" Aubrey was genuinely glad to see her friendly face, but even more pleased for the distraction. She spontaneously gave her a hug.

"You're looking wonderful," Gigi gushed.

Sarah sidled up beside them, smiling. "Hello, ladies."

"I was just telling Aubrey how wonderful she looks."

"You do," Sarah said. "I don't think I realized, until now, how much you resemble your mother."

"Thank you." Aubrey was flooded with relief when, out of the corner of her eye, she saw Asa get pulled into a conversation on the other side of the room.

"Is that a new member of the Elks?" Gigi asked, glancing over to the cluster of people talking with Asa.

"That's Asa Kavanaugh," Molly said, loving her knowledge. "He's a K-9 officer with the county. Aubrey's going to be interviewing him for TV."

Both Sarah and Gigi asked in unison, "Really?"

"That's one fine-looking man," Gigi said, with a twinkle in her eyes.

Sarah shook her head. "Don't mind my friend here, Aubrey. She's the bad influence our mothers warned us about."

"Hey"—Gigi feigned indignation—"you can't blame me because I have eyes that can see. I mean, look at him."

Sarah gave her friend a playful swat, and instantly Aubrey missed her own best friend, Joanie. She made a mental note to call her former roommate to catch up.

"I heard you were at the elementary school covering Pet Day. That true?" Sarah asked.

"I was."

"That's different."

"It's, uh, for Mid Shore Live. They're considering me for a host spot in their Sunday program line-up."

"What's it about? Pets?" Gigi asked.

"Yes."

"So, you're a pet lover," Sarah said with appreciation. "How ideal for you then, huh?"

"Um." Aubrey's mouth couldn't form the *yes* that would have been the logical response. She made a mental note to appeal to her boss again. Perhaps there was another way for her to get a host spot. She simply could not be known as the *pet lady*.

****

Asa barely heard what the local committee members and their wives were talking about. Forcing himself to tune in enough to respond, and not appear rude, was a feat. His eyes kept wandering to Aubrey Donner.

It was better when she had looked like tumbleweed had landed on her noggin. Tonight, with her hair sleek and shiny, that dress fitting her curves, the heels, the legs…This was what his buddy Dylan would call a *conundrum*—just what appealed to him, yet the worst thing for him.

Aubrey Donner was a double shot of Kentucky bourbon. Tempting, great in the moment, but with regrettable after-effects.

Aubrey's gaze flitted from the conversation in which she was involved, and he caught the amber-colored eyes seeking him. Whiskey eyes. His mouth went dry. Somewhere deep, he stirred.

"So, I'm going to head out," he said to the people chatting around him. "Early day tomorrow."

They said their goodbyes, shook hands, and the whole time he was reminding himself that he was disciplined enough to keep away from Aubrey Donner.

In the past three years, any woman he'd spent time with had known just what to expect from him. He'd made it clear, up front, that he wasn't in it beyond the moment. Some nice ladies had bit the dust after one date. Others had stuck around a while, out of what he figured was curiosity. The end result had been the same.

But Aubrey Donner, this one-hundred proof fermented grain of a female, wasn't the carpe diem type. He could just tell. Too grounded, too immersed in her life.

His eyes glanced again at the appealing sight he'd have to work at getting out of his head. Her hand flitted to her earlobe where her long, tapered fingers clutched at the diamond earring that dangled there.

Asa pulled his gaze away, and his eyes landed on the eccentric-looking man named Ira who, too, seemed to be mesmerized by Aubrey. Ira studied her, and Asa was reminded of what he'd overheard. This guy proclaimed to be an actual clairvoyant? He shook his head. People were whacked.

As he made his way through the room, he noticed that Ira had joined a huddle of other men. With them were Sarah and her husband. Benny spotted Asa and waved a hand. "Asa, come here a minute."

"What's up?" Asa saw the worry on all their faces.

"We might have to call the police." Sarah's voice was a hurried whisper, panicky.

"What's going on?"

"There's been a robbery," Sarah said. Benny immediately put his arm around his wife.

"What was taken?" Asa looked around.

"Two guests had their wallets lifted," Benny said.

"Bert Raciopi and Ken Stang, here."

The two gentlemen were acknowledged with nods.

"And my wife can't find her watch," the one named Bert said. "And I know she was wearing it when we arrived."

"We want to keep this quiet, if we can," Gigi said. "The Cornelia is finally back on her feet after a disastrous year of remodeling. Is there a way not to have word get out?"

"We can't have any bad light shed on our establishment," Sarah said. "We've worked so hard."

The older gentleman beside Ira spoke up. "I'm Marcus Marzone, the Esteemed Leading Knight of our local lodge. I'm distressed that something like this could happen at one of our functions."

"This contradicts all we stand for," Ira added, nodding with concurrence to his leader. "We're a benevolent order."

"Our cardinal virtues are charity, justice, brotherly love, and fidelity." Marcus's voice nearly broke with emotion. "How could this happen?"

Ira touched his comrade's arm. "It's no one's fault, Marcus. Certainly not the Elks'."

"And you know for certain that these items have gone missing this evening?"

"Positive," the one named Ken said.

"In that case," Asa said, "here's what you can do. If you choose, you can hold off filing a report until tomorrow morning." He turned his attention to Sarah and Benny. "That way your guests will have gone home, giving you a better chance at keeping a lid on it."

"That's a good idea, honey," Benny said to his wife.

"It could be as simple as maybe the wallets and the watch fell out of jacket pockets. After everyone leaves you can do a clean sweep of the place."

"My wife's watch does have a finicky clasp. It's an antique."

"See?" Ira said. "Maybe your cleaning person will locate the items."

"I'm the cleaning person," Sarah said, then pointed to Benny. "He's the other cleaning person."

"Tomorrow when you call the department they'll send an officer out to take your statement. Meanwhile, he's going to want a list of guests, anyone that is, or was, present this evening, or here at the inn over the last day or so."

"I can provide that," Sarah said. She touched a hand to her chest. "But certainly no invited guest would have taken anything."

"Just to be thorough, Sarah," Benny said.

"Catering people, delivery individuals, anyone that would have had access to the inside of the inn. How about the guys parking cars? Would they have had any reason to be inside the premises?"

"Yes," Sarah said, "if they needed to use the bathroom. And one of the boys came in to tell me he was taking the place of a friend of his that was supposed to be working tonight, but got sick."

"Get all their names," Asa said.

"Thank you, Asa." Sarah patted his arm. "So glad you were here."

As he turned to leave, his eyes landed on Aubrey's curious stare. Without thinking he gave her a nod. She bit down on her lower lip. He'd have to erase that from his head, too.

"Asa."

He startled to attention to see Ira at his side, consternation pinching his face.

The man lowered his tone and leaned close. "I have no inclination of whomever it was that did this. In case you wondered."

"I don't understand."

"You know, no spirits have revealed the culprit although there are spirits here. The inn's namesake, Cornelia Vander Mark, for one."

Asa stared at him. It was obvious the guy was serious, so he kept his smirk at bay. "Good to know," he said.

"But," Ira said and leaned closer still, his head almost on Asa's chest. "I do know that you've lost a loved one. A woman. I've felt her presence. She was with child."

Asa's heart rattled in his chest. Was this a joke? His eyes, with new vision, surveyed the little man.

"Good night, Ira," Asa said, keeping his cool, but just barely. He didn't like people prying into his life, past or present. Who the hell was this clown?

"I just thought you should know," Ira called after him sotto voce. "I hope I haven't overstepped…"

Asa went through the door and didn't look back.

Chapter Eight

Aubrey still hadn't slept through the night and again three-eleven had come calling. Why that precise time? She was restless. The dream or whatever it was had engulfed her, stole her breath, making her sit upright panting.

Tonight, though, thoughts of another intruder swirled in her mind as well. Asa Kavanaugh.

She'd learned about the thefts at the Cornelia through hushed comments between Molly and the Elks' grand pooh-bah's wife, Nancy. It was Asa's reaction to the owners' dismay that stole any chance of slumber.

Asa had changed like a chameleon before her eyes. That stoic, distant action-hero-looking man had morphed into something close to human. She had watched Asa calm Sarah, touching a reassuring hand to her shoulder, his head bent, his attention rapt.

He was more than a robot. That was good for the county K-9 program and good for the WMSL series, increasing her chance at snagging the host spot. So, why did she not feel comforted? Why did the image of him—the seemingly genuine smile, the intent gaze, the palpable confidence—stay fixed in her head?

She grabbed her tablet and tried to focus on her inbox, tooled around on social sites, and finally decided she was up for the day. She shrugged out of her pajamas and darted down the hallway to the bathroom for a shower. She twisted the handle and waited for the hot water's steam to greet her skin. She waited some more. And more. No goddamned hot water.

She shut the water and pulled on her terry robe. Chanting a series of expletives, that rarely came to her lips, she charged down the stairs and opened the cellar door.

Snapping on the light switch, the evidence was clear. The cemented patch of floor where the furnace sat was at least two inches deep in water. The part where the floor was dirt had turned into a mucky mess of dark gooey mud.

The last repairman that had come to check the furnace had warned her that the hot water heater was also on its last legs. At the time she didn't have the money for a new one. And she still didn't.

There wasn't time for this. Her appointment with Asa Kavanaugh was scheduled for eleven this morning. She grabbed her phone to cancel, got his voicemail, and left a message.

She went to her bill file to locate the name and phone number of the guy that could fix her hot water. Ace Plumbing could come over in an hour.

She threw on an old pair of flannel boxers and her favorite *Welcome to Wildwood* sweatshirt with the frayed hem and wear-hole in the elbow. While she waited for the plumber she'd get some work done.

The plumber, a guy named Jimmy, arrived and after a quick assessment gave Aubrey the news that the water removal and replacement hot water heater would cost her upwards of six hundred dollars.

"Will you take a credit card?" She wondered how much credit she had left on her damned plastic lifeline.

Even Jimmy's confirmation that her form of payment was acceptable didn't ease her worry that her flooded basement might do her in.

Ira Tobias called while Jimmy worked his magic.

"Good day, Aubrey," he said. "I've called to tell you that Tuesday's the ideal day."

"I'm sorry?"

"For the séance. Tuesday evening at seven. Have you obtained a memento like I asked you?"

"Ira," she said holding the bridge of her nose. "I'm going to have to cancel. My hot water heater—"

"Oh, no, no, no. That won't do," he said. "It is imperative that we meet that evening. I have been called out of town at the end of the week. When I return, it may be beyond the ideal time to summon your spirits."

"Spirits? Can there be more than one?"

"Absolutely."

Aubrey's eyes scanned the room, her mother's kitchen, with the rooster wallpaper border above the chair rail and the dotted Swiss curtain on the window above the sink. This was her home now, her responsibility, her heritage.

This cottage at 44 Fisherman's Road was her mother's brick-and-mortar tribute to the tears and triumphs it took to overcome Grandfather Montgomery's banishment, and to give Aubrey a good life.

No stupid-assed ghost—or two, or three, or a thousand—were going to swoop in and demolish her inherited treasures, rob her sleep night after night, or mar her home's goodness.

"What time did you say for Tuesday?" she asked.

"Seven o'clock."

"I'll be ready."

She hung up the phone. The tidy room beckoned her scrutiny. The plates were stacked neatly atop the cupboard, the ceramic teacups were displayed on Mom's maple hutch. Were there any clues here, in this place she'd known as home all her life? Had she lived among and walked amidst what this ghost wanted?

The attic. The last time she'd been up there, a couple of weeks after Mom's funeral, she'd observed nothing remarkable. There were a few old pieces of furniture that Mom had sworn she'd someday find the time to refurbish, the old box of Christmas ornaments, and such. But clues? Maybe.

Jimmy's pricey project was complete, her credit card stripped of whatever was left on it. Now that she'd cancelled her appointment with Asa, she had the time to search.

Her mother had taught her many things, the most important of which was that she love and respect their home. And now that was all she had left to honor her mother.

The ladder was stored in the garage. Maneuvering the clumsy aluminum device through the hallway was not easy, and there were a few new nicks in the paint that showed its previous sojourns.

Aubrey positioned the ladder under the hatch cut out of the hallway's ceiling. She tested it by taking one step and jostling herself to make sure it was sturdy. Satisfied, she slowly climbed the narrow slats.

Near the top, she braced her legs against the frame and reached up to slide the hatch door away from the opening. She climbed the rest of the way to the top and hoisted herself into the attic on her knees, cussing herself for wearing boxers and not something to cover her legs.

It was dark, cold, stale, and thanks to the recent strange happenings, Aubrey was jumpy. She breathed out loud into the darkness, willing herself to *settle down*. Slowly standing upright she groped around above her head for the pull chain to the light bulb she knew was affixed to a beam. Why hadn't she thought to bring a flashlight?

Her hand found the chain. A forceful tug made the metallic links sound a loud crunch and the lit bulb cast a cone of golden light. The glow barely reached the corners of the attic leaving the objects stacked and stored against the rafters and tucked in the eaves in shadow. She stepped carefully over the makeshift floorboards, keeping in mind the exposed areas where one step onto the plasterboard could damage the hallway's ceiling below, not to mention send her sailing.

Her mother hadn't been a true packrat, but Caroline Donner did have a penchant for saving treasures. Aubrey found the old wooden highchair that had been hers and the wicker bassinette lined in droopy, faded gingham, as well.

Suddenly the air changed. The chilliness had turned frigid, and Aubrey could see her breath. She felt it again, that presence. Heart racing, she searched the articles, too curious to retreat. She needed to find something, anything that might give her insight, provide her with answers.

Tucked back against the pitched wall she spied a large leather suitcase. She shoved it closer to the beam of light. The brown leather was worn and cracked, and the brass corners were darkened with age. She pressed her thumb against the nub near the lock and it sprang open with a slap.

The interior was lined with a threadbare plaid fabric. Whose valise had this been? She'd never seen it before.

She lifted a small wooden box with a slide top. It contained a gentleman's sleek dark wood carved pipe with a swooping black stem. The aroma of tobacco was still present, but stale and displeasing.

Aubrey took a deeper whiff. The scent reminded her of the smoky smell that had been permeating her home inch for inch. She stared at the object in her hand. Certainly a dried-out old pipe hadn't the power to overtake her house. Tobacco had to be lit and burning to produce smoke.

A sudden chill ringed her neck, like malice-intending fingers. She dropped the pipe and shook off the feeling, determination in her gut.

She rummaged through the rest of the contents of the suitcase. An assortment of old frames holding black and white photos were stacked upon each other. There was one photo taken of the family when Aubrey's mother had been a small girl, maybe five. The three of them, in summery casual dress, posed in front of a natural rock wall, a vista of mountains and pines beyond.

How sweet and innocent Caroline looked. Cherubic cheeks and a twisty little grin showed a happy child, unknowing what sadness would befall her a decade or so later. The idea cut Aubrey, and she winced. Grandma Edith was so pretty in a cotton frock and wide-brimmed hat. The stern-faced man beside her wrenched Aubrey's insides—Montgomery Donner, II—this was her grandfather.

Montgomery stared into the lens, neither smiling nor frowning. His eyes pierced from the old photograph right to Aubrey's heart, so overpoweringly that she dropped the frame onto the floor. The photo stared back up at her, a crack of broken glass now cut across Montgomery Donner's stoic face.

A loud bang rang out from downstairs. Aubrey was frozen, the eeriness in the attic enveloping her. An old iron bed frame, leaning against the front wall, suddenly clanged to the floor, and she heard a sharp cracking sound.

An urge to flee from the space struck her, like a slap. She bolted to the hatch opening. One foot slipped off the plywood flooring and slammed down onto the plasterboard between two studs, sending a splintering of cracks over the area. She fell to her knees and crawled to the opening.

Peering into the aperture she sucked in her breath. The ladder had fallen down in the hallway, splayed like a dead body. *Shit!*

Chapter Nine

Asa was late for his eleven o'clock appointment with Aubrey Donner. The briefing at headquarters, regarding tonight's investigation in Neptune Junction, had run long.

Scout and he had a mission, a surveillance that would eat up most of the evening. This was what he was cut out for. Not posing for some nonsensical TV show.

The small house was tucked at the end of the road. It was a cute cottage, one Asa recognized as a craftsman-style typically built back in the twenties and thirties.

The shrubbery was overgrown and the shutters flanking the front window were off-kilter. Just like the unsolicited flip-flop that happened in his gut when he had caught sight of Aubrey Donner at the Cornelia.

He put his truck in park and sat in front of the house for a moment. He pictured Aubrey as she had looked at the Elks' event, sweet yet sultry, fire in her eyes, warmth on her lips, defiance in the way her chin tilted up to his deliberate and admittedly unwarranted rebuffing.

He spent too much time thinking about her, dangerous conduct for a guy like him.

He went to the door and rang the bell, then waited. While waiting, he reminded himself to keep the meeting brief and to keep his goddamned distance.

His eyes wandered over the aged façade of the small house. The window box affixed below the front window was rotted, its paint chipping. The place looked as if it needed a ton of repair, but it had good bones. Asa's in-born knack for fixing things enjoyed listing what he'd do to the place, if it were his.

Did he just hear the muffled sound of a female voice calling "Help"? Instinctively, he twisted the doorknob. It was locked.

"Hello?" he shouted. He knocked hard on the wooden door. Silence. Then he heard it again. "Help!"

Asa took a step away, charged forward with all his weight and rammed the heel of his boot against the door. It didn't budge, although he'd managed to produce a nasty gash across the oak. He stepped back again, removed one boot, held it firmly in his fist and slammed the stacked wooden heel against the windowpane that flanked the side of the door. It crashed into spiked shards. Careful not to get cut, he removed enough of the pointed pieces of glass to give his arm enough room to fit inside the opening. He reached around, gave the deadbolt a shove and withdrew his hand. He turned the knob, and the door opened.

"Hello?" he called from the entryway.

A hesitant female voice called, from somewhere deeper in the house, "Yes? Who are you?"

"Asa Kavanaugh," he replied. "I'm looking for Aubrey Donner. Is that you?" He paused for a moment waiting for a response. When none came he added, "Aubrey?"

A disgruntled voice sounded. "Yeah, it's me."

He took a tentative step toward the voice. "Are you

all right?"

"Not exactly."

She sounded pissed again. Was she always pissed?

"I heard you yelling for help. I had to break open your front door."

"You what?"—she groaned, paused again, then—"Can you come down the hallway, in front of you, and turn to the left?"

Was this legit or was it some type of trick? Was someone holding her against her will? He watchfully ventured down the hallway, his boot still in his grip in case he needed to whack somebody with it.

He eyed the furnishings as he walked. This seemed like an older person's house, with its outdated fussy wallpaper and a dried floral thing on the wall. A heavy smell of burning vanilla clung to the air.

At the place where the hallway turned, a fallen ladder was splayed across the narrow space. He craned his neck and eyed the square open hatch in the ceiling. The area around the opening was splintered and looked precarious.

In the dark cavernous space inside he saw the outline of a crouched female. He took a step closer and her face came into full view.

Aubrey Donner peered out at him. Her eyes were wide, her hair dangling long on either side of her head, her lips parted. Something in his gut flipped over like a pancake on a griddle.

****

Aubrey closed her eyes. Was this really happening?

"Well, hello," Asa said. He continued to stare up at her. His mouth quirked with a half-grin. "We keep meeting in the oddest places."

"Yes." She attempted to sound casual, as if she wasn't uncomfortable to be found on her hands and knees gaping out a hole in her ceiling. "But, why exactly are you here?"

"You mean besides having to rescue you?"

She closed her eyes again wishing she could vanish, better yet, wishing he would. "Yes, well, I'm not in the habit of needing rescue, although it must seem that way. By the way, why are you holding one of your boots?"

He looked at the leather boot in his hand as though he'd forgotten it was there. He met her gaze again. "I rang the bell and no one answered. When I heard you calling for help, and the door was locked, I had to break the side window. Let's get you down from there, then we'll talk."

He hoisted the ladder with ease and braced it at the opening. Her mouth went dry at the image of him standing at the base of the steps. For some reason her feet wouldn't move.

"Come on down."

She didn't move. What was wrong with her? This wasn't a trapeze. She eyed him again.

"I don't bite, I promise."

Ignoring his comment, Aubrey maneuvered her body and took the first step. She willed herself not to think about how her backside looked as she descended the ladder.

When she felt a hand on her back, it sent a charge of electricity through her clothes, under her skin, and right to her veins which whirred hello to the blond guy that didn't bite. *Oh, this is ridiculous.*

"You've done quite a job here." His eyes perused the cracks around the hatch.

Aubrey looked up and winced at the web of fissures. "Man, that can't be good."

He laughed.

It was a nice-sounding, easy kind of chuckle and was so contagious she felt a laugh bubble to her throat. "This stupid old house will be the death of me yet."

"Uh-huh, stupid house." He chuckled. "I'd say you ought to get that fixed sooner than later. It's not looking too sturdy."

Aubrey raked a hand through her hair, reminded suddenly of how she must look in her baggy boxers and ratty old sweatshirt. She tugged at the hem.

His mouth bore a nice curve, his dimple a deep pinch. That mouth teased her and the man didn't even know it. At least she hoped he didn't.

"Um, okay, well, thank you for, you know, helping me." She uttered a silly laugh that appalled her. "But, I cancelled our appointment. Didn't you get the message?"

"You did?" He checked his cell phone. "I put it on vibrate while I was in a meeting. I guess I didn't feel it. Ah, it does say I have a missed call." He met her eyes. "Sorry."

"I guess that's a good thing. Who knows how long I'd have been stuck up there."

She wracked her brain as it became more and more scrambled every time she looked into his chocolate eyes. "How's tomorrow morning before the first taping? Could you show maybe fifteen minutes earlier and we'll go over the segment before we roll. Would that be possible?"

He shrugged. "That'll work."

"Okay, good."

Asa turned from her gaze and walked down the hallway.

Aubrey followed him, noting his shoulders were nearly the breadth of the space. Instead of going to the door, he sat on the bench in the entry. *Oh, please get out of here before I stop hating you.*

She gave him her best "What are you doing?" face. He just smiled; the dimple blew her a kiss.

He waved his large leather boot at her. "Just putting my boot back on." He busied himself sliding his foot into the boot. "Wouldn't want to cut myself."

It suddenly occurred to her that they were standing amidst shattered bits of glass. Her gaze found the gaping hole in the side window next to the door.

"Well crap." She put her hands on her hips and surveyed the damage. She groaned. "Ugh, I don't know the first thing about fixing any of this, let alone the mess in the hallway." She faced him. "Did you seriously need to demolish my entry?"

Asa stood, eying her silently. He put his hands on his hips, too. "You were yelling '*help!*'"

She didn't like the way his mouth did a one-sided twist. "I realize that." She took a deep breath and let it expel. She fought to keep her temper in check, reminding herself that she needed this guy, needed his cooperation at the TV station.

Asa inspected his boots then met her gaze. "And, not for anything, but why didn't you just call somebody on your cell phone?"

"I didn't have my cell phone with me."

"Well, that was just stupid."

"*Stupid?*" She fumed. "Hey, I believe I know someone who did have his cell phone with him, but couldn't bother to check it for messages. Don't go calling me stupid."

"What I'm saying is to be home alone and go in the attic without a cell phone is a stupid thing to do. And my not checking my messages is what saved you from yourself. So, you're welcome."

"Okay, we're done here. Since you apparently know where the door is, how about you go use it?"

She held her tongue when he narrowed his eyes, his brows diving in on themselves. She wanted to let all the steam blow, but knew better than to make a total enemy out of this jerk.

But, oh yeah, she was mad as hell—at him, at herself, at the mess, this decrepit house of hers, the ghost, and the goddamned *Pet Parade* program.

****

As he strode to the door, Asa decided he was done trying to smooth this chick's feathers, and his captain be damned.

However, eyeing the broken window beside the door, he stopped. Even an unreasonable person like she didn't deserve to be vulnerable to God-knew-what might intrude through the gaping hole. Chances were there was an opportunistic thief on the loose in Ronan's Harbor.

Besides, this crazy-assed woman had a link to the media that, for some reason his bosses were convinced of, their unit needed to be part of. If he walked across that threshold with her in the spin she was in now, there was a good chance the TV show could do more damage than good to the K-9 Command. Damned to hell or not,

Mike would have his head.

Asa let his hand fall from the doorknob. He faced her. "Look, hold on a sec. You have anything I can block this opening up with?"

Aubrey folded her arms.

She looked kind of crazy in that getup of hers. Her hair all spilled out of the clip, still chomped on top of her head, holding not much more than a few out-of-control strands.

He did his best to keep his eyes from the length of her shapely, elegant, and smooth neck. Instead his eyes slid lower catching the way her curves were still evident despite the sack-like clothes on her frame. He squeezed his eyes shut, cursing them.

"Look, I may be a cop, but I'm also a pretty good handyman." His eyeballs behaved for the moment. "Before I leave, how about if I rig something here?" He pointed to the broken window. "Do you have any wood anywhere?"

He could almost see the wheels turning in her head. She was fighting with her urge to kick him the hell out. But he knew she'd eventually have to take him up on the offer. What choice did she have? He waited.

"I don't have any wood," she said finally, grudgingly. "At least I don't think so."

"How about out in the garage?"

"Maybe." Her attitude was that of a belligerent kid. "I don't know."

"I could take a look. If I don't find anything, I can run back to my place and find something that'll do, until you can get it repaired."

Her pretty eyes lingered on the hole by the door, her mouth pulled into a pout. "Okay. Let me get the key."

She disappeared down the hallway. He heard the phone ring and his first thought was, again, how stupid it was that she had gone up in that attic without it.

He heard her part of the phone conversation. The tone of her voice indicated that she liked whoever it was on the line. He'd yet to hear that pleasantness in her intonation when speaking to him, which was just as well. He liked it more than he should.

Waiting wasn't his strong suit. His eyes scanned the area around him. The house was a true craftsman with its unique nooks and crannies. The wide molding was in pretty good shape and he was sorry to see it had been painted over, and not left natural.

So this was where, according to the eavesdropped conversation last night, she convinced herself she'd seen a ghost? His eyes found a beat-to-shit rocking chair by the window in the living room. Its upholstery was a torn-up mess. Asa's old man, the best at furniture refurbishment, could turn that piece into something worth having.

But none of this was any of his business. The sooner he could block the broken window and get the hell out of Aubrey Donner's house, the better.

****

"Joanie, I still can't believe you called," Aubrey said again into the device braced at her ear.

While she talked with her best friend, she continued to rummage through the contents of the ceramic cookie jar that was ever-present on the counter since she was a kid.

Back then, of course, there had been cookies in the jar. Now it was a catch-all of rubber bands, used twisty-ties, and coupons she'd cut from Sunday newspapers when she'd had that going-to-start-using-these-things mindset. The key to the garage must be in there because it wasn't in the junk drawer, and it wasn't on the wooden key rack by the back door where it should have been in the first place.

"I've had you on my mind for days." She fisted things from the jar and laid them on the counter for perusal.

"Same here," Joanie said. "But that's no surprise. Even living apart this past year, we're still in sync. I miss you."

"Me, too," Aubrey said. "Listen, I've got so much to tell you. Tons. Crazy stuff. But, at the moment there's a guy here—"

"Oooooooo—"

"No, no, no. Not a 'guy' guy, a jerk guy, actually. But he's going to fix the broken window by my front door. He wants to look in the garage to see if he can find something to rig it with. I'm looking for the key. I never use the garage because it's so decrepit. I don't know where I left the key."

"Who is this guy and how'd the window break?"

"He's a cop, and he broke it."

"What? Why?"

Aubrey blew out a breath. "It's a long story, wrapped up in a whole bunch of crazy."

"You sound flustered, Aubrey. You're talking a mile a minute. Not going to lie. You're making me a little nervous."

"Eureka!" The key had been entangled in a cluster of paper clips so entwined it was like one of those brain-teaser puzzles she could never solve. She cradled the phone to her ear while she tugged at the metal clog.

"I was thinking of coming down for a visit for a couple of days," Joanie announced. "Is now a good time? I have a few vacation days I need to use, or lose, before the end of the year."

Unable to free the key from the tinny jumble it was in, Aubrey groaned. "Freaking key, freaking goddamned key." She remembered she had the phone to her ear. "Joanie, I'm sorry, what did you just say?"

"I said I'm coming down to see you, tomorrow, and don't tell me no."

****

Asa watched Aubrey emerge from the kitchen and stride down the hallway. It was obvious she worked at the sculpting of those legs. He forced his gaze to her face.

"Sorry it took me so long." The smoothness of her voice was gone now that she'd ended her phone call.

"Not a problem."

She held out the key which dangled from a paper clip, their fingers touching in the exchange. She yanked her hand back like she'd touched fire. The quick gesture surprised him. Wasn't she the fire?

"Be right back." He turned and went to the door. His head was scrambled with her, and he needed to stop this. "Do you have a hammer and some nails?"

"Under the sink?" She said it like she knew the question to an answer on *Jeopardy*. "I mean, yes."

"Okay." His eyes lingered on hers. The space between him and this slip of a woman seemed to close in on him. The air fused with an energy that begged for him to step in her direction, dared him...*just one little step.*

But he didn't do it. He stomped his way to the leaning structure standing at the back corner of the square yard. The garage had seen better days. If Aubrey hadn't found the key, it would have been nothing to just rip the door from its hinges. He felt like doing so anyway even though he had the key.

A square piece of particle board, warped and ragged-edged, would have to do. He locked up and went back to the house.

Aubrey was waiting for him in the entryway with a hammer in one hand and a mason jar of assorted nails in the other.

It was nothing to nail up the board, but the holes the effort put into the clapboard siding and the window frame would eventually have to be filled, sanded, and painted to ward off moisture seeping in and rotting the wood.

He slammed the hammer harder than necessary onto the last nail. His hand just needed to whack something.

"That should do it for now." He handed her the hammer, being careful not to touch her in the exchange. "You need to get an estimate for the rest of the damage around here. I know a guy, if you need a reference."

Aubrey put a hand to her hair and fiddled with the clip at the top of her head. "Do you know a cheap guy?"

Something inside him did that flip thing again. What was it about this woman?

"He'll give you a good deal. He's a buddy of mine, and he owes me."

"Then I guess I'll owe you." Her voice was warm like it had been when she was on the phone.

"Nah," he said. He pulled his eyes away from hers, hot like warmed whiskey, and his gaze flitted again to the living room. "What's the deal with that chair in there?"

Aubrey zeroed in on the chair. "That's my next dilemma." She shook her head. "I've got a slew of them these days."

"Well, I know a guy that does that, too. He comes with a solid endorsement."

"Um, thanks, but right now I'm overwhelmed with it all." She ran fingers through her dark, spicy-colored hair. "My world is crumbling around me."

Asa fought the urge to comfort her. His hands itched to console. *Don't invest.*

"I guess I'll see you tomorrow before the taping," he said.

"Um, yes."

He turned from the woman and left her house, wondering how the hell he was going to get through several impending encounters and keep himself from wanting her. Christ, he already did.

Chapter Ten

On the way to the station the next morning, dressed for success in her best suit, with all of last night's paperwork in her briefcase, and every duck in its row, Aubrey didn't feel ready.

This was it. The moment the light on the video camera blinked red could be the beginning of her future, if all went well. Her head swam with what-if's.

Would Asa Kavanaugh cooperate and loosen up on camera, be engaging, or would he continue to do his rendition of a two-by-four?

She remembered the way he looked at her at the house, his eyes shining with something other than that stoicism she'd come to expect. There was warmth in there. She'd seen a hint of it.

It would be good if that warmth were visible to Mid Shore Live's viewers, and certainly it would benefit her boss's faith in her capability as a show host.

That look of his had sent a shot of liquid heat through her veins yesterday which continued to warm her now just thinking about it.

And then there was Scout. Would his big, scary dog spook her in some way, tip her hand, expose her true raw fear of the beast right there for everyone to see?

She didn't know what made her more jittery— Asa's German shepherd, or Asa himself.

The moment she walked into the building, a production assistant escorted her to a room for make-up and hair.

The stylist, Patsy, a brown shaggy-haired, middle-aged woman sporting a powder blue smock, tapped the back of an awaiting chair. "Let's get you gorgeous," she said.

Aubrey plopped into the seat, staring at her reflection in the mirror on the wall. Her eyes were saucers. She looked like a scared rabbit, one of but a few animals that didn't freak her out. Why couldn't she be interviewing a bunny owner today?

"This'll be easy." Patsy swiveled Aubrey's chair a quarter turn, studying the image in the mirror. "Everybody's got good bones today."

"Yeah, right," Aubrey said. "I did the best I could with the hair."

"Your hair does have its own character." Patsy lifted a handful, and let it cascade back down Aubrey's back. "We're not going to fuss too much with your look. Wouldn't want to take away from your own uniqueness."

Aubrey felt herself relax. She didn't know what she'd been expecting, but was glad that it didn't appear Patsy had studied her trade at clown camp.

"Your interviewee was just here getting his glam on." Patsy laughed at her own quip. She made a sound like she'd just bitten into a double-fudge brownie. "Mmmm, mmmm."

A flush started somewhere at Aubrey's center and billowed along her skin, up her neck, to her face.

Her gaze caught Patsy's in the mirror. Patsy's smile quirked. "Now that's a man." Patsy winked.

"Poor me. Had to spend part of my morning touching him."

Aubrey laughed, though nothing about that felt funny. She remembered the way a touch of his finger branded her with a kind of zing she hadn't felt in a very long time. She was in no way in the market for a guy, having learned a long time ago that she had to go it alone until she was established enough to not need.

When, and if, that day came, then maybe she'd let the guard down. But not now, and certainly not with Asa Kavanaugh.

She had a half hour before she had to sit alone with him for their pre-interview meeting. *Deep breath.* She pulled one in, released it. Her chest was still a girdle.

****

Through the window in the conference room door, Aubrey saw Asa seated at the table with Scout sitting on the floor beside him. Thankfully, there was a black leather leash tethered to his collar.

The dog sensed her. His thick neck turned to the door, black eyes focused on her. Scout's ears twitched, his eyes pinned her. Aubrey's heart stammered in her chest.

In a flash the old memory flooded back, the unyielding clench on her leg, the slick black gums, pointed teeth, the bright red blood on her torn faded jeans, her own high-pitched scream. The twenty years since the attack evaporated, and the K-9 officer and his partner disappeared. All she saw was the wild-eyed Great Dane charging after her twelve-year-old self, seizing her, harming her, ripping away her peace forevermore.

Aubrey sped down the hallway toward the ladies'

room. On the way she bumped into her boss, Dean Manning.

"Hey, Blitzen, aren't you going the wrong way?"

"Uh, no, I…" She managed a laugh. "Ladies' room."

Dean lifted his hand and circled it in the air in front of her face. "Don't mess with whatever Patsy did here. You look great."

"I wouldn't dare."

Aubrey started to walk away, and Dean grabbed her arm. She looked at him.

"You okay, kid? You got stage fright?"

"No, I'm fine." She pinned on a smile. "All gussied up and ready."

"Good. Ace Ventura's waiting in the conference room."

"I'll be right there."

She was relieved to be alone and paced back and forth on the tiled floor. Arms folded across her chest, she breathed in and out, in and out. She could do this. She could do this.

****

Asa's back was to Aubrey Donner when she opened the door. He turned around and met her eyes. *Shit, she looks good*, great if he were honest.

The face-painter, make-up lady had tried putting goo on him and he had managed to convince her to leave well enough alone. "I'll admit you're pretty enough as you are," she had drawled, "but, trust me, Mr. Kavanaugh, the camera tells no lies, and you're going to need some concealer."

Right now Asa wished he had taken Patsy up on the concealer. He needed something to hide the way every cell in his body was reacting to the woman in the room.

Aubrey's make-up only served to accent what Asa already knew she had—beautiful cat-like eyes, a kaleidoscope of facets that wooed him. She stole his breath.

"Hello," she said. "Are we ready?"

There was something in her voice. She was nervous. Asa was paid a good wage to spot those nuances. He slid his gaze to Scout whose eyes were intent on her. Scout smelled her leeriness.

Her eyes fixated on Scout and her mouth, painted an appealing, glossy tone, was pulled down at the edges.

"Scout and I are. How about you?"

Chapter Eleven

It was hot under the lights, and dampness formed under Aubrey's arms and at the back of her neck. Eleven minutes. The entire segment was just that long, and yet one minute in she felt like it had been an eternity.

She could see the dog wasn't comfortable in this bright place surrounded by cameramen and the stage crew. Aubrey watched his eyes dart to all the strangeness around him. Her insides jumped every time he adjusted himself in his seated position at Asa's feet.

Asa, handsome in the light, sat like a mannequin propped in the upholstered seat. The small coffee table between them acted as a proper buffer from her inward pull to the man.

Aubrey tried. Her questions, the very ones they had gone over in the conference room, were direct and pertinent.

After a forty-five second introduction, in which Asa had responded like a robot, she asked, "Tell us about life as a canine handler for the police department."

"The principle duty of the police canine is to serve as support in general law enforcement. They can be used to track lost persons or fleeing suspects, search for discarded or lost evidence, hidden contraband, detect illegal drugs, search buildings, and help protect officers."

"The dogs live with their handlers?"

"They do."

"Can you tell us why that is?"

"To better facilitate bonding and the working relationship between the canine and the handler."

Aubrey had to extend herself to the animal. Her knees knocked as she regarded him and gave him an appreciative smile.

"He sure is handsome." It wasn't a lie.

The dog was as striking as his handler. Scout was regal, his markings—from what she knew of markings, which was almost nothing—seemed perfect. She pulled her eyes from his black ones when his ears quirked.

Asa patted Scout on his firm back. She waited for Asa to take the agreed-on cue of her words, as they had discussed in the conference room, as his opportunity to expound. The mannequin just sat there.

"Tell us what it's like having a dog in the house that's not a pet," she prompted, hoping he'd grab the lead-in. A bead of sweat trickled down her spine.

She bore her gaze into his, ignoring the jiggly affect of woo in his liquid chocolate orbs. *Speak*, her mind screamed at him. *You-hoo!*

"So, since Scout is not a household pet—a part of your family, as most people regard an animal in their homes—how does that differentiate in the maintenance of the dog?"

Asa spoke, finally, "Well, first off Scout is a working dog."

She thought she caught an apology in his gaze, but if it had been there, it zapped away in a flash.

"The canine is regarded as specialized equipment.

Scout here has been provided by the department to assist me in carrying out my job effectively."

The eleven minutes somehow drew to a close, and Aubrey ended the segment with the announcement that there would be three more segments with Officer Kavanaugh and Scout. *God help me.*

Her blouse, her only pure silk garment, was surely ruined by her own perspiration. For the next taping she'd be sure to wear cotton.

****

Alone with Dean in his office, Aubrey fidgeted. She hated the feeling it gave her to be seated in front of him waiting for his critique of her first go-round of *Pet Parade.*

She wasn't kidding herself. It had been more like a pet funeral than a parade, with the low energy of the interview. What was she supposed to do with a mannequin? Make him a rock star?

"Okay, give it to me straight," she said. She wanted to get it over with so she could go home and take a shower, rid herself of her own stink.

"Not bad." Dean lifted his gaze to meet hers. "What you've got on your side is that Melanie Robertson thinks Officer Ace Ventura is the best thing since the Scooter Pie."

"She does?" It shocked her. Asa had been just shy of a nuisance. "How's that possible?"

Dean wiggled his bushy eyebrows, two caterpillars doing a jig.

Anger charged up her spine where not long ago perspiration had made its trail. She bolted upright in the chair.

"Are you seriously telling me this guy gets a free

pass because Melanie likes the way he looks? Why doesn't she just send women's equality in the workplace straight to the guillotine?"

"Calm down, Blitzen. You're starting to blotch. Listen, I happen to know she's kind of crushing on the guy, but don't get me wrong. Melanie wants *Pet Parade* to score big, and even a pretty face ain't going to magically make it a hit."

"Well, maybe she can get him to speak up, then. Tell her to give it a whirl. Apparently I render him lifeless."

"Sheesh, you're your own worst enemy. You did a good job pulling the words out of him. I know that, and Melanie Robertson knows that, too. Also, the footage of the pet day at the elementary school was good. Melanie liked it. The audience response was positive. You're better than you think. All you've got to do is loosen up Ace. I'm convinced you can do that."

"I can't turn a two-by-four into a human being. I am not Geppetto."

Dean's eyebrows danced again, and he batted his eyelids. "Sure you can."

"Will I get fired if I throw something at you?"

Dean laughed. "Ah, you kill me, Blitzen."

****

"You have no choice, Kavanaugh. Get over it."

The captain sat at the edge of his desk. Asa was in the guest chair opposite him, leg crossed with one booted foot resting on his other knee. "I'm not cut out for this, Michael." He shook his head to toss away the miserable memory of his poor performance. "I'd rather get a root canal."

"Asa." Michael leaned in. "Buddy, the program's

on the line. I told you the county's giving us heat on the cost of what we do here. If they scrap the division, where will that leave all of us?"

Asa looked at the ceiling. "I've asked you before, a dozen times. Why me? I suck at this. Dylan Grant should have been your guy."

The captain shrugged. "The top brass chose you. What can I say? More importantly, that producer, Melanie Robertson, chose you."

"Don't joke about it. I seriously am not good at this. I'll hurt our program more than I'll help it. Wait 'til you see the video. I was awful. Really bad."

"The station said you need to lighten up a bit, so that you're"—Michael consulted something he'd jotted on a white legal pad—"more engaging, and more relatable."

"I don't engage. I don't relate."

"For crap's sake, fake it then. You going to tell me you can't play pretend for a couple of minutes?"

Asa opened his mouth to speak, but a sudden thought slapped a vise-like clamp on his jaw. *Am I already playing pretend?*

His chest was taut with self accusation while his mind rained with maybes. *Maybe* he was pretending to be happy with his life the way it was. *Maybe* he was fooling himself that he'd accepted the fact that Cheryl and their unborn child had been taken away by one miscalculation of an oncoming tractor trailer.

The thoughts would not be halted. Worst of all, *maybe* he was pretending that his body hadn't outrun his spiritual mourning. It was true. His body, his senses, his instinct all wanted to *engage and relate* to Aubrey Donner. And, yes, damn it, he'd been pretending those parts of him didn't want the same.

****

At home Asa kicked off his boots and gave Scout a fresh bowl of water and a biscuit. He dug into a mound of paperwork, hoping to officially shut his fickle brain off from maybes.

Recounting the lack of results of the empty warehouse inspection in Neptune Junction absorbed his attention. Scout had detected that drugs, cocaine specifically, had been present in the space, but it wasn't there upon their examination.

Believed to be a kingpin dealer's place of operation, the department had surveilled the site on two different occasions. One theory speculated the dealer was gone for good from that particular site, but hadn't gone far. How could he? His clientele, his runners, his contacts were all right there.

Oh, this guy was still in Neptune Junction, all right. And, damn it, he and Scout were going to find him. Then, perhaps, the department would release him from all these promo ops and just let him do his job.

The phone's ringing broke his concentration. The caller ID's display caused him to utter a groan. He knew this call was overdue. Thanksgiving was just a week away. He was surprised she hadn't called sooner.

Asa picked up the receiver. "Hi, Mom."

"Asa Kavanaugh, I am not speaking to you."

He knew the tone, playful with undertones of a zing to the sorry fact that he hadn't picked up the phone to call his parents down in Florida in several weeks, probably longer.

"So, you're calling me to say you are not talking to me?"

"Ha-ha. Never mind, you. How's my grand doggie? Put Scout on the phone. I'm not mad at him."

Mom still didn't get that Scout wasn't his pet. But, he knew enough not to bring that up again right now.

"Scout's napping, Mom. How are you? How's Dad?"

Mom sighed into the phone, the rush of her sorrowful breath meeting his ears with purpose.

He could see her now, standing in her bright yellow kitchen. She was most likely at the granite countertop that she loved so much she had actually leaned over and kissed the glossy surface when they'd first bought the Bonita Springs house.

Asa pictured her in the active adult community called Pelican Walk. Right now she was probably in her signature golf getup, that half-shorts-half-skirt thing and a polo shirt, a colorful visor tucked in her graying blonde hair. She and Dad had likely walked through a quick nine holes before the Florida heat had made their sport of choice unbearable.

Dad, he suspected, was now at the back door appearing to be focused on their small tidy backyard, though actually listening intently to every word his wife of forty-plus years was saying to their only son.

Mom sighed again into the phone. "We're fine, Asa. Your father's got plaque, but otherwise fine. We just miss you. We know you have a big busy life, but still."

His heart tugged. "I know, Mom. I'm sorry. I'll do better at calling. So, Dad's got plaque? Okay, so he's got to floss more or something?"

"The plaque is in his veins, but the doctor's convinced lifestyle and medication will curb the problem. We're both going on a diet starting right after Thanksgiving."

"Sounds good."

"Dad and I were thinking…"

Historically, those were dangerous words. God only knew what clause would be attached to that lethal lead-in. Asa waited, a thumb and forefinger pinching the bridge of his nose where a headache was destined to begin.

"…of coming for Thanksgiving. I'd like to make you a real Thanksgiving dinner with all the things you love."

Part of this was his fault. To avoid upsetting Mom, who had toiled through all the preparation of the grand meal, Asa had led her to believe he enjoyed all the offerings. Only he knew this wasn't true.

"Mom, that's a nice thought, but seriously the trip's a lot for you two. Isn't it?"

"Nonsense. We'll come up on Monday. That will give me plenty of time to shop and prepare. I know how much you enjoy my mashed turnips."

Asa especially hated the mashed turnips. But, he loved his parents. "If you're sure, Mom. That would be great."

"Really?"

Mom wanted more. She had him in her clutches, just the way she'd always liked it. He recalled her smashing him, just like the turnips, against her doughy self for a Mama Bear hug despite his groans. *I'm in it now,* he thought, *might as well relax and let her Mom me up.*

"Yes, really. It'll be terrific to see you and Dad."

"Okay, then. Louie, Asa wants us to come."

Asa also knew Dad's "Great!" with the perfect inflection of surprise, was no surprise at all. He and Dad were in the same boat when it came to the wants of Jenny Kavanaugh.

After the phone call ended, Asa was surprised that Mom had forgotten to bring up the topic of his dating. That was usually number one on her list when they spoke. He suspected, though, as he reached for a beer in the fridge, that she was saving it for Thanksgiving.

Chapter Twelve

Joanie smelled like rose petals, and Aubrey savored the floral scent that emanated from her best friend as the two embraced for a long moment while standing in Aubrey's entryway.

"God, I missed you," Joanie said. "So much."

Aubrey pulled away and stood at arm's length, the two women clasping hands. She couldn't believe tears were brimming in her eyes. She tried blinking them away, but the salty droplets tumbled down her cheeks.

"Sweetie"—Joanie gave Aubrey's hands a squeeze—"what's going on?"

She laughed, despite the tears. She swiped the back of her hand over her cheeks. "It's five o'clock. And it's Saturday."

A big infectious grin broke out across Joanie's mouth. "It is, indeed."

"Leave your stuff here—you can settle in the guest room later—because now it's martini time. Let's go into the kitchen, and I'll catch you up on the whole story."

"And that's going to require vodka, huh?"

"Top shelf."

The two friends sat at the kitchen's maple table while Aubrey poured the icy concoction from the tumbler she'd filled nearly an hour earlier and stored in the freezer.

Cheese and crackers and a cluster of red grapes were already on a ceramic tray in the center of the table. Aubrey carefully handed a filled martini glass to Joanie, complete with a fat green olive nestled at the crux of the glass.

****

Aunt Molly was due to arrive at six o'clock, to discuss the séance. The two friends were still sipping their same martinis and nibbling at the tray of cheese and crackers. The grapes were gone.

"A ghost *and* a TV show. I agree this *is* martini news." Joanie took another sip of her dwindling drink. She fished out the olive and tucked it into the pocket of her cheek. "I don't know about you, but I think both are cool as hell."

"Yeah, wait until the middle of the night when something goes smashing off a table or something. We'll see how cool you think it is then." Aubrey sipped her drink.

"I need another olive."

Aubrey poked a toothpick into the small bowl of olives and gently placed another into Joanie's martini glass. Then she poured what liquid was left in the shaker into Joanie's glass.

"Do you think it's your mom's ghost who's been showing up?"

"I guess so. We didn't have one when she was alive. I don't know what to do about any of it."

"Well, I do." The comment came from the entrance to the kitchen. Aunt Molly stood in the doorway, oversized black felt hat, with one sweeping brown feather poking out from the ribbon trim, on her head.

Approaching, Molly began a slow unwind of the

106

magenta-colored scarf from its intricate twist at her neck.

She sat at the table and flung the scarf with a diva's hand over the back of the chair. "Is there one of those for me?" She nodded to the stainless steel cocktail shaker.

"Hello," she said to Joanie. "How have you been, dear?"

"Great. Good to see you, Aunt Molly."

Molly let her eyes cast a blatant sweep. "Don't you girls eat?"

While Aubrey fixed another shaker-full of martinis, Aunt Molly and Joanie, acquaintances for all the years Joanie and Aubrey had been friends, caught up with each other.

"Were you referring to the séance when you said you know what Aubrey should do about this ghost stuff?" Joanie asked.

"Indeed."

"Aubrey says your man friend is a clairvoyant."

"Ira. He's coming here to perform the séance on Tuesday night. You'll join us, won't you, dear? The more the merrier."

"Awesome," Joanie said.

Aubrey could tell her friend's martini was doing the talking at that point. Joanie didn't use the word *awesome.*

"I'm not going to lie, Auntie. The whole business makes me nervous." Aubrey settled into her chair. "I almost want to cancel."

"You've no other choice, Aubrey. This ghost won't quit until it's heard, so you can't quit on the séance."

Aubrey shook her head. Could she really allow this

macabre ritual to be performed in the home she promised to protect and cherish?

The only sound in the room was the toppling of ice cubes as they clicked against the metal cocktail shaker while Aubrey poured the measure of vodka with a splash of vermouth into Molly's awaiting glass.

"Did you even notice my four-legged little love bug isn't with me?" Molly took a delicate sip of her drink.

"Where is Roscoe?" Joanie asked. She delicately placed a gnawed olive pit onto her napkin. She sucked the salty residue from her thumb pad.

"I hope you haven't banished him, have you?" Aubrey asked.

"Banishment, heavens no. But after his wig-out of the other day I thought it best for his nerves, and yours, that he not come here until after Ira works his magic."

Aubrey uttered a groan. "Why me? Why now?"

"Relax. Your ghost will be no match for my Ira."

Just over an hour later, Molly began the process of twirling her scarf back into place at her neck. She adjusted the hat on her head and grabbed her clutch. "So I bid you ladies good evening. Roscoe's bladder calls, and my squeeze is coming by for a while." She winked a blue eye-shadowed lid and quirked her rosy lips.

"Why is it that, of the three of us, Molly's always the only one with a man?" Joanie gave Molly a hug, another symptom of vodka. Joanie was usually more reticent with her PDA's. "You are so awesome."

Oh yeah, Aubrey thought, *Joanie's buzzed*.

The two friends walked Molly to the door and said their goodbyes. Joanie and Aubrey cleaned up the kitchen in comfortable silence, each with their own thoughts.

Aubrey's mind zoomed with the idea of a séance. All she knew of the ritual was what she'd seen on TV or in the movies. Were they ever really legit?

On some level it seemed like bunk. Even if it wasn't, would believing it to be bunk create a detriment to the whole damned thing? Like would her doubt short out a psychic wire or something? Her head spun, and not because of a few sips of vodka.

Later, after they had shared a sandwich and talked until they were spent, the girls carried Joanie's stuff up to the guest room across the hall from Aubrey's room. Joanie turned after entering the doorway. "It's too late now, but we still need to discuss Officer K-9."

"What?" Aubrey let out a scoffing laugh. "Why?"

"When you told me about him, you sounded all flustered and, I don't know, exasperated." Joanie's hands were flailing. "And we both know what that means."

Aubrey emitted a tired laugh. Joanie's vodka buzz was too endearing for her to combat, plus she, herself, was exhausted.

"What?" Joanie lifted her hands. "No comeback?"

Aubrey placed her hands on Joanie's shoulders and turned her around. She gave her a gentle shove. "Go to bed. You're tired. I'm tired. We'll talk in the morning."

"Okay," Joanie said, as she sashayed to the guest room. "But it just struck me—exasperate sounds like masturbate." She giggled, another byproduct of her evening's beverage. "I can't wait to lay eyes on this guy."

Aubrey slipped into her bedroom vowing to keep

her best friend on the planet from being in the company of Asa Kavanaugh. One look at the guy's blond hair, no-nonsense stature, soulful brown eyes, and Joanie would think Aubrey had hit an *awesome* jackpot.

A little while later, lying in bed and staring at the ceiling, a nightly ritual these days, one question burned in her head. *When did I decide his eyes are soulful?*

****

When sleep eventually came, Aubrey dreamed. In the dream, someone, an imprecise figure, was there in her room. Her eyes strained for focus. The vision did not speak or even move.

In her dream she called out "Who are you?" to which there was no answer. Her dream self sat up, threw the covers away from her body and charged out of bed. She was irritated. She breathed heavily. She demanded an answer and received none.

"Aubrey," the figure said. The voice was muffled as though coming through gauze. It came again. "Aubrey." Just her name, that's all.

Again she asked, "Who are you?" Adding, "What do you want?"

She was angry. Her hands clenched into fists and her arms fought the urge to start swinging at the gray shadow.

"Please, Aubrey," she heard. "Wake up."

"What?" Her eyes shot open, and she blinked away the dream.

Aubrey stood in the center of her bedroom. Joanie was there in front of her. Even in the darkness, Aubrey could see that her face was stricken with anguish.

"Are you awake now?"

"What's going on?" Aubrey whispered, feeling out

of sorts, nervous, jelly-legged.

"You had a wicked dream," Joanie said, relief trickling into her tone. "You woke me up. You were shouting at somebody. What the hell were you dreaming about?"

Aubrey sat on her bed and turned on the small lamp on her nightstand. A low beam bathed the space.

Joanie sat down beside her.

"You okay?"

Her eyes slid to the face of her digital alarm clock, but she knew she didn't have to. She already knew it was three-eleven.

"So, you up for a séance?" she asked her friend.

"Hell, yeah."

"No turning back now."

"Awesome."

Chapter Thirteen

Asa was called in to review the Neptune Junction drug case and had no choice but to send a car to the airport to pick up his parents. He was already prepared to catch hell for that.

While at the department, waiting for the meeting to commence, his mind mulled the arrival of his folks. He hadn't told them, Mom particularly, about his PR gigs with WMSL. He knew exactly how she'd react—over the top, sky high, rockets in flight. Praise over such idiocy was the last thing he wanted.

On second thought, there was one thing he wanted even less. Mom prying into his personal life, or lack of one. She'd bring it up. She always did. And considering that Cheryl was killed just before the holidays, December 3rd specifically, Mom was sure to have his period of mourning on her mind.

It would be four years. Hard to believe. Was he actually still in mourning? Mostly it didn't feel that way. His life, his day-to-day existence, felt fine—time spent, time lived.

Was he happy? Mom would ask. How would he respond? He was fine. Was fine *happy?* Maybe not. But nothing was worth another chance at agony. That dark intruder's clutch, woven along happiness's vibrant stem, was ready anytime to strangle it lifeless. Living *fine* was better.

Dylan came into the meeting room with their supervisor, Mike—the lead on the drug ring case.

"We've got word of a rendezvous that we'll be in place for. There's the chance we can bust this thing wide open," Mike said. "Kavanaugh, Grant, both of you are on for this one."

"What's the timeframe?" Asa asked. A spark of excitement enlivened him, reminded him of his calling.

"Friday night at ten."

"Black Friday," Dylan said. "We'll get them this time."

"This is it, boys," Mike said. "We'll meet again Friday afternoon. Enjoy your Thanksgiving, guys."

****

They'd already arrived. Asa knew it the minute he pulled his truck into the driveway. Scout did not let go one of his typical barks at the sound of his master's wheels hitting the gravel drive.

And Asa knew why, too. Mom had to have given him some crazy treat, a bone with steak still on it, a plate of scrambled eggs, a pot roast…who knew? It was inevitable. Mom fed all her men.

"There he is!" Jenny Kavanaugh said the moment Asa walked through the door. Scout sat at Dad's feet chomping on a rawhide bone the size of a femur. At least the dog had the courtesy to look up and acknowledge Asa, just before clamping his jaw back onto his prize.

"Scout." His voice was stern, the order direct. On cue Scout let the rawhide cylinder fall from his mouth. Lithely, the dog shot up from his lounged spot on the rug. He charged to heel at Asa's side, awaiting his next command.

"Oh, big shot. Let the poor boy enjoy his treat." Jenny came up and wrapped her arms around her son.

"Mom, we've discussed this. Scout's a police dog. A tool specifically used in important investigations."

"Oh, boo. You're a tool." She laughed at her own reference. She pulled away and gave him a scrutinizing once-over. "Handsome." She shook her head. "What beautiful grandchildren you're going to give me."

"Jen, you starting on the poor kid already?" His father pulled himself up from the overstuffed chair. He lumbered over and extended his hand, which Asa grabbed in a firm handshake. "Hey, Pops. You're in charge of Mom for this whole visit."

"Yeah, okay." He laughed and slapped Asa on the back affectionately. "Then I'll fly a rocket ship to the moon."

This was going to be a long holiday.

Chapter Fourteen

"So, while you work on your hot new television career today, I'm going to Franklin's Finds to console myself for still not being named Veep at my ho-hum company." Joanie slipped into her denim jacket, part of a bagel clamped between her teeth, as she fastened the buttons.

"Don't go turning my job into a Disney movie. That hot new TV spot, may I remind you, involves me—me!—being in the company of all things animal. And, that includes dogs—big, scary ones." Aubrey took the last sip of her coffee. "Trust me this isn't glamorous. It's insanity, beyond compare."

Joanie cocked her head. "Do the big shots at the station know that you're, um, not exactly a pet person?"

"No, because if they did, I'd be out of the running. So, many prayers have been lifted up, by me, that everybody behaves and there's no biting involved."

"Are we talking animals now or big, hot cops?"

"Oh, my God, Joanie. Who said he's hot?"

"You did."

"When did I say that?"

"Last night when I asked you what he looks like. You made that face you make, when you don't want to say the truth. So you just give the pat 'interesting.'"

"I don't do that."

"Yeah…you do."

"Since when?"

"Um, how about, 'So Aubrey, how do you like the color I painted my bedroom?'" Joanie changed her tone, doing her best rendition of Aubrey's voice, which sounded deep and ridiculous to Aubrey's ears. "And you say, 'oh that eggplant color is *interesting.*"

"Well, what did you want me to say?"

"The truth," Joanie taunted, pointing the half-eaten cinnamon raisin bagel to accentuate her point.

"Okay, fine. I'm not a fan of the eggplant paint. It's too dark."

"I agree. I already repainted the room. Now it's taupe."

Aubrey laughed. "You're crazy."

"So, now that we're being truthful. I'll ask you again. Is the K-9 cop hot?"

Aubrey stared her down. "Define hot."

"Would you go so far as to say scrumptious? The kind you want to jump, perhaps, and have your way with?"

Aubrey blew out a breath. "If I say 'yes,' will you go shopping and leave me in peace?"

"Yes."

"Okay then. Yes."

"Ha!" Joanie headed to the door. "Oh, how I know you, friend of mine."

****

While Louie Kavanaugh took a nap, the man loved naps, Asa offered to take his mother to the grocery store. She had a list a mile long, and he just knew turnips were on it.

Asa pulled his truck into the parking lot at the Acme. Mom's store of choice was across town. The

116

local food market just "didn't have everything."

After the yam selecting process, which felt to Asa like she'd taken an hour choosing one by one, Mom headed over to the bulbous unappealing turnips. She lifted one up for inspection.

"Look at these things." Mom held it out to him.

"Yeah, uh, I see."

She made a face when he failed to meet her expectation of equaled admiration.

"I'm going over to the liquor section; I'll meet you by the registers. And don't check out without me."

Mom had a way of not letting him pay for anything. And this lavish Thanksgiving meal was on him, whether she liked it or not.

"While you're there, grab me a bottle of those low-calorie cosmopolitans made by that skinny lady on TV."

He stopped and gave her a raised eyebrow. "Since when do you drink that stuff?"

Mom waved a hand. "The girls from the club introduced me. It's divine."

"Okay. *Divine,* huh? In that case maybe I'd better get two bottles."

"Good idea." She went back to the large bin to continue tackling turnips.

Asa grabbed a shopping cart and headed to the liquor aisle, beer section first. Loaded with a case of Dad's favorite brew—Asa could drink any beer, so it didn't matter that the old man liked domestic—he went in search of girlie cocktails.

The selection was chock with varieties. Which to choose? He picked up two different brands of the lower calorie cocktails and tried to compare the ingredients.

What did he know?

He craned his neck to see if there was an available clerk anywhere in sight. And that's when he saw Aubrey Donner moseying around the corner of the aisle. He cursed the calisthenic muscle pumping in the middle of his chest.

Her whiskey eyes found him, a flash in them betraying she wished she hadn't. A nanosecond's pause of her cart's wheels, and then she forged ahead in his direction.

"You know anything about this stuff?" he asked, surprising himself.

"Depends. What is it?" She came closer. A waft of something spicy and appealing met his nose.

"It's for my Mom." He laughed. "My parents are here for Thanksgiving. And my mother requested a bottle of cosmopolitans made by some lady on a TV show."

"Ah." She looked amused. A crinkle fought to settle at the corner of her mouth. Full glossy lips worked hard, he could tell, not to smile. His eyes feasted on that area of her face. He swallowed the idea that taunted his mind.

"This one." Aubrey pointed to a narrow bottle of pinkish liquid still on the shelf near him.

He put the bottles he was holding back where they came from and selected the one with the ridiculous brand name, Simply Savvy.

It made him laugh. "This stuff any good?"

Aubrey shrugged. "Who knows? I mix my own, if I'm so inclined."

"Okay, well, this is what the lady wants, so this is what she gets."

An awkward pause befell them. His eyes darted and, before he could mouth a good-bye, he heard his name coming from somewhere behind him.

"There you are. Come help me lift a bird out of the case. They're like bowling balls when they're frozen." Jenny Kavanaugh sidled up to her son's shopping cart and immediately took to eyeballing his companion.

There was no way to avoid what would come next. "Oh, hello," she said all sweet and charming. She slid her sly eyes to Asa, expectancy beaming in the brown orbs.

"My mother, Jenny Kavanaugh," Asa said, motioning a hand, palm up. He then directed it toward Aubrey. "Aubrey Donner."

"Hi," Aubrey said. The crinkle beside her mouth was back and, like that, a full grin broke across her mouth.

Jenny's face was bright, her grin broad. "Nice to meet you, Aubrey. What a pretty name." Her gaze took Aubrey in.

"This what you wanted me to get?" Asa held the bottle by its neck and tilted it for inspection.

"That's it," she said. She addressed Aubrey. "Ever try this?"

"No, but I do like cosmos."

Jenny leaned in conspiratorially, as though a shared like for pink drinks had made them fast friends. "Aren't they divine?"

Aubrey laughed. Her whiskey eyes danced with flashes of light.

If Asa stuck around much longer, he'd get goddamned drunk right there in the liquor department of the Acme without benefit of a single sip of anything.

"Thank you for helping me find the right stuff," Asa said. "And I guess I'll see you tomorrow at the station. Ten a.m., right?"

"Yes," Aubrey said. "See you then." She directed her gaze to Asa's mom. "Enjoy your holiday."

"Oh, the same to you, Aubrey."

Aubrey steered her cart past the two Kavanaughs.

Asa braced himself for an interrogation as he and his mother went to pick out a frozen heavier-than-a-bowling-ball turkey.

****

Surprisingly Mom waited until after they had loaded the hatch of his truck, and after they were buckled into their seats, before she began. "She seems nice."

Asa concentrated on maneuvering out of the parking space while an oversized SUV, with its blinker winking like an eye, waited nearby for the spot.

"Aubrey Donner. Pretty girl, don't you think?"

Asa blew out a long breath. "Mom, what are you getting at? She's just a woman that works at the TV station. She's the one who's interviewing me about the K-9 program. End of story."

"So, you two aren't an item, then?"

"No, we most definitely are not." He fought the visions that nudged his memory.

"Okay." Mom thrummed her peach-colored fingernails on the luggage-sized pocketbook on her lap. "Then it won't be a problem if I invite my friend Linda's daughter to join us for Thanksgiving."

His head snapped in her direction. "Time out. What?"

"My friend Linda. You met her when you were

visiting us in Bonita Springs. The redhead at the golf course. You remember. The woman with the furry leopard club covers in her golf bag."

At the moment, all his mind could conjure was an image of Aubrey Donner, soaking wet, with her leopard bra exposed through her gaping blouse.

Mom continued. "Her daughter, Amy, lives right here in New Jersey. She's a nurse at Mid-State Medical Center."

"Mom, why are you telling me all this?"

"Because Amy can't go to her parents' in Bonita Springs for Thanksgiving. She'll be alone, and I told Linda that we always get a turkey that's too large for the three of us, and…"

"Mom, no."

"What do you mean 'no'? You'll like her. I have her picture on my phone. She's adorable."

His mom fished her cell phone from her bag and began a frenzied search with rapid wags of her index finger.

"Oh God." Asa pulled into his gravel drive and put the truck in park. Before opening the door, he turned in his seat to give his mom his most pointed stare, and he knew it to be imposing.

"I am thirty-eight years old."

"I was there when you were born, so, yes, I know."

"If I want to be in the company of a woman, that's up to me. I'm not in eighth grade, with no date for the dance."

Mom recoiled in her seat, the pout on her face so pathetic he almost acquiesced. "Mom." He softened. "Okay? You'll let me handle my own personal life?"

"That's the point, Asa. You don't have one."

They unloaded the groceries in silence. Dad came out to assist, totally unaware that mother and son were in what Mom would call a "tiff."

The silence hung between them. Asa knew the woman enough to know the debate was not over.

Chapter Fifteen

By the time Aubrey reached her house, from her trip to the Acme, the rattled feeling had subsided. A residue, however, clung to her nerve endings like icicles. Asa Kavanaugh had found his way into her marrow. It was a cold fact.

The exchange between the man, who could have been made of tin, and his mother had been nothing short of endearing. Just seeing that someone on the planet had the soft side of his heart worried her. She was a sucker for his big, blond looks, but the antidote had been that she had every reason to think of him as a mannequin named *Ass Kavanaugh.*

That glimpse of sweetness—the way his mother beamed looking at him, the cute way his mouth screwed sideways when he acted annoyed—did not fool her. But those eyes of his, those deep brown portals, showed love. That was bad. Very, very bad.

She lifted the martini makings from the backseat of her car and slammed the door closed with her butt.

Inside the house, Joanie was in the living room staring at the garishly disturbed rocker.

"Hi?" Aubrey said, cautiously entering the room. Had the chair started up again? Had the ghost made a visit in her absence?

Joanie snapped around, and slammed a hand to her chest. "Don't freak me out, would you? After that dream of yours last night, just being in this place alone is scary."

"I hear you." Aubrey put her purchases on the side table.

The lines of fear disappeared from Joanie's face, and she offered a bright smile. "Listen, I'm not here to make you even more spooked."

"Well, good. I can't take any more."

"I have decided what we need to do is embrace the séance. Embrace the experience. It might resolve all this."

"Embrace the séance…" Aubrey mulled the words.

"Yes. Now, ready?" Joanie clapped her hands.

"For?"

Joanie darted to the ottoman, where she'd placed a white paper bag from Franklin's Finds. She withdrew an object from the crackly bag. She unfolded a large square of fabric, a tablecloth of dark purple brocade accented with ropey red fringe. It reminded Aubrey of a magician's cape.

"Do you love it?" Joanie said.

"Um, it's *interesting?*"

Joanie's hands fell in defeat. She flipped the cloth over her arm. "It's perfect for a séance. When I saw it hanging on a blanket rack I just had to have it. Come on. Please love it."

"Um, love's not exactly how I'd put it."

Joanie screwed her mouth.

"But, I have to say, it does seem perfect for a séance."

Joanie brightened. "I know, right? Ira the Elk guy is going to think this is great. Where are we doing this thing? The dining room?"

Aubrey hadn't thought about it, but that sounded appropriate. Every séance she'd seen on TV, or in a movie, had taken place at a table of some kind. "I guess."

"I'm starting to look forward to this voodoo event."

"That makes one of us."

"Embrace," Joanie reminded her.

"It's kind of tough to embrace what's been going on around here, Joanie."

"Okay, sure. But the way to deal with this is to blow it out of the water. Hit it between the eyes, and your weapon of choice is your Aunt Molly's boyfriend."

Joanie's face, alight with anticipation, struck Aubrey with a rush of memory. There were all the times she and Joanie had rallied for each other— through finals, and the disappointments over screwed-up boyfriends, and times like when the sober one nursed the not-so-sober one after a zealous frat party.

Aubrey pulled her friend into an embrace. "You are my weapon of choice. You cure me of all my ills."

Joanie squeezed her back. "Well, that's good, because my next diagnosis involves the big, blond symptom I saw in a clip on Mid Shore Live just a few minutes ago."

Aubrey pulled away. "What clip?"

"Your station is advertising *Pet Parade* by giving teasers, and I purposely accent the word, with footage of Pet Day at the elementary school. It was you talking with the Ken doll in the fatigues."

Aubrey grabbed the bag from the grocery store. "So, how do you think I looked?" She headed toward the kitchen.

Joanie followed her. "Gorgeous. When are you not gorgeous? But let's discuss this Asa Kavanaugh."

In the kitchen Aubrey unloaded her parcel. "Let's not." She put the bottle of vodka on the counter and set a bottle of olives beside it.

"Are you going to say he *exasperates* you again, because—"

"I wouldn't dare."

"Aubrey," Joanie said, in that lilting way she did when she'd decided she was onto something. "You yourself know, when it comes to the measure of liking anything, it's not what you say but what you don't."

Aubrey faced her friend and folded her arms across her chest. "I admitted that he was my type, physically, didn't I? On the outside, sure—yum, yum, give me some. But, he's an oaf, Joanie. A jerk, a crab ass. He looks like the Russian that killed Apollo Creed, and he's about as nice. Okay?"

Joanie held up her hand. "Okay, Lady Macbeth. Listen to yourself."

"I mean it." Even as she said the words, a new dread trickled into her veins.

Tomorrow she was going to the K-9 Training Headquarters to film Asa for the next installment of the series. At the moment, she could not shake the vision of the man and his mother as they'd been in the aisle of the Acme. In truth, he hadn't been a crab ass at all and he and his mother were charming.

But no way would she mention that tidbit to Joanie. Aubrey grabbed the empty grocery bag from the counter and crumpled it in her fists.

Chapter Sixteen

The county K-9 training facility was a low-lying building, its façade dark gray cinderblocks. Flanked on either end by two fenced-in pens, it sprawled across a wide grassy lawn dotted with browning leaves fallen from a grand oak tree.

Aubrey and Joe, with his recording equipment, made their way through the front doors and went directly to the check-in desk. A young officer had their visitor passes ready. Another officer, a woman named Regina, came out from a doorway and introduced herself as their guide.

Aubrey wondered where Asa was. They were scheduled to start filming at eleven and it was already ten-thirty. Anticipating a face-to-face with Asa was like being in the dentist's office waiting for them to call her name. *Just get it over with already.*

Regina, a tall, lanky woman with a tightly held yellow blonde ponytail, guided them down the hallway, past open offices where officers and staff sat at desks or milled about the spaces. Phones were ringing, machines were humming. Regina gave Joe and Aubrey a wink. "The hub," she said with a motion of her head, ponytail swinging.

Aubrey and Joe followed Regina through double doors at the end of the hallway, and they found themselves in a kennel. It came to life with barking the moment they stepped in.

"Don't mind the troops," Regina said in a raised voice. "They know you're company."

"Do they know we're *good* company?" Aubrey asked eying the gated cubicles and the large dogs contained in them.

"Oh sure," Regina said. "They know."

"I can take the *good company* from here, Reggie," came a voice from around the corner of a row of kennels.

Aubrey lifted her gaze, and it landed on the blond head and broad shoulders poking above a low wall. Her insides were a jumble. She could almost hear a dentist's drill.

Asa strode along the partition and uttered a "settle down," to which the barking dogs, in each compartment, silenced themselves as though they were privates in the military and their commander had arrived to inspect their bunks.

"Good morning. Joe, wasn't it?" He addressed the cameraman, who gave him a nod.

"And how are you today?" he said to Aubrey.

His eyes beamed with something she could not identify, a kind of flash that was distracting, unsettling. She looked away.

"We're good," she said to the wall. "Ready to get started."

"I'll leave you to your business then." Regina gave them all a swinging-ponytailed nod.

Asa led them through the kennel. When the dogs got a glimpse of Aubrey and Joe, with his somewhat imposing black duffle of equipment, another ruckus erupted. Aubrey jumped, grabbing her cameraman's forearm.

"You okay?" He cast a gaze to her vice-like grip on his arm.

"Yes!" Aubrey said the word too loud, sounding too happy, punctuated by an absurd-sounding chuckle. Her eyes were on Asa. She knew he was aware of the exchange. Her heart thumped in her chest.

She chanted what she hoped would calm her nerves. *Eleven minutes, eleven minutes.* The segment was just that long—shorter than a root canal, that was for sure. It would be over in a snap.

Asa brought them outside to the penned area and its training maze. Exercise apparatus dotted the patchy lawn. After Joe set up his camera equipment, they began to film the segment.

Aubrey, after studying her notes last night and again this morning, was prepared to nail the interview. She knew, in advance, that the staircase apparatus was crucial to the dogs' agility training and the tunnel structure was there to provide simulation of searches through sewer lines and confined spaces. She was ready.

Regina, and her swinging ponytail, appeared and gingerly stepped around Joe and his camera. She handed Asa what looked like a soft brown cast, the kind people wore when they had a bad sprain, and then departed quickly.

Aubrey watched the exchange with breath held. She knew what that was. She'd read about that sleeve in her research, but nowhere in her script had it mentioned it would be part of their filming.

Asa met her gaze and went right into an explanation of the device. It was a sleeve the trainer wore to protect himself while teaching the dog to bite the hell out of a perpetrator.

Aubrey felt sick, a wave of nausea powerful enough to overturn a cruise ship surged through her.

"This here is a vital part of the training process," Asa said, holding up the sleeve. "I guess now would be a good time to demonstrate its use?"

"Uh…" Aubrey's eyes flicked to the camera, then pulled back to the thing her mind wanted to call the *sock of death*. Her head screamed "No!" With the camera lens pointed at her, and just knowing that Melanie Robertson would be watching while sharpening her guillotine blade, Aubrey smiled nice and said, "Yes, absolutely."

If her voice had been any higher sounding, she'd have airlifted and flown away like a hot air balloon. Before she could process what was happening, still thinking about how flying away wouldn't necessarily be a bad thing, Asa was slipping that *sock of death* onto her arm and tightening the Velcro straps.

It felt like a wrist-to-shoulder version of a blood pressure cuff. If it had been, she figured her numbers at the moment would get her a free trip to the emergency room.

"Wait a second." Her brain finally registered that she was now dressed as a chew toy. "You're not going to actually sic a dog on me, are you?" For the sake of the camera she chuckled, when what she wanted to do was lose her breakfast.

"Trust me, there's no danger. Scout is trained to relinquish hold upon my command."

She swallowed hard. The camera on Joe's shoulder was aimed at her and the lens did not lie. Was there a remote chance that any pair of eyeballs watching this segment wouldn't see that she was scared shitless? For a nanosecond she debated refusing the demonstration. That would certainly screw her bid for the host job.

"Okay?" Asa's eyes implored her. A sudden flash of what looked like concern glazed bright in the chocolate orbs. "I, uh, could call another officer to stand in."

"Nah," Aubrey said with a wink into the lens, or was it a tick that had developed from her nerves? "Let's do this."

Scout had been directed to stand at a pace of what looked to be about twenty feet. He sat tall, patient, eyes focused on Asa. All in a day's work.

Asa touched a hand to Aubrey's wrapped elbow and guided her to stand sideways on the grass, her sleeve-bearing arm facing the K-9 jaw waiting to charge her. Her heart thundered in her chest. The microphone in her other hand wobbled in shaky fingers.

"Ready?" Asa asked. He leaned down, his lips nearly brushing her ear. His breath was warm on her skin. "You'll be okay. Trust me."

She met his gaze. The reassurance in his eyes was apparent and sent a liquid charge through her system. "Ready," she whispered.

"Scout." Asa's voice was a deep, commanding call. The dog stood up, eyes intent, ears perked up. "Advance."

The dog bolted to her in a flash. Aubrey morphed into a victimized twelve-year-old, unable to breathe. Scout clamped his alligator-sized jaw onto the sleeve and thrashed his big head back and forth, as though trying to tear her limb from its socket.

It was an out-of-body moment, her eyes watching the dog's attack though not feeling it. Someone was screaming an ear-piercing call that reverberated to her spine and threatened to snap it in half. The pitch hurt her ears, her throat, her jaw. *Shit, shit, shit.*

Before she had a chance to faint, or die, or vomit, Asa called "red" and the dog let go.

Asa grabbed hold of Aubrey's shoulders and tucked her close. "Hey, it's okay. See? Look. Open your eyes."

Aubrey hadn't even realized she'd had her eyes squeezed shut. When she released their clench, she saw that Scout was sitting docile, content, happy as a goddamned clam, though panting from his exercise. She, too, was panting, gulping air.

"Don't worry," Joe said. "I cut the camera when you first started wigging out."

"Wigging out?" Aubrey karate-chopped Asa to free herself from the hold of his big arm. "You had no right to spring that on me. That wasn't in the script, you ass. I hope you had fun scaring the crap out of me."

"Whoa," Asa said, his body tensing. "I offered to have an officer stand in. Calm down. You're the one that gave the go-ahead. I told you it would be okay."

"Aubrey," Joe said. "Let's take a break. I've got all day, you know, unless I get *the call.*"

Aubrey eyed the officer and his dog. They both watched her intently. "No," she said. "Let's roll. We need to have shots of the dog running the maze."

Aubrey was shaking, her nerves protracted like claws. She couldn't pull her eyes from the calm, unassuming dog.

Scout tilted his head as he studied her, then he took

a step in her direction, another. She was frozen. When had Asa removed the apparatus from her arm? At her feet, Scout sat and angled his head, and waited.

She had begun to breathe more evenly.

"He's a smart dog. He knows you're upset," Asa said.

"Yeah, well, thanks to him." She flashed Asa a look. "And you."

Asa shook his head. "I thought you were running this show." He uttered a scoffing laugh.

The dog nudged her leg, his forehead tapping her kneecap. He was a beautiful animal, as far as his outward appearance was concerned. But so were tigers. No one would ever guess that just minutes ago the dog had had a grip on her arm.

It really was amazing how Scout gave no indication that he wasn't in complete control and under the command of his handler. She tried to relax.

"Waiting on you," Joe said, his voice kind.

Scout tapped her kneecap again. Then he looked up at her with big black eyes, soft like velvet.

"Okay, let's finish this," she said.

Camera rolling, Scout trotted alongside his master. Asa prepared the dog for running the stations in the maze. He spoke in sharp-toned commands to the animal.

The dog's black eyes held Asa's with discernible intelligence that, to Aubrey, was unsettling. Whoever had coined the phrase *dumb animals* hadn't seen the acumen in this dog's glistening eyeballs.

"Asa, tell us about what Scout is going to perform for us," she said into her microphone.

"The entire course involves twelve stations, kind of

like a fitness trail. Scout, here, holds the record for completing the exercises in remarkable time."

Although Asa's voice gave no hint of admiration at the dog's prowess, Aubrey could see the tell-tale signs of pride in his expressive eyes. She was getting good at reading the man/beast duo, but it comforted her nil.

Scout dashed to the first apparatus, a low-lying piece of fencing braced over a ditch. It was Scout's job to scrunch his hefty self under the fence without displacing it.

Asa told the camera that if the dog were to dislodge the fence's position a buzzer would sound. No sound came from the canine's effort, and he dashed to the next station.

Asa provided appropriate commentary as Scout performed the routine in what seemed like a blur of time. Afterwards, the dog pranced to Asa's side and sat obediently at his heel. He gave the dog a perfunctory pat on the head.

Aubrey and Asa discussed the show in stilted, though polite conversation, after the segment was complete. She needed to pull relaxation from her well of ease hidden deeply inside. Ease and Asa Kavanaugh just did not mix for her.

Calm now, she knew her earlier lashing out at the officer had been an expulsion of fear. Mortification was a seed in her belly beginning to sprout. Asa Kavanaugh was onto her. She saw it in his eyes.

Fleetingly, the conversation with Joanie about the man's appearance came to mind. In today's perfectly-fitted cargo khakis, black tee, and lightweight black jacket—with its collar turned upward—he was a specimen.

She sighed aloud. Maybe Melanie Robertson would be so enthralled with his good looks on camera that she'd fail to notice Aubrey's ineptitude.

Her cell phone vibrated in her pants pocket. "Excuse me a minute." She withdrew her phone and clicked it on.

"It could be your ghost has it out for me."

"Joanie, what happened?" Aubrey turned away from Asa to avoid those brown eyes watching and reading her.

"I had just taken a shower and went downstairs to make myself a cup of coffee. When I was in the hallway, bam, a hunk of plasterboard clobbered me on the head."

"Holy crap." Aubrey whipped her own head around to see if either Asa or Joe were watching her. They both were. "Are you okay?"

"I'm okay, but there's a hole in your ceiling. I can see pink insulation. I'm not convinced it's done falling either. There are cracks all over the place."

"I know." Aubrey blew out a long breath. "I should be home in a little while. Stay out of the hallway, if you can."

Joanie started to laugh. "You know that metal tray you have on the side table? I held it over my head so I could go in the kitchen. I really wanted coffee."

"For crying out loud, Joanie. I'll be home soon."

As she hung up, Aubrey saw that now Joe was on his phone. Both Asa and his canine companion were staring at him with their heads cocked.

When she met Scout's gaze, he offered a soft bark of acknowledgement. It made her jump. Everything did these days.

"Problem?" Asa asked, eyes peeled.

"The, uh, ceiling in the hallway, from when I was up in the attic, is crumbling."

"I put out a call to my buddy, but haven't heard back yet. I'll give him a shout again today."

She rubbed her forehead which had started to throb at the temples. "Thanks, but I still don't know how I can, you know, swing it at the moment. I'll figure something out."

"Holy Moses!"

Aubrey turned to see Joe, cell phone plastered to his ear, had started to jump up and down.

"Holy Moses!" he shouted again. "It's time. She's on her way to the hospital." He went back to the device. "Charlotte? Char, you there?" He turned back to Aubrey. "I have to get out of here. Her—my wife—her pains are back to back. Nonstop. That means this is happening now, doesn't it?"

"I think so." Aubrey turned instinctively to Asa.

"Sounds like it," he offered. "How is your wife getting to the hospital?"

"What? Oh, um, her sister Jackie. She's calling from Jackie's car. I have to go."

"Go!" Aubrey said, getting wrapped up in his frenzied energy. "Don't worry about us here."

Joe trudged off with his equipment flopping on his back. He turned around. "I'm going to be a father *today!*" His eyes were saucers.

"Good luck, Joe."

He disappeared around the corner. It was then that Aubrey realized she had come here with Joe and she was now stranded, alone with Asa Kavanaugh, his pony-sized dog, and Fate—her cruel companion.

Chapter Seventeen

Asa eyed Aubrey Donner. *She's terrified of Scout.* It was evident. Every time Scout moved a muscle she jumped. He'd seen the fear in her eyes, witnessed the magnitude of it during the demo debacle.

Having regained her composure after the troubling phone call, followed by her cameraman's excited departure, she said, "How exciting. For Joe and his wife, I mean."

Aubrey fiddled with her earring. "About the segment...they'll edit it, you know, so it will be fine."

"Sure," he said without much conviction. "We're halfway through with the series now."

"I see you're thrilled about that." She uttered a chuckle. "Since my ride just left to go have a baby, I'm going to have to call for a lift. Can I wait in the reception area?"

Before he had a chance to think it through, Asa opened his mouth. "You going home? I can give you a lift."

Her face fell. He saw her eyes flit to Scout. She was probably freaking about being closed in a truck cab with the dog. "He goes in a cage in the back."

"What?" She laughed, putting a hand to her chest. "No, that's not it. Thank you, but I can call my friend who's visiting. She'll be more than happy to come get me."

"Anything to avoid falling plasterboard, you mean?"

She closed her lips and studied him a beat.

The sunshine brings out the amber-like flecks in her eyes. He shook the thought.

"Yeah." She tilted her head in, what looked to him like, dismay. She was hard up for cash. That much he had figured out. She knew jack shit about renovations. He had grasped that, too.

"Look, let me drop you home. I'll check out the recent damage, and make things safe. Then I can let my friend know everything that needs doing."

She was about to protest. He could see it in her eyes, the set of her jaw, the way her teeth bit down on her lower lip—*moist, plump, pink.* He pulled his eyes away.

"Okay." The concession in her voice tugged at him like a leash.

****

Asa guided Scout into the backseat of the truck, where the crate's door swung wide open for the dog's easy entrance. Scout crept into the space and Asa flipped the latch. Feeling Aubrey's eyes on his effort, he gave the lever an extra, unnecessary, jiggle for the sake of her nerves.

The silence in the cab of his truck was thick, and it made Asa edgy. Finally, his racing mind came up with something he could say to cut the pudding air between them. "Are you afraid of dogs, in general, or just Scout?"

The way she turned her head, sneaking a glimpse to the crate in the backseat, he now decided it would have been better to suffer the silence.

Her eyes were on the hands in her lap, fingers entwined. "I was caught off guard," she said.

That was all she said, and he decided prodding would only increase the tension, not alleviate it. He drove on in silence.

Out of the corner of his eye he saw her hands busy in a tangle of worrying fingers.

"He's not going to hurt you."

"Doesn't everybody say that about their dog?"

Asa shrugged. "I don't know. But what I can tell you is that Scout is as disciplined a being as anything, or anyone, I know. You can trust me on this one."

"Okay." She offered a smile he didn't believe.

"He would never harm you. But I'm willing to guess something, or someone, did."

Aubrey flashed him a look before focusing her gaze on the road ahead of them. Finally, a soft question came. "Am I that transparent?"

"No. I'm that perceptive."

She rolled her eyes.

Aubrey Donner was on the fence about him. The disdain she exuded when it came to him had softened over the last couple of interactions. He felt like tipping the scale even more so in his favor.

He set his jaw. Two minutes locked up in a truck with the woman made him think all kinds of ridiculous things. Thankfully, he was just two blocks or so from where he would turn onto her street.

Quiet befell them for the rest of the way to her house. He pulled into her driveway and cut the engine. Why had he offered to assess the damage inside her house? A piercing thought shot through his mind. *You do not invest. Leave well enough alone.*

Her grip on the door handle, Aubrey turned to him, whiskey eyes dotted with worry.

"You won't give me away, will you?"

The sound of the request bored a hole in his heart, flooded his chest with warmth that he didn't expect, or want.

"How long have you been afraid of dogs?"

"Since I was twelve. A big monster of a dog decided to chase me home from school."

"Did he catch you?"

She released a raggedy breath. "Twenty-seven stitches." A hand brushed over her pant leg on the area of her thigh. "A lovely reminder."

Asa blew out a whistle of air. "Out of curiosity, how'd you wind up with this job then?"

"A crazy twist of fate." She shrugged. "It's my one chance to get out of the copy edit pool, and use my college training. And as you may have guessed, I could use the pay increase."

She motioned her head in the direction of her repair-starved house. "I have to hold onto my mom's house."

They held a long glance. There was strength in this slight woman who'd resemble a drowned rabbit the first time he laid eyes on her. She was still a skittish rabbit when it came to being in the company of her greatest fear, but the strength in her wouldn't let it stop her.

Another thing Asa had figured out about Aubrey was that her *crazy twist of fate,* as she'd called it, had put her in the best position to conquer what held her back.

His breath caught in his chest as he finally broke the lock on her whiskey eyes. Aubrey Donner wasn't the only one being navigated by fate.

"So, you coming in?" she asked.

Asa swallowed hard. "Yes."

****

Asa opened the back door of his truck and reached in to free Scout.

Panic made Aubrey's voice weaken with each word, leaving her last syllables a whisper. "Wait, what are you doing? He's not coming inside, too, is he?"

"Scout will be fine," he said as he watched the dog hop down onto the ground. "You know, I've also been trained in techniques to help overcome cynophobia. We could go over some of them, if you're game."

She blew out a half laugh. "You mean now?"

"Sure. It's easy." He reached back into the truck and withdrew Scout's leash, latching it to his collar. He extended the hand loop to Aubrey. "Here you go. You can lead him into your house."

She took a step backwards. She half-whispered, "Not a good idea. Really. But thanks."

He kept his voice low, but firm. "Take the leash, Aubrey." He held the black leather strap out to her.

Her eyes were saucers as they flitted to the dog and then back to Asa. A tug of her lower lip told him her mind was holding court. He waited.

****

Aubrey eyed her front door. Thirty footsteps. Maybe less. Not a far walk from where she was planted on the driveway, her feet blocks of cement. She hated this, hated the absurd requirements of this job. And she hated Asa Kavanaugh for being human.

Scout's black eyes waited and watched expectantly. She slid her gaze to the officer whose face had softened from the stoic angles and planes that had served her so well as a deterrent. His mouth quirked up at one corner in an appealing curve of encouragement.

Swallowing the protest that formed in her throat, Aubrey extended her hand for the leash.

Scout walked alongside her, his prickly fur brushing against her leg. She focused on her front door. The gash across the wood grain was a reminder that Asa had burst into her home when she'd been stranded in the attic.

Her life lately had been one disruption after another, beginning with the appearance of that damned ghost. She was sure the ghost couldn't possibly enjoy being suspended between what was and what is. She knew she didn't.

Aubrey looked down at her hand with the coil of leather strap wrapped around it. Her fingers were so frozen in place they might fall off and she wouldn't even notice.

Chapter Eighteen

The moment they entered through the front door, Scout tugged at the leash. He uttered a low-throated sound that made Aubrey jump. His head was angled toward the living room, his ears poking up straight, like arrowheads.

Aubrey swung her head around to Asa who had come into the entryway after her. "Here." She thrust her leather-wrapped hand out. "Is he nervous or something?"

Asa took the leash, his fingers brushing her skin as he unwound the strap. Her skin pricked with gooseflesh.

"He's fine. Scout's trained to immediately assess his surroundings. That's all." He reached to unlatch the dog.

"You're letting him go?"

"You did well, by the way. Walking him in, I mean. How'd it make you feel?"

"Okay, I guess."

The last thing her nerves wanted was Asa Kavanaugh asking her how she felt. Her thoughts and her nerves were a big jumble, but she wasn't about to let him in on that.

Asa stepped closer to her. She felt the energy coming from his body, his heat. "Take this," he said softly.

His fingers unfolded to reveal a cylindrical object on his palm. "It's his favorite. He obeyed you, and it would be good if his reward came from you."

She peered at the tan-colored biscuit.

"Go ahead. Say his name. Be sure to tell him he did well. Pat him on the head, too."

She swallowed, took the treat into her hand. "Scout," she said, the word squeaking from her clenching throat. "Here, boy."

She flashed a look to Asa whose chocolate eyes shone with approval. Something stirred inside her; it wasn't just the approval in his gaze. It was something more.

Scout turned away from his view of the living room, his black nose wiggling as he sensed the smell of the morsel she held between two shaky fingers.

"Put it in your palm. Let him take it from there."

She did as Asa said, rolling the cookie into her palm. Her hand quaked in the air as she waited for Scout to take his treat. Her eyes locked onto his oversized jaw, a glimpse of pointed teeth, the glistening dark gums, the protrusion of his tongue.

"Good boy," Asa said. "Go easy."

The command only made her nerves jump again. Did the dog need reminding not to pounce? Is that why Asa said what he did?

She wanted to drop the food and run. A little voice inside her, one that sounded like herself as a preteen, urged her to flee, to hide, to seek safety.

Scout lowered his face to her palm, his movement graceful and slow, almost poetic. His pink tongue lapped up the treat.

Aubrey felt his moist heat bathe the skin of her

palm. It tickled. Instinctively a smile broke out on her mouth, and she enjoyed the ease it brought to her face. She turned her hand over and let her palm rest on the bony top of Scout's head. She massaged the tightly-packed fur of his brow.

"Good boy, Scout," she whispered, the words catching in her throat.

****

Joanie came trotting down from the second floor, but stopped when the line of the wall along the staircase opened up to the view of Aubrey, the officer, and his dog standing in the entryway.

"Wow! Hello." Joanie continued down the rest of the stairs, her head cocked as she eyed Aubrey with a side glance.

Aubrey made the introductions.

After Joanie's lingering look at Asa, her eyes flashed to Aubrey.

"Say 'hi' to Scout," was what Aubrey decided to say in response to Joanie's quizzical gaze. She'd always been able to read her friend like a textbook page.

Joanie bent close to the big dog, with a kind of ease that Aubrey envied. "Hey, boy. Aren't you handsome?" She rumpled the dog's ears. She fixed her gaze back on Aubrey. "So very handsome, huh?"

"Yes," Aubrey said, her jaw tight. She silently hoped that Joanie was as adept at reading her as she was of Joanie.

Under normal circumstances it might have been funny for Joanie to wiggle her eyebrows at Aubrey regarding the fine specimen of manhood standing in her house. But this specimen was trained to decipher nuances, a sharp-eyed reader of people's actions. She hoped her eyeballs conveyed the big *don't* that she planted there.

"I hear there's some falling plasterboard to contend with," Asa offered.

Joanie pointed down the hallway. "It's a minefield down there."

"Asa's offered to get a friend of his to give me a reasonable price quote on the work that needs to be done."

"I see," Joanie said, with a tone that indicated she saw more than just a price-quote offer.

They went to the hallway. Scout followed closely behind them, sticking oddly close to Aubrey's side. Powdery chunks of drywall were strewn across the hardwood floor. Dusty bits littered the side table and the edges of the picture frames that now hung crooked on the wall.

"Well, this is just terrific," Aubrey said.

Asa gave out a low whistle. His hands were on his hips and his discerning eyes scanned the space. "You might need to have this entire ceiling re-plasterboarded."

Aubrey groaned. "Seriously, I can't even think about what that'll mean." Tightness clenched her chest as numbers rolled around in her head. Would she qualify for a loan? Would a carpenter take time payments? Did she even have the room in her budget for monthly payments?

"Where's that ladder you had the other day?"

"In the garage."

"Okay, if I go get it? I want to take a look up there." He pointed to the attic.

"Sure," she said with a shrug.

"Down this way, right?" He pointed through the kitchen doorway which led to the back door.

Aubrey nodded.

As Asa stepped away, Scout proceeded to follow him. Asa stopped and turned to the dog. "Stay here, Scout." His voice was filled with authority, and the dog plopped onto his haunches, just like that, and waited while Asa disappeared out the back door.

"So…"

"Joanie, not now."

Joanie laughed. "Not now, what?"

"Please. I can't deal with anything else right now."

"You do have your hands full. I'll give you that." Joanie's face was a mask of amusement. "So full." She spread her two index fingers to indicate something big and satisfyingly large.

"I will not engage in this line of conversation."

"Okay, fine. But I just want to go on record as saying that if you don't want to climb that manly man mountain, I've lost all faith in you."

"Are we done now?"

"He's like the perfect-looking guy for you. This would be like, say, a Latin football player wearing a black leather jacket, carrying, I don't know, a box of chocolate-covered cashews maybe, showing up at my door. I mean, come on, Aubrey. Accept this for what it is. It's a Thanksgiving miracle."

"Shhhh…" She heard Asa coming back into the house.

He was carrying the ladder with both hands, while talking into his cell phone wedged against his ear with his shoulder.

"This conversation is not over," Joanie whispered.

Aubrey shot her a look of warning while holding her index finger to her lips.

****

Asa spoke louder into the phone at his ear. "Yes, I can hear you."

"Are you solving crimes right now or anything?"

"Not at the moment, Mom. I am kind of busy, though. What's up?"

"Two things."

"Okay."

"First, what happened to the big roasting pan I brought you last year from Florida?"

"I have no idea."

"Asa, it's a gigantic speckled pot with a lid. Think."

"Ma, how about if I look around for it when I get home, okay? I'm in the middle of something…"

"Fine. The other thing, though, is about Amy, the nurse."

He groaned into the device.

"Oh, be quiet and listen. I talked with her mother, my very dear friend Linda who happens to be my golf buddy and mahjong partner, this morning. Linda's just so concerned that her Amy won't have homemade turkey for Thanksgiving. She's scheduled to be on duty at the hospital on Thursday, I think I told you."

"Yes, you did. But I'm pretty sure they'll have turkey dinner in their cafeteria for the staff that day."

His mother *tsk-tsked* into his ear. "It's not the same as homemade. Besides, she's a lovely girl, and it's time for you to socialize. I won't take 'no' for an answer."

He put the ladder down and switched ears with the phone. "Mother, I do not want to argue with you. We don't get the chance to see each other that often. Let it go. Please don't let this upset our holiday."

"Me? You're the one. I am serious. I'm going to invite Amy to join us for Thanksgiving unless you can convince me right now why I shouldn't."

He groaned again.

"And there is no valid reason unless you already have someone in your life, which you don't, so…"

He was desperate. He did not want to meet Amy the nurse, no offense to her or her mother, Linda. "Well, maybe I do." He had to stop this before she made that phone call.

Mom harrumphed into the phone. "Since when?"

"I don't tell you everything. Let's discuss this later, okay?"

"Are you lying to your own mother?" she accused.

"Mom. Please?"

"What's her name if you have someone you're interested in? Huh? Tell me her name."

He carried the ladder through the doorway into the kitchen, careful not to let it scratch the wall as he turned the corner. While his mother silently waited on the other end of the call he came face-to-face with Aubrey.

Chapter Nineteen

Aubrey didn't know who Asa had on the phone, but either something they said freaked him out or the ghost had been hanging out in the garage. He was looking at her with saucer eyes.

A loud cracking sound startled her and, in an instant, Joanie was at her side clutching her arm. A string of crashes sequentially followed like a fireworks display—*bam, bam, bam.*

Asa had shoved his phone into his pocket and dropped the ladder onto the floor with a loud pinging sound. Scout let go of a vicious-sounding growl. The cacophony stripped Aubrey's nerve endings, rendering them raw and bouncing around like live wires.

"What the hell?" Asa came closer to Aubrey and Joanie.

"It's coming from in there." Aubrey pointed to the kitchen.

Asa made a motion with his hand, and Scout darted ahead of him as they went through the doorway.

"This is nuts," Joanie whispered, as she continued to clutch onto Aubrey's arm.

"I can't take much more of this crap."

"Aubrey, it's okay. Come in here," Asa called.

Aubrey and Joanie went into the kitchen. The cupboard shelving, where her mother had displayed her collection of teacups, had collapsed. It looked like a scene of bone china homicide. The antique collectibles were demolished, strewn across the old hardwood floor in bits.

Aubrey reached down and picked up a chunk of a handle she recognized as the cup that had been her favorite—hand painted with delicate pink tea roses around the rim and the belly of the cup. Tears stung her eyes.

What little she owned was being smashed piece by piece. Memory after memory was being erased from her life. She pressed a clenched fist to her mouth.

"Let's get a broom and dust pan," Asa said.

"I'll get them." Joanie dashed from the room.

"This isn't trash," Aubrey said against her fist. Her throat was clogged with a sob that needed and deserved escape.

"Aubrey." Asa was at her side, his strength and calm like radiant heat, an antidote for her goose-bumped flesh.

Scout had sidled up beside her, pressing his body against her legs. His heavy-muscled self was almost a comfort, or at least she was still too flipped out by the damaged goods to think long enough about a massive dog being nearly on top of her.

She met Asa's concern-filled gaze and attempted to say something, anything, to chase away that brown-eyed sympathy. When her lips parted, all that came out was a squeak.

A big, solid arm wrapped around her shoulders, his fingers kneading her shoulder. Overtaken by the touch, the feel, the pressure, and the appeal of his nearness she did the unthinkable. Aubrey Donner grabbed a fistful of his shirt and tugged him closer.

On tiptoes she pressed her mouth to his, a zoom of excitement careening through her. His lips were sweet, lush. She'd regret it later, certainly, but right now all she wanted was that mouth.

Asa's arms encircled her and the kiss deepened, knocking any thought to stop right out of her head.

Joanie reentered the room carrying the broom with its attached dustpan in one hand and a waste basket in the other.

"I'm thinking poltergeist," she said. "A cranky-assed poltergeist."

Aubrey gulped air into her lungs now that the kiss had broken in a rush. Her betraying eyes filtered to Asa who looked about as shocked at her behavior as she was.

"You really think this is ghost-related?" Asa asked. His tone carried the deep warmth of a man who'd just been kissed.

Aubrey was mortified.

"I'm just going to gather the pieces so that no one steps on them, okay? I'll put them all in this container."

How quickly things change. Aubrey watched, as if suspended above the scene, while Asa took the broom from Joanie. He commenced clean-up with light-pressured sweeps of the broom that, to Aubrey, seemed almost gentle. The bristles fanned while gathering the fragments of teacups; his careful movements were reverent.

Her heart lurched. Kiss aside, there was just so long she could deny the kind aspects of Asa Kavanaugh.

The doorbell rang, startling both Aubrey and Joanie, the two friends sounding a unanimous sucked-in breath. Scout barked—not in response to the doorbell, Aubrey suspected, but at the palpable fear coming from the two of them.

The door opened. Aubrey spotted the squared edge of a pizza box before she saw Ira Tobias carrying it into the entryway, now preceded by a pungent smell of oregano and basil.

"We're here!" Aunt Molly's voice was a sing-song as she followed behind. "We've brought some pre-séance sustenance, slathered in cheese and pepperoni!"

"Did she say séance?" Asa asked, halting the movement of the broom.

"Um, yeah." Aubrey didn't know whether to laugh or cry at the way Asa's head quirked sideways as he eyed the latest arrivals.

"Just in freaking time," Joanie said.

Molly appeared in the kitchen with Ira, each dressed for séance success.

Ira's getup consisted of a too-shiny black suit, a white silk stringy-fringed scarf draped around his neck, topped off by a fedora sprouting a purple feather from its ribbon band.

An urge to giggle bubbled in her throat and, although she silenced it, she welcomed the way it relaxed her tensed muscles.

"Goodness, Aubrey, what happened?" Molly eyed the mound of broken china on the floor. "Are those your mother's teacups?"

"They were."

"Oh, Ira,"—Molly turned to her companion—"your expertise comes not a minute too soon. You do have your whole bag of tricks with you, I hope."

"It's not trickery, my dear."

He smiled. "Hello, Aubrey." He gave a slight bow. "So sorry for your misfortune. But, please, for the sake of this evening, I ask that you not remove the broken pieces from the room."

"Um, we're just going to put them in a container. That okay?" Aubrey asked.

Ira nodded, while his beady eyes surveyed the fragments and the collapsed shelves now leaning against the wall. "My, my," he said. "We do have a restless spirit, don't we?" He shook his head.

Ira faced Joanie. "And who have we here?"

"Joanie Pritchard. Hi." Joanie gave a demure wave of her hand. "I'm Aubrey's friend from college."

"Will you be participating in this evening's exercise?"

"Are you kidding?" Joanie laughed, the sound of levity a welcome break in the room's tension. "I've been dying to be part of a séance since I was a kid. So, yes, if it's okay that I join in. I mean, I won't be upsetting the vibes or anything, will I?"

"Only nonbelievers upset the apple cart, dear girl," Ira said. His mouth curved into a smile as he found Asa's gaze. "I believe the name's Kavanaugh, am I right?"

"Asa Kavanaugh, yes."

"The officer from the other night at the Cornelia," Ira said. He shifted his gaze to Scout who continued to sit at Aubrey's side. "A member of the K-9 Command, as I recall."

"Right again," Asa said. His mouth was turned into a grin, but there was no smile in his eyes.

"We spoke briefly." Ira's furry brows pitched together at the center of his forehead forming a bushy

"V" on his face. "I mentioned your lost loved one."

Lost loved one?

Aubrey and Asa's eyes met for a brief hold before he pulled his eyes away. He leaned the broom against the wall and dusted off his hands. "Mind if I wash up?" he asked.

"Powder room's down the hall, on the right," Aubrey said.

He disappeared through the doorway.

Ira handed the fragrant pizza box off to Molly. She, too, was dressed even more outlandishly than her norm. A white flower was tucked behind one ear, and her multi-colored broomstick skirt, swishing around her small frame, gave Aubrey the idea that the beloved woman might secretly wish she were a flamenco dancer.

Ira surveyed the room, his head tilted upward, nostrils flaring as though he were sniffing. Did ghosts have a scent? And if they did, how could the man detect it over the pungent smell of tomatoes, garlic, and pepperoni that swirled in the air?

"Yes," he said, satisfaction clear on his face. "The time is prime."

"Then let's take this into the dining room and dig in, shall we?" Molly said. She exited the room. "Aubrey, I have a bottle of cabernet in my bag."

Joanie touched Aubrey's arm. "Come on. Let's have some pizza and a glass of red."

"In a minute." She gave her friend a reassuring smile. "Do me a favor and get out the plates and pour some wine for everyone."

"Will do."

Ira offered a gentlemanly bow and followed Joanie

down the hallway.

It was just she and Scout, who continued to sit guard at her feet, in the room now. For the first time that she could recall, Aubrey was comforted by the presence of an animal.

She eyed the contents of the black plastic waste pail. The chunks of Mom's china collectibles lay like a pile of rubble. Ragged-edged pieces and halved handles were a sorry cache of brokenness.

The brokenness spoke to Aubrey, called to her heart. It was her job, her legacy, her promise to her only parent that she guard their home. She was blowing it.

She'd spent too much time lately cursing the old house, its high-cost needs, and how it all negatively impacted her existence. And now something, or someone, already dead was only compounding her broken promise.

Damn it. This was her house now, her life, and nothing living or dead was going to get in the way of what mattered.

"I think you've found a friend."

She startled to attention, finding Asa standing in the doorway of the kitchen. He was studying her, and her gaze fell to the third button of his shirt that just minutes ago was held fast inside her eager fist. His face, so handsome, was warm, his eyes shone while peering at the scene of Aubrey and his dog Scout.

She hadn't even noticed that one of her hands had drifted to the bristly place between the big shepherd's ears, her fingers kneading and burrowing into the fur.

"You think so?" She eyed Scout. He craned his neck around to look at her, his open mouth almost a smile, big pink tongue flapping out one side.

She tried to picture this beast chasing criminals, biting them, tearing their pant legs perhaps, but the image would not form in her head. All she saw was a pony-sized lump of fur so intuitive that he knew just how to win her over.

Her eyes found Asa's again. This was a kinder-looking guy. These big brown eyes were torches, melting her resolve to dislike him. Had the man taught the dog how to attain her turn of affection? Or had both man and beast accomplished it on their own?

She suddenly noticed that Asa had shrugged into his denim jacket. "You're leaving?"

Asa nodded. "Scout and I are going to leave you and your company to your, uh, event."

She cocked her head. "Are you taunting me about the séance?"

"Not at all," he said. "I, uh, just, you know, don't have much experience with crazy ghosts. My specialty, as you know, is living, breathing crazy folks."

She nodded, a smile finding itself onto her mouth. "Speaking of that, and since Ira mentioned the night at the Cornelia Inn—did they find the guy who pilfered people's belongings?"

Asa shook his head. "Not yet. But there's been a string of robberies from here to Beach Haven down on the island. They're following some strong leads. They'll nab them."

"Them? They thinking there's a ring of robbers?"

"Possibly."

"How do they determine that?"

A smile broke out across Asa's mouth. "Careful, Ms. Donner, your reporter is showing."

She laughed. "Yeah. Okay. These days I'm

concentrating on furry friends, remember?"

"At least now you can say it with a smile. That's progress."

His comment silenced her for a moment. Was that true? Was she smiling? Was she feeling less disdain for *Pet Parade?*

"Say goodbye, Scout." Asa came over and patted the dog on the head. "Time to go, buddy."

Scout nudged his wet nose against Aubrey's leg. Was this how he said goodbye? She patted his head awkwardly. "'Bye for now, Scout."

"Listen—"

"Please, don't even talk about it. I don't know what prompted me to, uh, you know, plant one on you. But, really, right now I'd rather forget it."

"Well," Asa said slowly. "I'd rather not forget it. It was nice. But what I was going to say is in regard to the repairs around here—"

"Oh," she said, and laughed. *This must be what it's like to sink into quicksand,* she thought. The more she thrashed to get free, the deeper she was pulled. "I guess this latest disaster sidetracked things." She took a breath and willed herself to think of anything besides his mouth.

"Oh, I know. This latest disaster got in the way." Aubrey shrugged. "But I've been thinking. Is there a way your friend could give me an itemized list of what each job would cost? That way I can kind of cherry-pick which things to tackle first. You know, so as to not break the bank."

"About that…" he said. Asa's mouth pulled into a thin line of hesitation.

She worried that maybe there was too much to be

done, the jobs too big for his buddy to perform, too costly. What the heck would she do then? A mocking *For Sale* sign jabbed in her lawn would kill her.

She folded her arms across her chest, bracing herself for what would come.

****

Aubrey's whiskey eyes implored Asa to finish what he started, though his conflicted head continued to debate. He was fighting the urge to offer to do the work for her, sans payment.

The expense of the work around her place would be mostly man-hours. He could charge her for the materials, which wouldn't be much. Fitting the work into his off time would be easy enough. What kind of door would that open, though?

Scout was still plastered to Aubrey's side. It was almost laughable to see the dog so smitten with the lady. Scout had good taste.

Asa watched her arms unfold and one hand float to the top of Scout's head again. Her long, pretty fingers rumpled his ears. Scout's eyes were slits of ecstasy. The word gave Asa a twinge.

What would ecstasy with Aubrey Donner be like? He shook the thought.

"Well?"

Her one-word question broke his reverie. The look in her eyes smashed his hesitancy like another china teacup thrown to the floor.

"Let me do the work for you. You'll just have to pay for the materials, but I'm pretty sure that won't cost much."

Aubrey blinked at him several times.

Shocking the shit out of himself, he tried and failed

to conjure his old motto—*don't invest. Trust me*, his mind implored, *I'm as surprised as you are*.

Aubrey's tone was tinged in wonder, her words a near whisper. "I can't let you do that."

"Why not?"

She shrugged, opened her mouth, but nothing came out.

He thought of his mother's latest attempt to match him up with her friend's daughter. He just didn't want to endure another tedious attempt at small talk and polite banter that would eventually go nowhere.

He was just finding out that all the time he'd been spending on what he didn't want had been keeping him from thinking about what he did, or could, want. He wished his own mind would stop working against him. "How about we strike a bargain?"

Aubrey narrowed her eyes. "What kind of bargain?"

"What are your plans for Thanksgiving?"

Chapter Twenty

"I don't understand," Aubrey said. "What's Thanksgiving got to do with it?"

Asa blew out a long breath. "My mother."

"Your mother?"

"You met her at the Acme."

"I remember. But…"

"She means well, but she's rather relentless in trying to match me up. At the moment her matchmaking efforts involve the daughter of a friend of hers, a woman she refers to as 'Amy the Nurse.' She'd like to have *Amy the Nurse* join us for Thanksgiving dinner."

Aubrey eyed him. "And?"

"And the only way to get her to back off was for me to intimate that there was someone I'm already interested in."

Aubrey's heart took on propellers and whizzed around her chest like a helicopter with no place to land. Her mind went right to the words *interested in.* Her brain recited it again and again. Was Asa Kavanaugh *interested in* her? And why would the mere thought of that send her heart into orbit?

Aubrey hated the idea, liked the idea, detested it, was intrigued by it. She was appalled at the yin and yang of her own life force.

How she found the words around the clog in her

throat she did not know. "I still don't understand."

"If I invite my own guest to the dinner table, my well-intentioned mother will cease her manipulations."

With a laugh that released air held captive in her lungs, Aubrey said, "I see." Relief—wait, was it relief?—flooded her chest, halting the whirling of her heart.

Asa just needs a favor. One favor in exchange for another. Simple. That's what he's interested in.

But did she have that in her? As it was, the wall she'd so expertly erected around her feelings was cracking, like the miserable plasterboard down the hallway, with each occasion spent in Asa's company.

"I usually spend Thanksgiving with my Aunt Molly. I couldn't abandon her."

"I understand."

She turned her gaze from the disappointment in his eyes.

Ira came into the room. "Aubrey, dear, come. We're discussing the evening's event. And if you want pizza, you'd better hurry. It seems our Molly has a penchant for pepperoni."

"Come, boy." Asa snapped his fingers at Scout who came to attention and trotted over to his master's side.

"You're not leaving, certainly?"

"We are," Asa said, with a nod.

"Oh, no, no, no." Ira wagged his head. "You must stay. We cannot perform a séance with an even number of participants. It's bad luck. We must be odd."

Aubrey, against her dwindling will, let her gaze filter to Asa. His all-but-talking eyes were telling Ira not to worry. They were, indeed, *odd.*

"Um, Ira, Asa can't stay. But the rest of us are anxious, eager to get started. Doesn't that make up for our even number?

"Eagerness is good, but openness is the key. All must be open. Those who are closed, unwilling, or unable to discern a presence would stunt the event, possibly render it useless." Ira turned to Asa. "Are you open to summoning spirits, sir?"

Ira's eyes bored into Aubrey's. "But it is imperative we have an odd number of us, and the séance must be tonight." His eyes closed and with a dramatic wave of his hand in front of his nose he breathed in, as though he were trying to guess the type of soup in a pot just by its smell.

"Oh yes, the conditions are ideal. Do you smell it, Aubrey?" Ira's eyes were still closed.

The same pungent aroma that had haunted her home before had crept into the room

"Vanilla Cavendish."

Aubrey whipped her head to look at Asa. Ira opened his eyes.

"Tobacco," Asa clarified. "I had a professor in college that smoked a pipe. That's definitely the blend."

"Oh, you'll do fine." Ira beamed. "Splendidly. This evening we're seeking to make contact with a spirit who's passed on. It happens to be the one-year anniversary of Aubrey's mother passing to the other side, so it is likely she is attempting to communicate something of importance."

Molly came into the room. "I can't find matches. Aubrey, Ira needs matches for the candles. Where are they?"

"Uh, yes, matches." Aubrey darted to the sideboard

and pulled open the top drawer. She fished around until her fingers located the lighter wand she kept around for her own candles. She handed it to Ira.

"I'd like a minute with Asa," she said.

Molly and Ira exchanged a look, then left the room.

Aubrey and Asa stared at each other, there in the kitchen surrounded by what Asa had determined was the scent of vanilla-flavored tobacco.

"Listen, Asa…" She laced her fingers as she tried to calm her nerves.

"I'm sorry you lost your mother."

It came out as a whisper. "Thank you."

"Sounds like you're looking for an answer of some kind."

She nodded, feeling foolish. "As crazy as that sounds, yes."

"I could stick around. But I'd have to run Scout home."

"Really?"

"Ira"—he pointed to the doorway of the kitchen—"said you can't do it without another person."

"True."

He smiled, the dimple in his cheek cutting deep. He slipped his hands into the back pockets of his jeans and offered a shrug. "Right now I'm all you've got then, huh? Looks like without me it would be a no-go."

Aubrey sensed where this was going. Her heart prepared for flight. She waited.

"So, about Thanksgiving…"

Chapter Twenty-One

On the drive home, Asa wrestled with the Aubrey-related scenarios that bombarded his thoughts. Pulling into his driveway he hopped out of the truck and released Scout from his crate.

"You like her, don't you, pal?" he asked the dog.

The dog wagging his big, strong tail, couldn't possibly understand the words, but Scout was an expert in tone. And Asa and his tone were screwed when it came to Aubrey Donner. Hell, he was going back to her house so he could participate in a séance. *Yeah, that would happen under normal circumstances.*

Inside, Scout charged ahead of him. The smells wafting from the kitchen were a succulent draw, particularly because the perpetrator of the aromas was an easy mark for doling snacks. Scout was sharp on that, too.

"Is that you, Asa honey?" Jenny called out. "I found the pot."

"Good." He'd forgotten about the pot, but was glad he wouldn't need to take any time to help find it. "Something smells good in here."

"Your mother's a mad scientist today," his father said from the doorway to the kitchen. Louie, in his kelly-green golf sweater, slouched against the doorframe, a brown bottle of beer in his hand. "I'm supervising."

"Hey, Pop." Asa tapped the old guy on his rounding belly.

"Blame your mother for that," his dad said, touching his own protruding midsection. "Best damned cook."

Mom was at the counter tossing a bowl of sliced apples in sugar and cinnamon, her fingers gloved in sugary granules.

"Pumpkin's in the oven." Pride gave her voice a deeper resonance.

"Man, we're going to be doing some good eating." Asa watched his mom's hands manipulate the apple mixture with practiced precision.

As much as he knew his next statement would get her going, Asa couldn't stall any longer. Time was running short. So, he took the plunge with as much nonchalance as he could muster. "You guys are on your own tonight for dinner, okay? I have to go out, and I'm not sure when I'll be home."

Mom ceased her tossing motion and wiped her hands on a spotted dish towel. "Uh-oh, nothing dangerous, I hope."

"No." He laughed. What would the old gal say if he told her he was going to be part of a séance? Certainly she'd think he'd lost his mind, because, after all, he had.

"Okay, but before you go…" His mother tugged a piece of paper from the front pocket of her pants using two still-sugary fingers. "Call Amy the Nurse and don't give me any of that bunk about somebody else. You don't fool me, Asa Kavanaugh."

"Mom, I actually do have a friend joining us for Thanksgiving. As a matter of fact I'm on my way to her house now. What time should I ask her to come for dinner?"

Jenny pressed her fists on her hips and eyed him sideways. She cast a sloe-eyed gaze to her husband. "What do you think, Louie? Is your son full of it, or what?"

Pops chuckled, then swigged his beer. "She's onto you." He pointed the bottleneck to his son. "Better off coming clean now. And while you two do your dance, I'm off to the television. It's almost time for the sports."

After his dad left the kitchen, Asa took a step closer to where his mother stood with the mask of doubt painting her face.

"I'm serious."

"Two o'clock. Tell your friend she can join us then. And now tell me her name."

"Aubrey Donner."

"The pretty little girl from the food store?" The misgiving melted away from his mother's face, replaced by glee that pinked her cheeks and settled in her dewy eyes. "I knew it!"

His mother knew nothing of the sort, or she wouldn't have been spinning her web about her friend's daughter. But Asa didn't argue. At least she was off his case.

"So, I'm going to clean up a little, then I've got to go." He turned to exit the kitchen.

"Oh no, you don't," she said. "I want some details. Like how long has this been going on? How come you didn't tell me sooner? How serious is this?"

"Mother, these questions you're throwing at me—they are precisely the reason I didn't mention anything to you."

Suddenly Mom flew to him and wrapped her arms around her son. "Asa, a mother never stops worrying about her children." She pulled back and looked him in the eye, her own gaze beaming with love. "Cheryl has been gone for almost four years. Happiness is overdue."

Asa gave her a reassuring smile and took a step away. He felt like a fraud. His mother, with her flashlights for eyeballs, acting all excited and relieved because he had decided to be happy sat like a hunk of stone in his gut.

For four years he had kept his distance from any type of connectedness with a woman. He'd told himself all that time that it was a kind of insurance policy against having to go through anything horrific like losing someone again. But right now his admitted interest in Aubrey Donner didn't feel like a step toward healing.

It felt like a thick, sickening presence filling his veins—a syrup of anguish. Newness would bring a permanent goodbye to what had been.

Could he do that? Could he put Cheryl behind him? Until now he hadn't been able to even think about such severance, but would he ever really be ready?

Chapter Twenty-Two

They stood around the heirloom dining table, another of her mother's garage sale finds, waiting for direction.

The lights in the room were off, a line of white candles flickering from the sideboard. Ira and Molly had drawn the curtains with Ira's statement that even at nighttime the windows must be covered to ward off *unwanted intrusion.*

The thought of that creeped Aubrey out, but there was no turning back now. Two nervous fingers drifted to her earlobe and when the cushiony pads had no metal to worry she sucked in an audible breath. "Wait."

"What is it, dear?" Ira stood tall at the head of the table, a patriarch to the unlikely gathering.

"My mother's earrings. Let me just run up to my room to get them."

"That won't be necessary, Aubrey." Ira indicated for everyone to take their seats. "When I initially asked you to bring a memento to the séance I didn't realize we would be sitting amongst so many. It's fine. Please, have a seat."

A triple-wick candle with its zealous flames had been placed in the center of the table. It cast a dancing glow over the purple covering Joanie had found downtown at Franklin's today.

"At this time we will place our hands on the table

and stretch our fingers out wide." Ira's tone was authoritative. His words' substantive quality only served to rattle Aubrey more. Her knees shook under the table.

"Touch your pinky fingers to the person's beside you," Ira continued. "We are making an unbroken ring. We do this to protect against negativity."

Aubrey placed her hands on the table, watching out the corner of her eye at Asa beside her. His big masculine hands were outstretched. His right pinky sought and found her left. A kind of vibration extended from their connected digits, and she was tempted to pull away. She knew better than to meet his gaze she felt on her, wooing her to turn her head.

On her other side, Joanie also placed her hands into position and pressed the tip of her smallest finger against Aubrey's right one. One by one, they all formed an unbroken ring of their hands.

"Let us begin," Ira said, the cadence of his voice clergy-like. "We close our eyes and still our minds."

Aubrey squeezed her eyes shut, trying to keep her thoughts still as Ira had asked. But there was a big man, with a teasing dimple, sitting beside her, his electric finger pressing onto hers. She shook her head and tried to dismiss the sensation that quivered through her veins.

"We invite only good spirits with pure intention to join us here," Ira intoned. "We pray that only white light enter this space and banish any and all ill purpose."

There was quiet among them. Aubrey's heartbeats thrummed in her ears.

Ira cleared his throat, then spoke again. "Are there any spirits here with us this evening?" he asked.

Silence.

"You that have made your presence known to Aubrey and to Molly, please return now to them. Reveal your desire."

Aubrey sucked in her breath at the sound of her mother's damaged rocker creaking back and forth from the next room. Her arms tensed, and her fingers curled down on the tabletop.

Beside her Asa pressed his finger harder to hers, as though reassuring her that he was there. That didn't help. Her mind zoomed.

"Caroline?" Ira said. His tone rose in excitement. Aubrey heard his pulled-in breath. "Caroline, dear, is that you? Answer yes by making a single sound or rapping a single knock on the table. One sound for yes, two for no."

The rocker stopped creaking. There was no other sound. Silence enveloped them again.

"Reveal your presence. Is this you, Caroline?"

Two loud knocks, as though someone had banged on the wall, boomed from across the room. Molly stifled a squeal.

"Gatherers, please do not break our sealed ring," Ira instructed. "Remain quiet, please."

Two knocks? Aubrey's heart quickened. Had her mom misunderstood Ira's directions? She felt a smile curl on her lips. Her poor mom probably couldn't think straight with all the hullabaloo, as she'd have called this spectacle.

"Caroline, again, is this you here with us now?"

Two knocks.

Ira cleared his throat again. "Am I to understand that you are *not* Aubrey's departed mother, Caroline

Donner?"

One knock.

"Reveal your identity to us. Give us a clue," Ira said, as silence enveloped them again.

After several minutes Ira sucked in such a raggedy breath that Aubrey's eyes snapped open. She scanned around the table. All eyes were on Ira. His eyes, too, were open.

"Ira," Molly whispered. "What is it?"

He did not answer. His eyes were glazed, staring. Finally he shook his head and blew out a lungful of air.

Ira pulled his hands from the circle and folded them on the tabletop, his fingers laced.

"There has been a message from beyond."

"What? When?" Molly asked. "You mean the knocking sounds? The rocker?"

"Yes, and no. What we've heard here tonight were signs of the presence. The message was delivered to me silently, in a whisper to my mind."

Aubrey wondered, *is that how this business worked*? Did Ira have a direct line to the apparently unhappy-to-be-dead? She slid her eye to Asa, whose indiscernible focus was on Ira. Then she turned to Joanie, whose face looked like someone had splashed it with ice water. Aubrey tapped her finger on Joanie's. "You okay?"

"Hell, yeah," she said. "This is wild."

"We must pause for now. I have received numbers from our visitor and when numbers are communicated during the preliminaries of a session it can indicate a date or a time when revelation can be expected."

"Is that what you heard? Numbers?" Aubrey asked.

Ira nodded. "I believe we have a logistical

dilemma."

"Okay, what's that mean?"

She couldn't help it; Aubrey pulled her eyes to Asa.

He sat there stoically, his face like expertly chiseled granite. He met her gaze, the melted chocolate of his eyes swimming with reassurance. He mouthed the words, "It's okay," then slid one finger back to touch her arm. Apparently, all his fingers were charged with electricity.

"The spirit is gone for now but will return later. We have no choice but to wait for that revisit. It's absolute."

"Is that normal?" Aubrey asked. She almost laughed at herself. Like any of this was normal. "I mean, have you had this happen before during a séance?"

"Oh yes. When a spirit is strong, obstinate if you will, they tend to make demands. Our guest of honor, shall we say, has requested that we reconvene later. Much later."

"Okay, so what time?"

"The message was specific. Three eleven."

"In the morning?" Asa asked with incredulity.

Ira nodded. "And not a minute before, or after."

"But why?" Molly asked again.

"It has some significance."

"I'm sure it does," Aubrey said. The sound of her voice was hollow to her own ears, like a call into a bottomless well. "I have woken up every morning at exactly that time in the last week and a half."

"See there?" Ira said. He pointed a finger in the air. "Three eleven it shall be, must be."

"Okay, so what do we do? All set our alarms and meet back here at, say, quarter to three? Oh, dear, this will be difficult," Molly lamented. "Poor Roscoe's clock will be thrown off when his mommy gets up and leaves at that hour."

"Leaves?" Ira said standing. He licked a quick tongue to the pad of his thumb and index finger then extinguished the three dancing flames of the candle in the center of the table. "We cannot leave these premises or all will be lost. No. We must all stay here until the hour."

"All of us?" Aubrey asked.

"Indeed. I'm sure you haven't the room to provide us with private accommodations, but fear not Aubrey. I've slept on many a sofa in my time. We'll improvise."

Aubrey and Joanie locked eyes. She could read her friend's baby blues. The pretty eyes flashed with the question her own mind bombarded her with. *What are you going to do with the big, blond guy?*

She swallowed hard and turned to Asa. His eyes were filled with consternation. Did he have a conflict with work? Was he worried about getting back to Scout?

Did it have anything at all to do with the fact that the two of them had glided away from ambivalence and danced toward curiosity? Hell, that's what it was for her. She couldn't imagine having the man under her roof, albeit a leaky one that he'd offered to fix, for all those hours. She'd never sleep or breathe.

"Asa, look, we'll arrange to do this some other time. I certainly won't expect you to stick around until…"

"Not a problem. I'll just text my parents that I

won't be home."

Molly got up from the table. "My mahjong partner has Roscoe. I'll just give her a call to let her know that I'll retrieve him sometime in the morning."

Aubrey felt panic climb through her, starting in her toes and winding its way up her entire body like a choking vine. They were really doing this.

"I wouldn't know where to put, uh, you." She stared at Asa.

He pulled his shiny eyes to Ira, then looked at her again. "Like the man said. We'll improvise."

****

Aubrey's look of horror was worth a million bucks. Asa knew, of course, that she'd react that way when he said he'd be okay with sticking around for the appointment with this punctual ghost of hers.

He wasn't sure what he really thought about it all. Certainly if there was such a thing as ghosts, he'd have been visited by Cheryl, wouldn't he?

He thought of her now. Was it true that loved ones looked down from their heavenly perch to oversee those they left behind? Was Cheryl watching him now? Did she know how often he thought of this new woman? The idea stabbed him somewhere.

He received no response from his text to his mother's cell phone. Not sure she knew her way around that technology, Asa punched in the numbers of his land line. Mom picked up on the second ring.

"Are you having fun?" She asked this as though her grown son was a fourth grader at a friend's birthday party.

"Hi, Mom. Listen, I won't be home until sometime in the morning. I'm not on duty until late in the afternoon, so I'll see you when I get home, okay?"

"You're having a sleepover?" Her voice was accusatory as though he was breaking curfew, like he'd done a million times when he was a teenager.

"See you in the morning, Ma," Asa said, and hung up the phone.

Chapter Twenty-Three

After it had been determined that Aunt Molly would take the guest room and Joanie would bunk with Aubrey, there was the matter of the two men, Ira and Asa.

"You take the couch," Asa said to the elder man. "I'm fine in the wing chair." He pointed to the chair positioned in front of an ottoman by the fireplace. "I'll just stretch out there."

"You'll have a tough time of it, sir," Ira said.

"I'll be fine."

"Okay, then. Since we'll be rising in the middle of the night, I suggest we all attempt to get some sleep. Shall we?" Ira said.

"It's not even nine-thirty." Aubrey held a stack of bedding for the two men. "I'm sure I can't sleep yet."

"That's what this is for," Ira said, pulling a bottle from his black doctor's bag. "Elderberry wine," he said, with triumph. "Aubrey, dear, get us some glasses, will you?"

Aubrey and Joanie found glasses in the dining room curio cabinet, and took them into the kitchen to rinse. While Joanie dried the glasses, Aubrey assembled a plate of cheese slices and crackers.

"You like him." Joanie's eyes were focused on the cloth she rubbed on delicate cordial glass, but her mouth was screwed in a playful twist.

Aubrey stopped her action, her hand in the box of wheat crackers. "I know you think I've spent my time coming up with pretend reasons not to go there with this guy. But trust me on this, Joanie, he's not for me. He's"—she thought a moment, while she lifted a handful of square crackers from the box—"detached."

"He's hot."

"Regardless, he's emotionally unavailable."

"Well, at least your eyes work, even if your logic's out of whack."

The cheese and crackers ready, Aubrey grabbed a stack of napkins from the holder on the kitchen table. Joanie cradled five petite glasses in her hands.

"What's elderberry wine, anyway?" she whispered. They exited the kitchen and headed for where the rest of the crew sat in the living room.

"Let's ask," Aubrey said. She put her tray onto the coffee table, then helped Joanie with the glasses. "Ira, we were wondering about the elderberry wine. What's an elderberry?"

Ira began pouring measures of the dark red wine into the glasses that had belonged to Aubrey's mom. A pungent fruity aroma immediately wafted through the air.

"Elderberries are small and dark, akin to blueberries. They're a fascinating fruit, and its wine is the perfect accompaniment to our type of gathering. Some say elderberries have a form of toxicity, or at least the possibility of it. However, cooking the berries banishes their poison, rendering it a splendid drink. Something wonderful from something toxic."

Ira lifted two glasses by their stems and handed one to Molly and one to Aubrey. He then offered one each to Joanie and Asa. He took the last and lifted it into the air. "To three eleven," he said, and waited for everyone to chime into his toast.

Aubrey said the words and reluctantly took a tentative sip of the wine. She didn't know what she'd expected, especially after Ira's talk about the berry's potential toxicity. It tasted to her like fermented prune juice, thick and sweet. The blob on her tongue was like taking a swig of pancake syrup, and she had all she could do to swallow it.

Ira did most of the talking, which suited Aubrey fine. She was spooked by the whole conjuring the ghost premise and the recent events that led up to this meeting. She was also baffled by Asa Kavanaugh becoming part of it.

Every once in a while she managed to steal a glance of him. When his eyes drifted to hers, she focused on the deep, red wine in the belly of her glass. Giving it a little shake, she watched the thick brew undulate from her movements. *Something wonderful from something toxic.*

By ten-thirty Ira had run out of steam. His lengthy talk regarding the spirit world had slowed to a near stop.

Aubrey declared she was going up to bed, with the offer that if anyone needed anything to just help themselves.

Asa set the alarm on his cell phone, as did Ira. Molly counted on Aubrey and Joanie to wake her up.

As the three women stood on the square landing outside the two bedrooms, Molly reiterated, "You'll be sure to wake me in time, won't you?"

"Yes, Auntie, I promise."

"Good. Ira's wine has me feeling a bit mellow. I'm sure I'll sleep soundly."

Aubrey gave the woman a one-armed hug. She kissed her temple. "'Night, Auntie. I'll wake you at two forty-five, as you asked."

****

The two girlfriends settled in Aubrey's king bed. Aubrey tugged the chain to shut the bedside lamp off.

"Aubrey," Joanie whispered, then yawned. "Can you believe we're doing this?"

"I know. I keep asking myself that same question. I mean, are there really five people sleeping here with the intention of waking up in the middle of the night to talk to a ghost?"

"Nobody would believe us, if we told them. And, you know what? I see what you mean about Asa. You have to steer clear."

Aubrey sat up in the darkness. "I do?" She hadn't expected that out of her friend.

She knew that from the outside Asa had it all in terms of what she liked in a man—the looks, the swagger, the intoxicating flash of tease in his eyes, the woo of the dimple. But as her deceased mother would have said, trust your gut.

And from day one her gut told her the sole reason Asa Kavanaugh had crossed her path was to help her snag the full-time spot on Mid Shore Live. Finito.

"Yes," Joanie said. Her shifting body rocked the mattress. She lowered her voice. "He's smoking, let's agree on that one. And before you start with how much you wouldn't go near him with a ten-foot pole, let me remind you that I'm the one who knows you better than you know yourself. If you really don't want anything to do with this guy, then you have to stop now." Joanie flopped back onto her pillow as though the gesture were an exclamation mark at the end of her statement.

"Stop what?"

"I see that little dance you two do. You fool no one."

Aubrey flopped back onto her pillow. She spoke up to the ceiling. "We don't dance."

Joanie chuckled in the dark. "It's so smooth you don't even know you're dancing, you silly girl. If you really think this guy's *detached,* as you say, or whatever other reason you come up with for why you don't want to entertain the idea of him, then by all means, I agree. Run while you still can. Because, you want him. And he wants you."

"I admit there's something kind of magnetic about the guy, but trust me, I'm not deluding myself that this could be romance, or that he's—"

"Your *real as real.*" Joanie finished Aubrey's statement.

That was what their college girl selves had termed the someday when they'd meet their soul mate or *the* guy. It had been a wine-cooler dorm-room coining of a phrase that would seem silly now if it weren't just Aubrey and Joanie alone in the dark discussing it.

"Yes," Aubrey whispered back. "I'm not even sure that love as *real as real* even exists. Besides, I'm well aware of my luck with men."

"Let's assess."

"How about we sleep instead?"

Joanie ignored her and began what sounded like reading from a bullet-point list. "You've dated some bozos. Guys have disappointed you from here to kingdom come. You grew up with a first-hand example of just how lousy a man can be, thanks to your tyrant of a grandfather. Why wouldn't you be conflicted?"

"Who said I'm conflicted? I'm going with my gut."

Joanie leaned up on one elbow and faced her. Aubrey could barely make out her friend's features in the darkness of the room.

"Bree-Bree," Joanie said.

The nickname pricked Aubrey's memory, the endearment Joanie had used at times when Aubrey needed a surrogate parent—times like when they were at college and some guy had turned out to be a lying creep, or the times in the city when Aubrey didn't get the job she wanted, and when she'd gotten the call that Mom had been diagnosed and she'd been summoned to *come quick*. In those times Aubrey had been Bree-Bree. Just the sound of it conjured moisture to her eyes.

"As long as it's your gut talking to you, and not your fear." Joanie yawned again. "Okay, Bree-Bree, how's this? You truly trust your gut, and I'll trust you."

Aubrey whispered, voice thick with emotion, "You are my family, you know that?"

"Real as real," Joanie said.

They were silent for a moment, the two friends. Then, Joanie uttered a preamble. "Can I say one more thing?"

Aubrey smiled in the darkness. "Can I stop you?"

"Do you think just anybody would agree to take part in this wacky soirée? Do you think it could be this Asa's just a good old guy? What's your gut say to that one?"

Aubrey was silent. She stared at the ceiling, wracking her brain for something to say that would end the debate. She settled for, "We better get some sleep. Quarter to three will be here all too soon."

****

Before one in the morning Aubrey startled awake. She was breathing heavily, and her mouth was parched dry. Joanie was sound asleep. Her breathing was even, steady, untroubled.

Aubrey swung her legs over the side of the bed and fished with her feet in the darkness for her mules. Locating them, she slid her feet into the soft slippers and stood up.

She slowly made her way across the room and gently opened the door. She knew it squeaked, but somehow managed to keep that to a minimum by slipping through a wedge of opening just big enough for her to fit through.

The trip down the staircase was soundless thanks to her slippers on the carpeted steps. In the living room, covered in the old comforter dug out of the linen closet earlier, she spied a large mound that had to be Ira. Her eyes strained in the dark to make out the wing chair where Asa would be asleep. She was rattled to see that the chair was empty. A light on in the kitchen told her his probable whereabouts.

Aubrey thought about skipping the glass of water she'd come down for and just going back upstairs to the bathroom and drinking from under the faucet with cupped hands. But, hell, it was her kitchen.

Asa sat at the maple table. He was still in his jeans but he'd shunned the plaid shirt and now just wore a dark brown tee leaving his toned arms bare and tan. His boots were off and his socks were white with yellow tips.

He had the black plastic bucket that contained the bits of her mom's china teacups at his side. He was busy laying out a design of the china chips on an open page of yesterday's Harbor Herald as though he were in art class.

The scene, blond head bent in consternation, big hands adding chips of china with almost delicate precision did something to her insides, causing cords of emotion, past and present, to weave together.

She shuffled across the floor and opened a cabinet with a territorial grip of the wrought-iron knob. She withdrew a drinking glass and poured herself a full measure of water from the filtered jug that sat on the counter, plopping it back on the surface with a definitive thud. She stared out the window to the blackness of the night, the only place in the room that wasn't consumed with Asa Kavanaugh. She sipped quietly.

"Can't sleep either, huh?"

Aubrey closed her eyes, but did not turn to the voice. "Nope."

"Did you have a favorite?"

She turned before thinking not to. Asa looked up from his project, a shiny broken bit pinched in two fingers.

"I'm sorry, what?"

He held up the piece of china. "Were you partial to any in particular?"

She took a step in his direction then another. "They were all pretty."

Closer to the project, the layout looked like the beginnings of a mosaic pattern, and a dichotomy of emotion swelled in Aubrey's chest. The bits were almost pretty in their arrangement, yet the array was a hodgepodge aftermath of brokenness.

"Sure," Asa said with the shrug of a mighty shoulder. "But that's not what I asked."

Her feet carried her closer. He had placed a chunk painted with a tiny buttercup into the pattern, like a puzzle piece. He reached into the bucket and withdrew another bit, a fragment of the one with the pale pink sweetheart roses.

She remembered when she'd had chicken pox as a little girl, miserable in a mass of oozing breakouts and itchiness she'd been forbidden to scratch. Her mother had made weak tea and jellied toast, cut in triangles. She'd allowed Aubrey to drink from whichever delicate cup she chose.

Now, a virtual stranger, in stocking feet, who was sleeping over to await a ghost, of all things, was making a design with its shattered remains.

The cool water sat like lead in her belly. Everything about her life, as she'd known it, seemed just like those bits in the bucket. Shattered remains.

Asa fished out another piece, a triangular shard adorned with a dot of the pink paint. "So," he said without looking up. "This one then."

Aubrey came up to the table, her heart suddenly waking from a kind of slumber, stirring in a rapid-winged flutter. "What?" she asked.

He held up the ragged-edged piece of white china decorated with a fractured little flower. "You were partial to the pink roses."

She sat in the chair to Asa's left and put her glass on the edge of the spread newspaper. "How'd you know?" She was either too tired to deny the fact or too curious to let his comment go unsubstantiated.

"The way your eyes looked when you saw it." Asa fished around in the bucket again, making a clinking sound with all the pieces. He withdrew another bit, this one an odd shaped piece that included the ropy handle of the rosebud teacup. He extended it toward her.

Unable to resist, Aubrey let him place it in her open palm. She brought it closer to inspect. What memories did the relic hold that had come way before her pocky tea party? Had Caroline sipped tea from that vessel, dreaming of a baby that she'd love enough to deny her old life? Aubrey closed her hand around the little nugget.

"It was," she said, looking down at her closed hand. She lifted her head and met his chocolate gaze intently watching her. "My favorite, I mean."

Asa pulled his gaze away and continued his work. He placed pieces in a ring and had begun to fill it in with more shards. "Your eyes do this kind of thing. I've seen it before." He looked up and offered a crooked smile. "When I've pissed you off."

Unable to help it, a little laugh bubbled up from her throat. "Okay, so what exactly is 'this thing' you say my eyes do?"

"They…"

She could see his Adam's apple move down, then up, his sturdy neck. She waited.

His gaze was steady. "Your eyes ignite, like flames around kindling."

Embarrassed, but not sure why, she pulled her water glass into her hand and fanned her fingers in the cool condensation.

She tried at humor. "You do bring out the blow

torch in me."

Asa shook his head.

"No?" she dared to ask.

He shook his head again. "You're a lit match, Aubrey Donner."

"And in that scenario you would be, what, gasoline?"

"Nope." Asa smiled, tilting sideways at her. "I'm November leaves on a sidewalk."

****

The silence was killing him. If it weren't for the hunks of broken china to occupy his attention, he'd go mad. Aubrey continued to watch him work, both of them quiet after his comment. *Brilliant*. Now that was all he could think about.

He was thirty-eight years old, and couldn't count the number of women he'd known, no less name them all. But no one, not one single lady had ever rendered him silent. In one little moment, this one—looking like a bag lady in that oversized miss-matched getup and her wacky hair that couldn't decide if it wanted to curl or just wave hello—had stolen his ability to speak. *Take that*, his mind taunted.

"I, uh"—she pushed her chair away from the table—"should go try to get some sleep." Her dangerous eyes looked up to the round clock positioned on the soffit above the cabinets. "It's almost two."

Asa swallowed, silently commanding his voice to step up. "Good idea."

She stood and carried her half-full glass of water to the sink. It was safe to watch her retreat from him. She was lost in that T-shirt that went down past her ass, and hung wide from her narrow frame. The huge, faded

187

plaid pajama pants were a joke, so long they puddled at her fuzzy-slippered feet.

The stunners he'd known, and had unwaveringly walked away from, would bludgeon him with the business end of their high heels if they saw who it was that compelled him now. All he wanted was that disheveled little too-nosy-for-her-own-good reporter. And he was unable to look away, let alone walk away.

He placed the bucket he'd been holding onto the floor and stood.

At the sink, Aubrey turned around. Twin lit matches surveyed him.

His feet carried him closer.

Aubrey's hands slid behind her back, but she did not move away. Her eyes held his, the flames in them beckoned stronger than a crooked finger calling him near.

"I think"—the words came to his mouth from some foreign place—"it would be a shame to just throw it all away."

Aubrey licked her lips. "Throw what away?"

"The broken pieces."

She shook her head and almost smiled. Relief could be seen on her slightly curved mouth, washed clean of lipstick, yet a prettier pink than the rosebuds painted on china. "The teacups."

He nodded. How had he gotten this close? He could feel her body heat, smell her scent. She was honeysuckle and sandalwood, sweet and savory.

"Sometimes brokenness can be made into something beautiful."

Aubrey was the first to move. That miniscule step closer kicked the air out of his chest, slammed away any hesitation. He reached for her, cupping his hands on her face.

They shared a look so deep he could see into her profound recesses. He wanted to be there with her, in that deep place. His lips came down on hers, claimed them greedily, as if they might vanish into thin air if he didn't declare them his.

The kiss lingered, calmed, and became less hurried. Their joined lips moved in a slow side-to-side dance, back and forth, yin, yang, me, you, mine, yours.

The connection broke, but Asa would be damned to know which of them had been the first to pull away. They each panted for breath, as though they'd run a far distance. And they had, he admitted silently, they had travelled far. In the darkness of the night, in that pre-dawn moment, he wondered if he'd ever find his way back.

Chapter Twenty-Four

Aubrey slipped into bed, the covers cool on her skin. She was hot, flushed, and stupid. But, man, she'd been kissed.

What had she done? The ceiling had no answer, despite her continued stare.

She decided to pray, something she didn't do often. But now on the precipice of something ominous about to happen, with a clairvoyant ready to summon something or someone unseen, together with her betraying urges, Aubrey needed guidance. Before she knew it, though, without a coherent plea to offer skyward, sleep stole her away.

****

Aubrey's body came to life with a heavy shove to her shoulder. She bolted upright.

"Did the alarm go off?"

"Yup," Joanie said. She stood at the foot of the bed, her bed head a frizzled nest, more rumpled in her flannel PJ's than the bedcovers surrounding a groggy Aubrey. "I hit the snooze button twice, my friend. We have fifteen minutes before show time. We have to wake Molly. Holy crow, she snores like a freight train."

"Crap." Aubrey kicked herself free of the covers. This séance had to happen today. She could not wait for the next time Molly's boyfriend decided the stars were aligned, or whatever, for conjuring ghosts.

"You were having a hell of a dream, kid."

"What else is new?" Aubrey yawned. "This has to stop today."

"You were saying the same thing over and over. *Leave me alone.*"

Aubrey shook her head. "Come on. We've got to hustle."

Joanie grabbed her clothes and darted from the room calling over her shoulder as she headed to the bathroom. "I'll be quick."

"I'll go rouse Molly."

Dressed and ready, minus any form of primping whatsoever, Joanie, Aubrey, and a still-befuddled Aunt Molly descended the staircase at five of the hour.

"Oh man," Joanie sniffed audibly. "The coffee gods are in the house." A waft of roasting Arabica beans met them at the base of the steps.

Asa stood at the kitchen counter pouring coffee into a mug. The silky brown color of the brew reminded Aubrey of Asa's eyes. She was certifiably screwed for noticing it.

A plate of muffins displayed in a kind of pyramid was there, too, with the telltale empty bag from Mulligan's Bakery beside it.

"Who ran to the bakery?" Aubrey did her best to avoid the man leaning against the sink trying to catch her eye over the rim of his coffee mug. Her body refused to cooperate, jolting her like she'd drunk the whole damned pot of java already.

"That would be me," Asa said, now making it unavoidable to connect eyes.

"Great!" She flashed a glance his way before quickly pulling it away.

191

"Where's Ira?" Joanie asked.

"In the dining room, getting ready." Molly pulled a knot of crumb off the top of a coffee-cake muffin top.

Beside her, Aubrey did the same. The morsel was sweet and satisfying, much like…

From her peripheral vision Aubrey watched Asa in kind of stilted clips, like movie film stuck on slow motion. A snap of Asa downing the rest of his coffee, a clip of his broad, strong, turned back as he placed the cup in the sink, a dash of his torso as he slid past her exiting the room and leaving the aroma of clean man to tantalize her nose. She closed her eyes when he was gone from sight. Oh, but he was not gone from mind.

"What's that?" Molly pointed to the arrangement of china chips displayed on the kitchen table.

"Oh"—Aubrey blew out a breath—"nothing." She shook her head, the jerky movement doing nothing to budge the memory of what occurred last night amongst the broken china.

Molly ran a soothing hand down Aubrey's arm. "You ready for this, my love?"

She nodded. "As I'll ever be."

The women made their way from the kitchen toward the dining room. Joanie sidled up beside Aubrey and crooked her arm into hers. She whispered, "So, here's what I know…"

Aubrey met her gaze.

"I know something's up with you and Officer Hottie in there."

Aubrey pulled her eyes away and did her best to twist her lips into a knot of denial.

"Don't even." Joanie smirked. "You forget I know you best."

Chapter Twenty-Five

The room was darkened. The candles had been relit, and Aubrey's heart stirred at the sight of the dancing light. It was hard not think of Asa's comparison of her eyes to a flickering flame.

It had probably just been an off-handed comment, her pragmatic self could be convinced. But this just-been-kissed idiot knew nothing of the sort. All she could see in her mind's eye was that tuft of dried leaves smoking from a haphazardly tossed match, flames forming, licking the leaves, consuming them, and converting them to their likeness.

Her heart pounded. Asa had compared himself to those overtaken leaves. She, though, at the moment, was not the fire. He was.

They resumed their same seats, at Ira's instruction.

"Place your hands onto the table." Ira's voice was again deep with authority. "Fingers spread wide, pinkies touching to recreate our unbroken circle."

Aubrey touched her right pinky to Joanie's, then in the interest of getting to the bottom of this craziness, she sought Asa's touch.

The softness of his finger pad met hers and although she had braced for some form of electricity, what happened was worse. Warmth, like bathwater on sore muscles, poured from his fingertip to hers flowing in her veins like a steady cascade of steeped tea poured into an unbroken teacup.

"Clear our minds of all thoughts," Ira said.

Easy for you to say.

"We close our eyes."

Aubrey shut her lids and worked at clearing her mind and forgetting the touch to her left.

"We, with our unbroken bond, banish any and all negativity. We welcome only pure white light into our presence. We gather again at this hour, in this very moment, at the request of the visitor who has made their presence known. I implore you now to acknowledge yourself. Are you among us? One knock to signify the affirmative."

One knock sounded, again like forceful knuckles on a wall, from somewhere in the house.

Although both her fingers stayed glued to their partners', Aubrey felt herself jump.

"It is our understanding that you are not the spirit of our passed friend, Caroline Donner. Is this indeed true?"

One knock. Everyone opened their eyes and all sent their gazes to meet the others. Aubrey and Asa's glance was brief. It had to be.

"Please assist us, then. Tell us who you are and what it is you've come to reveal."

The familiar scent of burnt vanilla, the tobacco smell as she'd learned from Asa, slithered on the air, teased their noses, surrounded them. One of the flames of the tri-wicked candle in the center of the dining table extinguished, perhaps at the wafting hand of the aromatic intruder, leaving two dancing wicks remaining.

"One lost flame. Am I to assume a significance of

the number one?"

Two knocks.

"No? All right, perhaps the number two for the remaining flames? Is that it? Something to do with two?"

One knock.

Ira sucked in an audible breath.

Aubrey kept her eyes on Ira's face, mesmerized by the transformation that overtook his expression. Eyes closed, bushy brows knit into a V like kissing caterpillars, his forehead pleated with wrinkles. His mouth pulled down at the corners into a deep frown that twitched, making his gray beard bob.

"I'm getting a message, but it's not clear." Ira tilted his head as though straining to hear a telephone conversation over a bad connection. "Mary. Is there someone named Mary that bears significance to you, Aubrey?"

"Not that I know of. My grandmother was Edith. Maybe it's her?"

Two loud knocks.

"Our visitor says no. Silence again, please." Ira's face resumed its overall pinch. "I'm hearing that the message is for someone named Mary. And, it says for Mary to go to the mountains, I believe. Any of this significant?"

Aubrey shook her head, her heart sinking to her belly in a slow dejected fall.

"I keep hearing it," Ira said. "Mount. Go. Mary."

"Montgomery!" The name shot simultaneously from both Aubrey and Molly.

"Oh my God," Molly said. "Of course. That old buzzard. It's Montgomery."

A question curved in Ira's bushy brows.

"My grandfather," Aubrey said. Her chest constricted, holding air hostage in her lungs. With a shallow breath she said his name. "Montgomery Donner, *the Second*."

One knock boomed loud.

"Well, son of a bitch," Aubrey said.

"Do not break our unity," Ira commanded. "Settle down, everyone.

The scent of tobacco was pungent in the air. The pipe she'd found in the attic had to have belonged to her grandfather, but why was he stinking up her house? She knew nothing about the man other than the fact that he had disowned his only child because of Aubrey's mere existence. Anger zipped through her.

"He wanted nothing to do with us while he was alive. What could he possibly want now?" The words were bitter on her tongue.

"Sir," Ira intoned. "Now that we know who you are. What is it you're here to accomplish? Tell us now."

A small wrought iron bracket holding up a corner shelf lost its hold, and fell to the floor with a metallic thud followed by the shelf and what had been displayed on it, Mom's painted wooden *Welcome* blocks.

Each thump to the floor shot at Aubrey's nerves, like gunfire. Molly squealed. Yet, they all somehow managed to maintain their connected pinkies.

"Tell us, Montgomery Donner, the Second, what does this signify?"

Aubrey heard the rocker begin to move in the other room. The old creaky wooden rungs clicked along the floorboards as though the chair were walking.

"Caroline's rocker," Molly's whisper an urgent

hiss.

Worried that her aunt would move, thus breaking the cosmic connection, Aubrey zeroed in on everyone's outstretched pinkies. That's when she noticed Ira's hands had moved into fists.

A breeze entered the room chasing away the scent of Montgomery's tobacco. Where the rushing air had come from Aubrey didn't know, but it was cold and goose bumps riddled the skin on her arms. She shivered.

The two remaining flames of the three-wick candle went out as did all five pillars that had been aglow on the sideboard.

In an instant the cold breeze vanished, having taken any scent of vanilla with it. In the next room Caroline's rocker had ceased its movement.

"He's gone," Ira said. "Our session has ended."

****

The five of them sat in the living room, Ira and Molly on the sofa beside Joanie. Asa had taken a seat on the raised brick hearth, and Aubrey had claimed a spot on the floor across the room, the furthest proximity. Whenever she looked over at him his eyes were on her, and there was no distance far enough in the room to avoid how it made her feel.

"We didn't learn anything."

"Well, we know who it is," Molly said. "What we don't know is what he wants."

"Whatever it is can't be good," Aubrey said. "And, truthfully, I don't care." She shouted loudly, "Knock it off. You don't scare me, not anymore anyway. I'll talk to you in words you'll understand—'go away and never come back.'" Her elbows poised on her knees, she put her head in her hands.

"Maybe if we give it one more shot, we'll get the answer you're looking for," Joanie said. "We could try, couldn't we, Ira?"

Ira twisted his lips. "When the time is right. Certainly I'll keep myself open for a sign."

"How long are you going to be gone for?" Molly asked.

"You're going away?" Asa asked.

"Yes," Ira said with a smile. "But just for a few days, right after Thanksgiving. My younger brother is out in Ohio. He's moving into a new home and needs a hand from big brother."

"Aubrey," Molly said. "I've been meaning to ask you. Would you like to join Ira and me for Thanksgiving dinner at the Elk's Lodge?"

"They put on quite a spread," Ira added.

"I, uh, that sounds nice, Auntie. Thank you." Aubrey flashed a quick side glance to Asa whose mouth bore that slanted half-smile. "I, uh, have been invited to join Asa for dinner with his family."

She silenced the room with that one. The only movement was the sight of Joanie's jaw dropping open.

"How nice." Molly's chin tilted down, one shoulder lifted.

"Isn't it, though?" Joanie said.

"My brother wanted me to come out in time to spend the holiday with him and his family, but I couldn't miss out on the Elk's bash. And didn't want to leave my girl, here."

Molly slipped her arm through his and hugged it close. "Remember what I told you, Ira. Don't be lifting anything. Your back, you know."

Ira smiled affectionately at the woman seated beside him. He cupped her knee and gave it a little squeeze. "I wouldn't dream of it."

"My dream!" Aubrey said.

"What dream?" Molly asked.

Joanie sat forward, and faced Ira and Molly. "She had a nightmare last night. She was talking in her sleep. She kept saying 'Leave me alone.'"

"What else, Aubrey?" Ira asked.

"I've been having this dream for more than a week now," Aubrey said, blowing out a long breath. "A shadowy figure appears, as if someone is standing in my room, but I can't make out who or even what it is. Last night, though, for the first time, he…it…whatever…said something."

"Do you recall what it was?" Ira leaned closer.

"*Falsehood is no ally.*" Aubrey recited the words like she were reading a blurb from a fortune cookie.

"Sounds pompous, and trust me, that was just like old Monty," Molly said. "Arrogant buzzard."

Ira wrapped an arm around Molly's shoulders and pulled her close. "There now, dear."

He directed his attention to Aubrey. "Dear girl, perhaps it was just your anxiousness working on your subconscious. Proof will be in the pudding, as they say."

"What's that mean?" Asa asked. "What proof?"

"We must have another séance when I return from Ohio." Ira said. "It is obvious that your grandfather has appeared for a reason, one that has not yet been satisfied."

"It's got to be something to do with this poor old rocking chair." Aubrey cast her eyes to the torn-up chair.

Ira pulled his lips downward. "Most likely that's just an attention device, the same as that shelf in the other room and the teacups. This is a restless spirit wanting to be heard."

"So then, why did he just disappear?" Asa asked.

"Ah, sir, if we knew the answer to that one…" Ira's mouth curved into a wry smile. "All we can do is work with what we're given."

Ira smoothed fingers over his beard. "For now, though, let us call it a day. I think we all need to catch up on some rest. You concur, my dear?" Ira beamed at Molly.

"Yes," she said. "I have to go retrieve my Roscoe now. I'm sure he's wondering where I am."

Asa stood from his perch on the brick hearth. "I've got a dog, and a work day, waiting for me, as well."

He cast a glance to Aubrey. "We didn't get the chance to go over the numbers for the supplies I'll need for the repairs around here. I've got a full boat today—meetings and such. I'll touch base with you tomorrow. Would that work?"

Aubrey rose. Standing beside him in her stocking feet, he seemed like more of a giant. To keep them from shaking, she shoved her hands into the back pockets of her jeans. Just his proximity reminded her of the feel of his arms, his body against hers, his taste, the sound of a soft muffled moan at the back of his throat.

"Tomorrow's fine. I've got a lot on the schedule today, as well." She looked at her watch and cursed under her breath. "I'm meeting my boss in an hour, then I've got an interview."

"Well…" Asa scanned the faces of those in the

room. "What can I say? It's been interesting." He gave a slight laugh.

"Thank you for being part of the session," Ira said, and stood to shake Asa's hand. "We couldn't have done it without you."

"Ira, help me with my bag. I put it in the kitchen." Molly stood from the couch, and Ira followed her through the doorway.

"It was nice meeting you, Asa," Joanie said. "Hope I see you next time I'm down for a visit."

"Odd circumstances, but good to meet you, too."

"Aubrey, I'm going to go on up and start packing." Joanie gave Aubrey a little eyebrow wiggle as she was leaving the room.

God, she'd miss Joanie. She loved having her around. The house would feel empty without her. At the moment, though, alone in the living room with Asa, Aubrey was consumed with the presence of the man beside her.

"I better head out," he said.

"I'll walk you to the door."

"Let me take a look at that shelf that fell in the dining room so I can see if I need to get a new bracket when I'm buying supplies."

"Okay."

She followed him into the dining room. It amazed her how it felt like her room again, in spite of the séance that had taken place just a short while ago. There was no sign of any spectral presence, except the telltale sign of the fallen shelf and the jumble of wooden blocks strewn on the floor.

Asa stood in front of the fallen items, hands on his hips. She came up beside him.

"Look," he said, pointing to the blocks.

She surveyed the blocks that had spelled *Welcome*. Four of them were faced down, their blond wooden backs blank. The other three blocks faced up, lined in a row, as though someone had placed them just like that. *E L C*.

"Like *elk*," Asa said. "How about that?"

"Hunh," she said. "The other day I noticed the blocks were turned backwards, the blank sides facing out. You think Montgomery somehow did this deliberately?"

"Maybe." Asa shook his head and uttered a soft laugh. "Now I'm starting to think like a ghost hunter." He shrugged. "Could be, though. You think?"

"But what's it mean?"

"Tell you what, Aubrey. Don't mention this to anyone else. Not yet anyway."

"Okay. But why?"

He shrugged again. "Just wait until we sit down for another séance. And keep a list of any other happenings."

She was too focused on his use of the word *we* to debate it any further.

At the front door Asa gave her a full, dimpled smile. "I'd say it's been fun…"

She laughed. "Yeah. Tons of it." She spied the plastic top of a storage bag peeking out from the opening of his jacket pocket. "You and your muffin have a good day," she said. Without thinking she reached for the bag and gave it a little tug. "Which kind did you take?"

"Uh," he said, his hand darting to stop hers.

It was too late, though, and what she pulled from

his pocket wasn't a muffin. It was a sloshy portion of the elderberry wine.

"What the heck?" Aubrey laughed.

"Yeah, well," he said. "I thought I'd bring a sample home with me. My, uh, father's kind of a fan of cordials and I thought he'd like this."

"Huh," she said. "Okay. But no muffin?"

"No," he said and smiled. "So, two o'clock on Thursday," he said. "You're good with this, right?"

"Sure," Aubrey said. "A deal's a deal. Okay if I bring a batch of low-cal cosmos for your mom and me? I remember from the food store that she really likes them."

"Oh, brother. You'll make a lifelong friend out of her, if you do."

His smile was infectious. His chocolate eyes shone with affection. Its voltage zapped through her.

In a soft, sensual voice, he asked, "Are we going to talk about what else, uh, happened last night? Would that be a good thing or a bad thing, do you think?"

She pulled in a deep breath and let it expel. "We could try pretending it didn't happen."

"You first." There was a challenge in his voice.

She matched the smile on his face and shook her head. It was a lost cause.

Chapter Twenty-Six

The bear hug felt good, and Aubrey closed her eyes breathing in the rosy scent of her best friend. She would miss this. "I can't believe you're going to leave me already," Aubrey said.

"I know. We can't wait too long to do this again. Promise?"

Aubrey nodded. They meant it wholeheartedly but somehow life had a way of keeping them planted in their own places. Her heart was heavy.

Joanie let go and took a step away. She reached for her glass of iced tea on the kitchen counter and took a long pull. "Can I trust you to not botch this up?"

Aubrey laughed. "Unfortunately, we both know there are several subjects you could be referring to. Be specific."

"We'll take it point by point," Joanie said, leaning against the counter. "The ghost. The minute you know when the next séance is going to be, you have to call me so I can be here."

"A given."

"Next, little Miss Pet Parade. You have to decide if you hate doing interviews with lions and tigers and bears, or if you love it. There should be no middle ground."

"Trying to love it," Aubrey said with a tilt to her head. "Does that count?"

Joanie shook her head. "Right track, but not quite. I've seen you with Asa's dog. He's getting to you."

"You talking about Asa or Scout?"

"Scout. Asa's the next point."

Aubrey laughed. She knew there was no getting around the Asa Kavanaugh factor. And that fact was true, whether she was in the kitchen with her best friend or if she was alone with her own thoughts.

"Well, I have to tell you. The big oaf is definitely worming his way into my heart with those big sad eyes and the way he wags his tail when he sees me."

"We talking Asa or Scout?" Joanie asked over the rim of her glass of iced tea.

Aubrey laughed out loud. "Ha-ha. I have yet to see Asa wag his tail."

"Which brings us to the last point. Thanksgiving."

"Ah, yes. There's no avoiding that discussion, I suppose."

"So, you've said this little holiday dinner is simply a deal you made with the fine officer so that he'd stay for the séance. And you'll be passing the gravy boat just so he can avoid his meddling mother's attempt at match-making."

Aubrey nodded. "Precisely."

Joanie twisted her mouth. "Be honest with yourself. Do you like him?"

Aubrey stared at her. How to answer that? A slew of smart-alecky comments swam around in her head. But the truth was that her best friend on the planet, the closest human being to her soul, was standing here in her kitchen ready to leave for God knew how long. The last thing Aubrey wanted to do was toss her a fib.

Was it true then? Had she even allowed her own

head to form that declaration? *Yes, I like him?* "I'd rather I didn't," is what came out of her mouth. It was not a fib.

"See that over there?" Joanie motioned her head in the direction of the kitchen table where the broken pieces of teacups still sat in their configuration. Aubrey fixed her gaze, and Joanie didn't wait for a comment. "You haven't moved it."

Aubrey shrugged. "So?"

"Because it would be a shame to disrupt something at its beginning?"

The friends locked eyes. "Don't you agree?" Joanie prompted.

Aubrey's chest rose with a deep breath, then fell when the air expelled. "I agree."

Joanie threw her arms around Aubrey and squeezed her tight. "Happy Thanksgiving, my love."

"Happy Thanksgiving," Aubrey said, with a tear biting the corner of her eye. "I miss you already."

Chapter Twenty-Seven

After rushing her, with his cryptic phone call, Aubrey wanted to throttle her boss for making her wait now. She was sitting alone in a booth at the diner, where he'd insisted on meeting.

Aubrey was running on minutes of sleep. Her head was fogged with the ghost of a dead man and the haunting of a very-much alive Asa Kavanaugh. Her nerves were shot, and the last thing she needed to hear was Dean Manning calling her with his, "We need to meet ASAP. There's an issue with the show."

Dear God, she thought, *could all this animal interaction I've had to endure been for naught?* Was she headed back to the ad copy department? She was too tired to ruminate over the effect of any of it. That was the only good thing about feeling like a zombie.

Finally, Dean breezed through the door, motioned to a waitress for his usual cup of coffee—black no sugar—and he slid into the booth opposite Aubrey.

"Traffic's a bear today." He took off his glasses and pinched the bridge of his nose. He fished a napkin from the chrome dispenser on the countertop and proceeded to massage smudges from his lenses.

"What's wrong with the show?" she asked, too anxious to wait for him to begin.

"Huh?" He halted his cleaning effort and tilted his head. "Look at you, Blitzen, being all energetic about

Pet Parade. Let's hope it's not too little, too late."

"What's that supposed to mean?" Warning signals clanged in her head like a fire alarm. She sat up straighter and leaned forward, elbows on the countertop. "Are you giving me the axe?"

"Me?" Dean shook his head. "Blitz, I wouldn't think of it. But, hey, that's me. I'm a sucker for your silly face."

She took a breath. "But?"

"The audience doesn't *relate* to you." Dean had put his glasses back on his face and waved his fingers in air quotes when he said the word *relate*. "This, apparently, a result of some internet sleuthing on Melanie Robertson's part. She's a hawk about numbers."

The waitress brought him his cup of coffee, and Aubrey ordered an iced tea. Dean ordered a BLT, extra crispy bacon, the way he knew Aubrey liked it. "Mayo on the side, right?" he asked Aubrey. She nodded dully. Like she could eat.

"Okay," Dean said leaning close. "Stop looking like we need to call the undertaker. There's been no death…yet."

"The audience doesn't like me." Aubrey was surprised at how quickly tears shot to her eyes. Fatigue was a pitiless companion. "The station would be nuts to keep me on as the spokesperson for *Pet Parade* under those circumstances."

"They want you to loosen up, act more like you care. Kind of tough, I realize, when animals tend to scare the bejesus out of you." Dean shook a sad head. "What am I to do with you?"

A lousy tear dribbled over the rim of her eye. Aubrey was quick to swat it away before it had the chance to parade down her cheek. The BLT arrived. She grabbed the pickle, minding its own business on the white ceramic plate, and bit the end off with a snap. "I need to fix this, Dean. I'm screwed without this gig. I can't go back to writing ad copy. Not unless I want to live in a tent."

"Let's go back to the station and watch some footage. We'll critique, tweak, and strategize. How's that?"

"Dean, you do know how much I appreciate the time you put into me, don't you? I promise I'll fix this. I won't let you down."

"I believe in you, kid. I watched the episodes last night and, got to tell you, you're stiff as a board in the spots with the K-9 cop. Whew! You act like he and his furry friend are poisonous. He do something to piss you off?"

Her heart squeezed like a fist. *Oh God,* she thought. How double-cruddy was it that her attempt to mask an attraction to Asa could be just what put her in the poor house?

"It's not him. It's me. I can fix this. Really."

"Your next spot involves the lady from the Insect Museum down in Toms River. Melanie is going to be there. Not to freak you out even more, but she's anxious for the ratings to spike." He twisted his mouth. "And she's going to decide if it's with, or without, you."

Taking the last bite of the dill spear, Aubrey pondered the irony of being in a pickle while a pickle was in her.

****

Asa felt better after the shower even though he knew what awaited him downstairs was a new-perm-headed Sherlock Holmes in an apron. When he'd buzzed past her, after getting home from the craziest night he'd ever spent, Mom was jumpier than Scout when he came through the door.

"Zero to sixty," she said with her mouth pulled sideways. "Not your style. Ever."

"I'm going upstairs to grab some paperwork before I head over to the department," he'd said. ignoring his mother's lead-in.

She called up the stairs as he bounded up followed by a wagging-tailed Scout. "We'll talk later." It wasn't a casual comment. It was a promise.

There was no time for a motherly interrogation. He was due to meet with his unit on the strategy of the drug operation they'd been working on for months.

"You're leaving so soon?" his mother asked, when she saw him with Scout's leash in his hands.

"Duty calls, Mom." He pulled a bottle of water from the fridge.

"What time can we expect you?"

"Not sure. Don't worry about me, though."

"I'm excited to get to know your girlfriend. Got my hair done yesterday. How do you like it?"

Asa blew out a long breath to the ceiling. "Mom, she's not my girlfriend. She's a friend that will be joining us for turkey dinner. Simple as that. And your hair's, uh, pretty."

"But you told me you are *interested* in this person. Isn't that specifically what you said, that you're *interested?* I know you, son of mine. You're not the type to use that word unless you mean it."

Mom turned away and patted the tight ringlets on her crown. "Do I look like a poodle? Your father's been calling me Fifi."

He couldn't help it, Asa let out a string of chuckles. "Pop's a comedian, Mom. Don't pay him any mind."

"I wanted to make a good impression on your girlfriend."

"Ma," he all but groaned. "Stop. She's a friend."

"Yeah, okay." She went to the sink, turned on the faucet, and squirted a stream of green dishwashing soap into the basin. "And I'm Santa Claus."

****

The guys meandered into the conference room, Asa's boss, Michael, at the podium in the front of the room. The white board behind him displayed a schematic of Neptune Junction's downtown main drag.

A red "X" marked the building across the block from the movie theatre—an old broken-down factory that had served as a ladies slip manufacturer back in the thirties and forties. Now, the brick edifice was a decrepit eyesore that the town had sanctioned for demolition. It was to be replaced by an apartment high-rise as part of their renaissance.

"Gentlemen," Michael said, calling them to order.

"This is it, pal," Dylan said from the seat next to Asa.

Michael went over the plan. Word was out that the drug kingpin was meeting with his people in the abandoned factory. It was an ideal opportunity to nab the whole slew of lowlifes and get their asses off the street.

Friday night at eleven. Asa slid his hand from his lap and let it rest on the crown on Scout's big head. This would be the culmination of what they'd worked on for all these weeks. This was what he and Scout were born to do. He massaged the short fur between his dog's brows.

Chapter Twenty-Eight

By Wednesday evening Aubrey had read up on insects so much she'd have thought that the idea of interviewing the keeper of things like eight-appendaged daddy long legs wouldn't make her squeamish. But, who was she kidding? A big fat *EEEEK!* waited on her lips like a canker sore.

How the hell was she supposed to impress Melanie Robertson during Friday's taping with the bug lady? There was so much on the line—her house, her career, and not the least of all, Dean's faith in her. There weren't too many people left on the planet that had invested in her the way Dean Manning had. She needed to keep this job.

After dinner, Asa arrived as planned to discuss the house repairs. Aubrey didn't even know if she'd be able to pay for the cost of the materials at this point.

"Hi. You look worried," he said, as he came into the house.

"No, I'm fine."

"Well, something's bothering you. Are you concerned about the work around here? Believe me, I know what I'm doing. And cost-wise, I'll go easy on you. Deal's a deal."

There it was again. The reminder that this big blond specimen was here in her house, and would be her Thanksgiving dinner companion, simply because they'd made a deal.

The kiss they'd shared had been what? She didn't know. Had it been a substitute for a handshake when they'd sealed their deal? *So much better than a handshake.*

"Work's driving me kind of nuts right now."

"I know what that's like," he said. "How are you doing with your phobia?"

Her face must have looked like he'd slapped it. She felt the blanching of her skin. Just saying the word *phobia* gave her a jab like a crazed dog had just broken his leash, or a tarantula had crawled across her arm.

"Hey, I'm sorry." He reached out a hand although he didn't touch her. "I didn't mean to, you know, bring up a tricky topic." He pulled out a notepad and an industrial-looking measuring tape from his cargo pocket. "Maybe I better just get to work and keep my big mouth shut."

"No, it's okay, really." She produced a laugh that she hoped was convincing. "Let me help you."

They went down the hallway. Aubrey assisted by holding the end of the tape measure and answering questions he had about things like paint preferences, three-quarter round molding, and scheduling the work.

"I'm going to take a look up there." Asa pointed upward to the attic's hatch. The ladder was still balanced against the hallway wall from when he'd put it there the other day.

He braced the apparatus under the hatch with impressive agility and hoisted himself up into the attic.

"I suppose you have a flashlight on you," Aubrey called out, hearing the snarkiness in her own tone.

"What kind of a fool do you take me for?" he shot

back, but his voice was coated in lightheartedness. Aubrey was getting to know the man.

"Hey." Asa's face appeared in the opening. "You want this pipe I found on the floor? And what about this picture in the busted frame? There's broken glass all around, but I can clean that up when I'm working up here."

Aubrey thought of the annoying scent that Asa had defined as the smell of tobacco. Now that she knew who the ghost was, Aubrey wanted to get a better look at the items.

"Can you hand them to me, the picture and the pipe?"

"I can bring them down. I suggest you stay away from ladders for now."

She shook her head. He really could be a wise ass. But he wasn't wrong on that point, so she kept mum.

In a while they moved to the dining room where Asa inspected the damage to the shelf that had fallen. The *Welcome* blocks were still on the floor in their strange arrangement of E L C.

"Still think that's interesting," he said, pointing the end of his tape measure at the blocks.

"Freaky actually," Aubrey said. "What scares me is how I'm starting to get used to this kind of stuff happening around here."

"Any news yet from Ira about when to do another séance?"

"Not yet," Aubrey replied. "But I don't expect to hear about that until after Thanksgiving."

Asa tilted his head. A smile grew on his lips, waking up the dimples in his cheeks. "You ready for Thanksgiving?"

She nodded while trying not to acknowledge the little buzz going on in her veins when the man looked at her like that. "Got two bottles of Simply Savvy cosmos. All set."

Asa whistled through his lower teeth. "Just warning you. My mother's got us picking out china patterns."

Heat climbed up her cheeks.

Asa's eyes studied her face. Something glistened in his brown eyes.

She turned from his gaze. "Can I get you something to drink? I've got iced tea, soda." There was beer in the fridge as well, but common sense told her bringing booze into the mix would be the undoing of what resolve remained. The offer had been a diversion of sorts, a way to fill the silence that hung between them like a web.

"Sure," he said. "I just need to go over this list before I leave. I should have the numbers by tomorrow. That good?"

"Great," she said, avoiding his eyes.

He followed her to the kitchen.

"I didn't, uh, get a chance to move this," she said when she saw Asa looking at the china chips still arrayed on the tabletop. "It'll just take a minute." She grabbed the bucket from the corner by the back door.

"Wait," he said.

She couldn't wait. Her heart raced as if she'd been running. Joanie's comment about not disturbing something that had just begun danced around in her mind.

Only, did she have it in her to give in to the feelings that had begun days ago, the quaking that now threatened to unravel her completely? At the moment all she could think of was to stop her plunge. There was just so much vulnerability she was able to handle.

With the edge of one hand, she slid the pieces back into the bucket where they clicked and clacked as they fell.

****

Asa had seen the look in her eyes, the chameleon oranges and browns of the orbs morphing like a kaleidoscope of amber. Aubrey wanted him. He saw it, felt it. A pulling sensation teased him deep inside.

What a mess it would be to act on what was happening between them. There was no room in his life or in his beat-to-shit heart for a woman like Aubrey Donner. She was too real. This was too real.

He hadn't felt this in a long time, had made sure not to. Yet, he betrayed himself with each glance, each inch he took in her direction. He looked at the pieces of broken china that had plopped back into the pail like a mountain of bones left after a feast. But there was no feast here this evening. Tonight there was only hunger.

Aubrey had washed her hands and was drying them on a dishtowel. Her back was to him, and while she gazed out the window above the sink he was free to indulge his eyes in her silhouette, despite his common sense.

He liked the slope of her shoulders, and it was just now, as he took in the delicate line, that he realized it. He admired her coltish legs in faded denim and the curvature of her bottom, envious of the good fortune of the patch pockets that caressed her there.

Aubrey's hair—that crazy mane that he'd first laid eyes on—was up on her head in a fastener, wisps hanging down on either side of her elegant neck. This woman would be the toughest one to keep at a distance. He wanted the total opposite. Tonight he just wanted her.

****

It was so black outside that Aubrey could see Asa in the reflection of the glass, behind her. He was staring at her. She felt the magnet of his eyes. Her body knew the path his gaze had taken.

What happened to the woman who not long ago might have spun around with indignation? Where had her resolve gone? That woman was not in her kitchen tonight. After a deep breath, she did turn around. But she did not flee, nor accuse.

Aubrey dared to smile. "How about a beer?"

"Sure," he said, with a steady gaze.

Standing at the fridge, Aubrey handed Asa a long-necked bottle and took one for herself. The skin on the inside of her thumb hurt as she twisted the cap off. She took a deep pull, surprising herself at how good the cold beverage tasted. She felt its chilly tingle as it traveled through her.

She was in trouble. Every little thing had come into focus. Especially the electricity between her and Asa. She watched him tilt his head back while he swigged from his beer, his strong neck craned back, tight.

"Hits the spot," he said, giving her a dimple.

Oddly, that tempting pinch in his cheek was not what made her take a step in his direction. It was the light in his liquid chocolate eyes—a beam of wanting, of caution, of question, of hope, of anticipation. All those lights flashed at her, called her. The warning that yakked in her mind went unheeded. All she did was follow the light.

"Aubrey..." There was hesitation in his tone as he put his beer down on the table.

She stopped. She waited.

Their eyes were locked, and they did not speak. It could have been a showdown, the way their stiff selves stood on either side of an imaginary line. It was her line to cross. They both knew it.

Aubrey took a step away and put her beer down on the kitchen counter. Her fingers lingered on the cool glass. She let them trail up then down the frosty bottle.

When she looked back at Asa, wanting so alive on his face it stole her breath. She moved closer to him then tilted her head to meet his gaze.

His tone was husky, deep. "Be sure...before you take that last step." His chest rose and fell as he breathed. "What do you want, Aubrey?"

As if suspended in time, Aubrey had a choice. She could retreat, deny the feelings. In this moment, she could stay here, a breath away, and guard herself from whatever lay beyond the pulsing want of this man.

Her hand, with a mind of its own, rose to touch his cheek—rough and smooth both. As her finger pads caressed him, an odd thought that he probably couldn't grow a full beard occurred to her.

Asa wrapped a big hand around her wrist and held it firm. Eyes burning, he almost looked angry. "Damn," he muttered under his breath. He tugged her close and planted a possessive kiss on her mouth.

Aubrey tasted the beer on his lips, or was it hers? Instinctively her arms wound around him and she pressed him even closer, her body melding to his, like two pieces that made a whole.

He groaned a low, sexy sound as he hands slid a slow path down her body, squeezing her waist then traveling to the curve of her bottom.

Aubrey pushed away, chest heaving with deep breaths, eyes pinned by Asa's fiery stare. "Take me there," she breathed, pointing an astonishing finger to the ceiling where her bedroom waited above them on the second floor.

In one swift move Asa swooped her up into his arms. She let him kiss away the *holy crap* that her mind chanted. Her life lately had been a series of hesitations. No more.

Chapter Twenty-Nine

They were a tangle of limbs, urgent mouths, and melded bodies—hasty, wanton, breathless. Aubrey's senses surged with every touch, every taste, and she matched Asa's passion with equal intoxicating fervor.

Spent, Aubrey lay panting, listening to the reliable, comforting thump of Asa's recovering heartbeats. She trailed a finger over the skin of the powerful arm that crooked around her. Snippets of the love they had made teased her brain, and a sheepish hand swooped to cover her eyes as though that would keep Asa from knowing where her mind was.

He jostled her with his arm, dipped his head and kissed her crown. "What are you thinking about?" he asked, his voice barely above a whisper.

"Mmmm, nothing," she responded. "Everything."

He kissed the top of her head again. "You're amazing."

She sat up, his arm falling away. The light in the hallway was on and its beam cast a swath across her bed. She pulled the sheet up over herself, suddenly shy at what exactly he meant by *amazing*. A host of things crossed her mind, all of which caused her blood to pump.

"I'm still rocked by what just happened." She raked a hand through her unruly hair and uttered a little laugh. "I mean, weren't we just measuring for how much plasterboard for you to buy?"

"Nooooo." He trailed the word like he was smarter than to believe her rendition of how they had come to be naked in bed together. "That's not quite how it went."

Aubrey flopped back onto her pillow. "Oh yeah, now I remember. You picked me up and dragged me up here kicking and screaming. I was Fay Wray; you were the furry guy that swats planes from the top of the Empire State Building."

Asa laughed a loud hearty sound that made her grin so wide her cheeks hurt. "Really?" he said. "That's really how you want to spin this?"

She shrugged a nonchalant shoulder. "Simply the way I remember it."

"Yeah?" He rolled onto his side, lifted himself up, and hovered over her. "Want to know what I remember?" His eyes were devilish, his mouth curved in an intoxicating tease.

With a light, feathery touch she trailed the tip of her index finger down the chest that lingered above her. "I'm listening."

His mouth crashed down on hers, and she wrapped her arms around his neck. Asa pressed himself against her, undulated a message from his body to hers.

She was completely wrapped in a blanket of feelings and touches, and the bonding of the physical. Yet, on some plane Aubrey was acutely aware that with each caress the difference between feeling and emotion had knit into one tight fabric.

Later, after Aubrey had dozed into a dreamless, satisfying sleep she awoke to a feathery sensation trailing along her skin. Her eyes fluttered open.

Asa, head supported on a bent arm, was on his side. His index finger traced the line of the scar on her thigh, the ugly, tight, shiny-skinned byproduct of her childhood disfigurement. A flood of loathing rushed through her, and she shoved his hand away. She pulled the sheet up over herself.

Asa grabbed her wrist. "Let me."

"No." Aubrey attempted to break his hold, but he tightened his grip. "Don't."

Loosening his hold, Asa leaned over and brushed soft lips over hers. "You're beautiful."

Ridiculous tears sprung to her eyes, and all she could do was blink at them.

"Every part of you." He slowly pushed the sheet from her body. He focused on the blemished skin, then met her eyes.

In a swift move Asa was there, bent over her. Slowly, methodically, he planted soft kisses along the snaking scar. Biting her lip, Aubrey held her breath, her muscles clenched in a kind of appall.

But the kissing continued, light touches of his warm lips on her skin.

Slowly, touch by touch, Aubrey's muscles softened and her insides went liquid. Her hand moved to rest on Asa's head. She caressed the blond crown, dug her fingers into the thickness and curled them around the strands, and held on tight.

****

Aubrey was in a plaid flannel robe. The big, belled sleeves swagged wide from her arms as Asa watched her prepare a pot of tea.

He wasn't a tea drinker, had always categorized the stuff as a remedy for colds and flu—right up there with chicken broth. But, tonight this woman could convince him to do anything. Even drink something called *oolong*.

Each time she looked up from her task—one time with a measuring spoon in her hand, another while placing a delicate lid on top of a china teapot—Aubrey had given him that smile. It was a pink curve of shyness, yet so succulent a mouth that it seemed to him a dichotomy of what burned inside her. It drove him wild.

Everything about her was like that. She was ferocious, but too, she was a skittish colt. She was headstrong, yet leery; assured, yet vulnerable. Aubrey Donner was a Tilt-O-Whirl. And, God help him, all he wanted was to ride that ride.

After drinking the *oolong*—which had a rich, woodsy taste that surprisingly appealed to him—it was time to leave. He had lingered as long as he could without giving in to the urge to repeat the King Kong routine, as the little smart-ass had jokingly referred to it.

"It's pretty late," he said.

"Very late," she said, with a smirk. As if the fact that he'd been with her for hours had been his doing alone. He liked when she teased him this way.

Women didn't usually behave around him like that. He knew he had the reputation of being sort of arrogant. He wasn't, not really. But the façade had served him well. It had worked just fine in cementing the fortress with which he surrounded himself. But, that wasn't the case with Aubrey. Not anymore. Not by a long shot.

"I should go," he said. He cast a glance to the clock over the kitchen sink. It was a few minutes before midnight. "It's almost Thanksgiving."

"Guess I'll be seeing you later today, then."

"Be prepared. My mother's going to drive you nuts."

"Hmmmmm, like mother, like son?"

He couldn't help it; Asa wrapped that smart-aleck into his arms and held her tight.

****

Aubrey's pillow smelled like Asa's musky, earthy aftershave she loved. She breathed in the scent, remembering the love they'd made.

This was new. She hadn't felt this way before. Not with the college boyfriends, certainly, nor anyone that had followed. Not even Charlie Alexander, Chaz as he'd preferred—the one she could have convinced herself to love, if she'd had her feet to the fire.

But when her mother had become so ill that Aubrey had to uproot, Chaz had decided it was the ideal time for the two of them to *reassess* where their relationship was going. To say it had been cruddy timing on his part was an understatement. It had been a deal breaker to Aubrey.

A man that wouldn't emotionally support a woman when she needed it wasn't worth crap. It was then, of course, that Joanie had begun to refer to him as *Up Chuck.*

As she drifted off to sleep, Aubrey thought of Asa and how each time he touched her or looked at her with that dimpled smile, it was like another silken thread pulling her into a web. Then she dreamed about spiders, and the impending interview with the bug lady from Toms River, until the witching hour of three-eleven—when the ghost of Montgomery Donner woke her again.

Chapter Thirty

A tenuous figure hovered at the end of her bed, a kind of billowy silhouette. Aubrey tried hard to find some resemblance to the stern man in the pictures of Montgomery Donner she'd seen.

There was nothing but shadow, no square jaw line, no sign of the thin seam of a mouth, no piercing eyes filled with disdain.

Tonight she was not afraid. She jumped up from her bed and with fists at her side made a demand. "Now you want contact, old man? Now? After torturing my mother all those years and renouncing me my whole life, you come calling? What the hell do you want, for crying out loud?"

She wasn't even concerned that there could be something seriously wrong with her. After all, she was talking to a black cloud of nothing. She expected it to dissolve, maybe, or at least fizzle away like the particles of dust in the sky after fireworks. But the stubborn gloominess lingered there at the foot of her bed, unmoving.

The hip-high bookcase in the corner of her room tipped over, spewing books and trinkets to the floor with a series of plops. Aubrey, angrier now, charged to the light switch while muttering a string of "Oh no, you don'ts." A flip of one finger bathed the space in brightness. And the ghost was gone.

"Yeah, that's right, loser. Bite the dust."

She righted the small shelf unit, all the while uttering a series of expletives that she normally saved for things like flat tires or having no umbrella during a typhoon.

The books, collectibles from her growing up—the Nancy Drew collection and a few children's storybooks—were splayed across the rag rug. Aubrey got down on her knees and reached for them.

The Secret in the Old Attic had fallen in a way that it had wedged itself into the pages of a vintage volume that her mother had given her as a little girl— *Cinderella.*

It may have simply been the way the two books fell that caused them to all but meld together in a kind of embrace of pages. But, these days, with all the crazy stuff that had gone on, and particularly because the spilled books happened with the appearance of the ghost, she was curious.

Aubrey sat on her rump and pulled the two books into her hands. Was there a message here somehow? She thought of the wooden blocks that had fallen in the dining room, their configuration spelling *E L C* right after Ira the Elk had performed the séance. Was she reading something into nothing?

She carefully opened the paired books. The pre-teen mystery involved clues in an attic. Aubrey thought of the pipe, with the signature scent, and the old photograph that had been retrieved from her attic and now sat on her kitchen table. Were these clues for her in this Montgomery Donner nuisance?

Cinderella, the book she remembered now that her mother had purchased at a rummage sale, creaked when she lifted the cover. Inside she read that the volume was one of a series of books called the *Threepenny Books* by George Routledge. Three pennies.

She dropped the books when her bedroom light went out, as if someone had flipped the switch.

Chapter Thirty-One

Sufficiently spooked, Aubrey grabbed her robe and all but ran down the staircase in the dark. She held her hands on the walls so she wouldn't tumble and break her neck.

Every light source in the kitchen was ablaze—the overhead, the tiffany lamp over the table, the stove light.

Aubrey pulled the pipe into her hands. She breathed in a deep whiff of the tobacco remnants that had been burned in the carved bowl of the smoke piece so many years ago. The scent was the same. *What was it about the pipe?* she wondered, as she turned it over in her hands.

The brass band that ringed the swoop of its neck was engraved. Her fingernail followed the etching in the metal. *Beaver Creek, Pa.* It meant nothing to her.

Aubrey put the pipe down and picked up the photo in the cracked frame. She was startled again at how normal the couple appeared, how contented her mother had looked as a small child.

What had made the man in the tweedy suit and skinny black tie dictatorial enough to ruin the stability of his family, bust it apart with a lack of humanity just as if he'd pulled the trigger of a loaded gun?

It saddened Aubrey to see her ancestors, posed as a family in front of someone's camera lens, knowing they had all died without each other. Eternally disjointed.

She tried to sleep on the sofa, to no avail. She wished she could call Aunt Molly and have her run the latest occurrence by Ira. She thought of calling Joanie. But it was the middle of the night. She decided to wait until she was at Asa's house for dinner, to get him alone, and tell him what had happened—get his take.

Her mind, refusing to rest, busily zoomed with thoughts of the day that would be upon her shortly. It was technically already Thanksgiving.

In a few short hours she would find herself having dinner at Asa's table. Now that they'd shamelessly rolled around together, the whole thought of spending a day under the scrutinizing eye of his mother gave her the willies.

The clock on the mantel told her there was plenty of time to get ready, prepare herself, and find something to wear that wouldn't tip her hand. Somehow timidity shrouded her. It was one thing to have a nighttime beer buzz and give into some deep-seated yearnings. It was entirely another to break bread with her horizontal cohort and his zealous cupid-prone mother.

Her lack of sleep would only make matters worse. When she wasn't rested enough to be on guard, she feared one encounter with the dimple might very well do her in.

****

Aubrey hoped the autumnal plaid skirt and bone-colored blouse she'd finally chosen to wear were appropriate. Standing at Asa's front door, her downcast gaze found her legs, exposed from the knee down.

Oh God, she wished she could get it out of her

head how those legs had been wrapped around her big blond host. Happily wrapped. And how he'd trailed a finger over the ugly scar on her thigh, then had stolen her breath with a trail of kisses along the unsightly line.

Asa opened the door. "Hi." His chocolate eyes shone with the familiarity of intimacy.

A flush of heat climbed up her face. "Hi." She couldn't pull her eyes away from him. She had wondered if, in the light of day, she'd be immune to the effect of the man. Nope. She lifted the satchel in her grasp. "Brought the cosmos."

He gave her the dimple.

Her heart thanked him, and she entered through the threshold. His musky scent filled her lungs, igniting thoughts of last night.

"Hello!" Asa's mother, dressed in a burgundy pantsuit, came up behind him. "Louis, come meet Aubrey. I just love your name, by the way."

"Thank you. Happy Thanksgiving, Mrs. Kavanaugh."

"You, too, dear. But please call me Jenny. And, this is Louie." Asa's father, a tall handsome man that looked like an older version of his son appeared before her.

"Nice to meet you," she offered.

"Hi, there," Asa's dad said. His smile was the same, though etched with age. He even had a dimple.

"Come in and make yourself at home," Jenny said. "Hope you're hungry!"

She linked her arm through Aubrey's. "What have you got there?"

"Simply Savvy Cosmos."

Jenny whooped. She turned to flash her son a look.

"She's a keeper."

****

The table was set so prettily that Aubrey wondered how much time it had taken Jenny to organize. She had to be one of those Martha Stewart-types that knew just how to arrange pinecones and dried leaves, as part of a centerpiece, without it turning out looking as if someone had left a window open and debris had blown in.

Aubrey touched the pad of her fingertip to a cluster of russet and gold oak leaves displayed on the table. Her mind again went to Asa's words when he'd told her she was a lit match and he the November leaves.

She snatched her finger away as if the leaves were ablaze. Did Asa really believe she had that effect on him? Together were they the two necessary ingredients to build a fire?

Despite her best intention, she stole a gaze. Asa's eyes were on her, luminous, afire. She didn't know how it was possible, but she was certain he'd read her mind.

If the aromas filling the home were any indication, Jenny was a terrific cook. The woman's talents were adding up, and Aubrey was a combination of awe and intimidation.

She'd loved her mother, but Caroline hadn't exactly been a whiz in the kitchen. An aficionado in the many uses of ground beef, Mom was no gastronome. But dinner had always been on the table and Mom had taken pride in their little house, their mini family.

Aubrey's heart ached with need. She had to keep the house. And that meant tomorrow, during the taping of *Pet Parade,* with all eyes on her she had to step up and be one with the creepy creatures.

"Tell us, Aubrey. How did you and Asa come to be?"

"Mom," Asa interrupted. "I told you this. Aubrey's been interviewing me for that show on Mid Shore Live. Remember? You saw the episode with Scout performing the maze routine."

"That was some demonstration, son," Louie said. "Scout's such an impressive dog."

Hearing his name, Scout meandered in from the living room and sat on the floor by Jenny.

"See that?" Asa pointed to Scout who strategically positioned himself by the softest sell in the room. "He knows you're going to slip him some table scraps. Please don't, Ma."

"You're such a party pooper," she said. "It's Thanksgiving, for crying out loud. Let the good boy have some turkey."

"He can have some turkey, but not from the table. And, to remind you, that goes for tomorrow's leftovers as well. Tomorrow's a big day for the two of us."

"Yes, we know. Something 'big' you can't talk about. I hate when you're hush-hush about an assignment. It makes me nervous." His mother shook her curly head.

Aubrey slipped her gaze to Asa. He hadn't mentioned the assignment to her. But, why should he? That would indicate some version of a relationship. Was there one brewing between them? Did she want that? Did he?

"You're pretty rigid with Scout. That part of the job?" his dad asked.

Asa nodded. "It's got to be."

Aubrey eyed the pooch sitting at attention, big dark

eyes glued on Asa's mom. He licked his chops while he waited patiently. She was surprised when an urge to give him a sample of something struck her.

She wondered about Asa's stoicism regarding the dog. Was it merely the rules of the K-9 program that kept him so rigid, as he'd said? Or was it that easy for the man to close himself off from becoming emotionally involved?

Again, her mind relived their heated entanglement. Visions of the two of them wrapped around each other, of his kisses, his daring passion stole her breath. Had it been presumptuous to believe they'd shared emotion, along with raw connectedness?

"Anyway," Jenny said. "Aubrey, so, about you and Mr. Don't Break The Rules…"

Asa opened his mouth to protest and Jenny held up a hand. "Yes, we know how you met. What I'd love to know is how you two kids decided to, you know, date."

Her eyes were on Aubrey, eyes lighter than her son's but just as penetrating. Aubrey's mouth went dry and she lifted her water glass to her lips, for both a sip and a chance to come up with something.

"Mom, come on," Asa said. "No more questions." He turned to Aubrey with a reassuring smile. "How about we clean up and let these two enjoy their coffee?"

"That's a deal," Aubrey said, with a smile of relief. She got up from her seat and quickly gathered dishes into her hands.

"Fine, you two," Jenny said with a Cheshire grin. "Just don't dare elope, or anything. I want to dance with my son at his wedding."

"You're relentless," Louie said with a laugh. "Good thing you make one hell of a pumpkin pie."

****

Asa washed, Aubrey dried.

Standing next to him at the double sink, their bodies grazing from time to time, Aubrey was surprised at how much she liked it. And how it scared the crap out of her, too.

"Let me ask you something…"

"Shoot." He handed her the wet gravy boat.

"Your Dad commented on the way you are with Scout. I see how good you are with him, and how well-reared he is. I mean, honestly, I never thought I could be around a dog that size and not need a tranquilizer."

"So, what's your question, Miss Pet Parade?"

She laughed. "I really haven't seen much outward affection. I mean, do you ever romp around with him or, I don't know, throw him a stick or anything like that?"

"Sure," Asa said. "On occasion. Scout knows when it's down time. But it's important to keep play and work well-defined, for the sake of the integrity of our work."

"Seems like a raw deal for Scout."

"Careful," Asa said handing her a serving tray. "You're starting to sound like you've got some affection for my business partner."

As if on cue, the big dog lumbered into the room. His jaw was working around something. Judging by the gleeful wag of his tail, Aubrey guessed Jenny had slipped him a treat after all.

"What are you smacking your lips about?" Asa asked the dog.

Scout trotted over and sat at Asa's feet, his tail continuing to wag and acting as a kind of sweeper on the wooden kitchen floor.

Asa touched the top of the dog's head and gave his ears a rumple. "Lucky for you, buddy, my mother doesn't listen to a single thing I say."

There it was, Aubrey thought. A light came into Asa's chocolate eyes and an affectionate smile claimed his mouth. The handsome officer was not immune to the dog's obvious love for him. She was surprised at how glad she felt.

Aubrey could hear Asa's parents' voices in the dining room and decided that she and Asa had a few minutes alone.

"The ghost came back again last night."

He stood up straight and his hands drifted to his hips. "Tell me what happened."

Asa's cell phone rang. "I'm sorry. I've been waiting for my supervisor's call. I have to get this." He grabbed the device and switched it on.

"Sure, go ahead."

"We'll pick this conversation back up later. Excuse me," he said, leaving the room.

That left her alone with a dog that probably weighed in about as much as she did, only with a whole lot more muscle and God only knew how many more teeth.

Chapter Thirty-Two

Scout stared at her, eyes steady, ears perked straight up. Aubrey swallowed hard as she dried the last handful of silverware. She looked down at the spoons in her grasp. Not exactly a weapon if she needed one.

He took a tentative step in her direction. She could tell he was well aware of her skittishness around him. Dogs knew that stuff. She'd read it a thousand times over the years. But, didn't that tend to aggravate the beasts? She swallowed hard.

What was it Asa had told her? Give him her hand to sniff? Palm up? Palm down? Smile. Definitely smile.

She reached out her palm and Scout came closer, sniffing her skin with his big black nose. His tail started to wag, slowly at first. When she put her hand on his head in the same place Asa had—the soft spot between his ears—Scout's tail turned into a frenzied metronome.

A smile, a genuine silly-assed grin broke out on her face. *That,* she decided, *deserves a treat and Asa be damned.*

She popped open the lid to a plastic storage container and snatched out a chunk of dark turkey meat.

Well, she couldn't throw it on the floor. She scanned the room and didn't see the dog's bowls. Maybe she hadn't thought it through. But it was too late. Scout was drooling, and his nostrils were wiggling in and out at the smell of the turkey in her fingers.

She laid the strip of meat across her palm and lowered it under his mouth—his big, slobbery mouth. She felt like one of those screwballs at the circus that put their head in a lion's mouth simply for the oohs and aahs of the crowd. On what planet had some idiot thought that that, or even this, was a good idea?

A silky-looking but surprisingly sandpaper-rough tongue lapped up the turkey from her palm, leaving nothing behind but a slick of wetness.

"How's that, huh?" she asked him. She found it easy to talk to the dog. Even liked it. There was no pretense with Scout. There were no nuances to worry about, no words to assess or analyze. Just a wagging tail and a bright-eyed look of gratitude. "That's good stuff, isn't it?"

Scout rubbed his head against her leg, a kind of nuzzle. She instinctively put her hand on his head again and rumpled his ears the way Asa had. Scout's eyes squeezed closed with bliss, at least it seemed like bliss. "I think you're nothing but a big flirt. Yes. You're a lover, aren't you?"

"Someone's got a friend," Louie said, as he entered the kitchen. "He's irresistible, huh?"

Aubrey looked at Asa's dad. It surprised her, but yes. Scout was irresistible.

"He sure likes you," Louie said.

This made her smile even more.

"I can tell when a guy's smitten. Trust me. There's another smitten fella around here."

She met his gaze, alight with a teasing glint much like the one she'd seen plenty of times in his son's eyes.

"Don't tell Asa, but I gave him a hunk of turkey."

Louie laughed a hearty sound. "Good for you."

"By the way, did you get a chance to taste that elderberry wine?"

"What elderberry wine?"

"Oh, Asa brought you a sample from my house. I thought he'd have given it to you."

Louie shook his head. "Not yet."

Jenny carried in the stainless steel coffee carafe in one hand and a pair of coffee mugs looped by their handles in her other. "What's going on in here?"

"Aubrey here just snuck somebody a hunk of meat," Louie said. He put a finger to his lips. "Our secret. Don't tell Officer Kavanaugh."

Jenny laughed, too.

It was a good feeling to be surrounded by the pair's joviality. It reminded Aubrey of what it had been like to have family.

Louie left the room, and Aubrey heard him saying something to Asa about the football game that was on the living room's TV.

"Forget it," Jenny said. "Those two will be entrenched in that stupid game for hours."

Aubrey was itching to talk to Asa about the ghost, and the way the books had fallen, but that would have to wait. "Can I help you with anything?" Aubrey asked.

"Sure, lend me a hand packaging up some of this food. And all these pies. I always make too many."

"All okay in here?" Asa stuck his head in through the doorway. "Aubrey, sorry our earlier conversation got interrupted."

"We're good." Aubrey flashed him a look to convey his mom wasn't drilling her, at least not at the moment. "We'll continue our chat later, not a problem."

"Going to watch the game with Pops, then."

"We'll be out there with you soon enough," Jenny said, sending her son back to the game.

Aubrey took the roll of aluminum foil and tore off a large piece. She followed Jenny's lead and wrapped a sizeable wedge of pie up into a neat package.

"I'm going to freeze some of this, but let's make you a goody bag to take home."

"Oh, no thank you. Really. It's terrific, but I shouldn't be left alone with pie."

Jenny laughed. "You're funny. Okay, I won't hound you. Just take one piece. Which is your favorite?"

There was no getting around bringing home some pie. "Coconut custard, but just a small slice, please."

"Asa's favorite, too. But I'm sure you know that."

She didn't, but she didn't tell his mother that.

"He likes you. But you know that, too."

Aubrey didn't know what to say about that. Did Asa like her? Yes. But how deep that went, well, that was the mystery. Another mystery was why it seemed to matter to her like it did.

"Look at you blushing." Jenny's grin was big and genuine. "My son's gotten to you."

Aubrey continued to wrap hunks of pie. She just couldn't elaborate on the woman's musings. Was she afraid any words would reveal too much of what she was thinking, feeling, wanting?

"I'm starting to think you'll be different than the others. You know, whoever he's dated since Cheryl died."

Cheryl?

"That was such a devastation for him. You know, it's horrible enough to lose your fiancée in a car

240

accident, but a pregnant fiancée is, well, beyond tragic."

Jenny was looking at her, had stopped wrapping leftover dessert. She was waiting for Aubrey's reaction, concurrence maybe, something. But Aubrey was so stunned that she couldn't find her voice.

"I'm sorry, dear," Jenny said. "This is no topic for a day of giving thanks."

"No," Aubrey said. "I understand. Uh, Asa's been through a lot."

"That's for sure." Jenny pointed the end of the box of foil at her. "But I've got high hopes. I see the way Asa looks at you, the way you both are with each other. Warms an old mom's heart."

Aubrey kept her head down, acted like making sure the tin foil was wrapped around the food, like a package going out with UPS, was crucial. Anything to keep from meeting Asa's mother's inquisitive eye.

She knew, without seeing herself in a mirror, that her own eyes would be beacons of truth. And the truth was she wanted like hell to believe every single thing Jenny thought she saw between her and Asa.

"God as my witness, Aubrey," Jenny said with glee. "I'm convinced you're not going to be like the few Asa's dated in the last four years that just faded into the woodwork." She fanned the fingers on one hand like something had gone *poof,* and disappeared.

Aubrey managed a smile, as if she appreciated what Jenny said. In actuality a cool stream of worry flooded her veins.

****

It's weird how Aubrey fits in, Asa thought, as he watched a replay of a questionable call on the field. Just a few days ago he wouldn't have been able to say he even liked the woman, and now here she was chewing the fat with Mom in his kitchen. He could hear an occasional sound of laughter coming from the two women down the hallway.

The craziest part was how comfortable he felt. How easy it would be to just go with it, continue to be in Aubrey Donner's company, to allow the chemistry between them to have its way. Could he do that? He turned his gaze to the open kitchen doorway. His heart thumped.

Mom and Aubrey joined them a few minutes later. Mom took the only available single seat in the room, leaving it necessary for Aubrey to position herself beside Asa on the couch.

"Who's winning?" Aubrey gave him a flash of her amber eyes.

"Nobody at the moment. Tie game."

They watched in silence for a few minutes, but Asa was acutely aware of the slender thigh pressed against his. He felt any minute movement of her body, the slightest pressure of the woman's touch sending signals to every region of his being.

They shared a glance of knowing, acknowledgement. He could escape what was happening about as efficiently as a pile of leaves touched by a lit match could. He was starting to believe that any hope in an about-face was, well, up in smoke.

At half-time Aubrey announced that it was time she went home. "I've got an interview tomorrow that I need to prepare for," she said.

She thanked his parents, even hugged Mom. Pops wrapped an arm around her shoulders and gave her one of his genial squeezes. Scout followed her like she had a turkey leg in her pocket. All of it gave Asa a clench in his chest.

He walked her to her car, Scout joining them.

"He's like your shadow, huh?" Asa motioned his head to the big dog.

"We've decided to be friends," Aubrey said, with an easy grin. "We had a chat."

"Did you? How'd that go?"

"I said 'how about some turkey?' and boom, we were like this," she said, with two fingers crossed.

Asa laughed. "Scout, since when are you so easy?"

He looked at Aubrey—so pretty standing there with her natural grin, and her bright eyes, and her hands full of a tin foil-wrapped package. He had all he could do not to fall in love.

Asa needed to focus on something else. "You were going to tell me about what happened last night."

She told him about the apparition and the overturned bookcase, the way two books fell in a way that sparked her curiosity, similar to the wooden blocks from the dining room shelf that had fallen in their peculiar way.

"I know I'm new to all this kind of stuff," he said. "But I wouldn't rule out anything at this point. Especially not since you've had instances where pennies have shown up in an odd way."

"Damned if I know what it means. I'll run it by Ira and see what he thinks," she said.

"Has he left for his family visit yet?"

"I'll find out later when I give Aunt Molly a call, see how their celebration at the Elks' went."

"Keep me posted."

"Thanks again for the invite today. Your parents

are really nice."

"It's hard to remember that your being here started out as a way of keeping my mother from fixing me up with somebody else."

She tilted her head as she studied him. A question sat in her eyes. She looked as if she was about to say something but, after a pause, she merely nodded.

"Good night." She bent to pet Scout on the head. "You too, Scout." The dog wagged a happy tail.

Before he could think it over or talk himself out of it, Asa shut his mind off and leaned down, planting a kiss on her lips. A split second froze, neither of their mouths moving.

He waited, heart thumping, and then in the next instant her mouth softened, opened, welcomed. He wrapped her up into his arms, pulled her close, and relished the fire.

Chapter Thirty-Three

Aubrey's answering machine blinked red as she walked into her kitchen. She pressed the button and listened to her Aunt Molly's resonant sound as she avidly detailed how "divine" dinner had been at the Elks lodge, and how she hoped Aubrey's had been as well.

Molly then went on to say that she and Ira were having some "private time" before his trip out to his brother's, and she'd talk with Aubrey tomorrow. The implication was apparent, and Aubrey fought hard to banish any saucy images that threatened to pop in her head. Truthfully, though, she was glad that her aunt had apparently found love, or a reasonable facsimile thereof.

She made a cup of tea, settled onto the sofa, and grabbed her phone. She punched in Joanie's digits hoping her friend would pick up.

"Happy Turkey Day," Joanie said into her ear, which made Aubrey smile against the device.

"To you, too. How was it?"

"You know, relatives, too much to eat, too much to drink. In other words, terrific. How was dinner with Officer Hottie?"

Aubrey was silent for a moment, caught off guard by the reference to Asa's level of hotness. *Oh God*, she thought. *Joanie has only been gone a few days and so much is different now.*

"Uh-oh," Joanie said conspiratorially. "You're speechless—either because it was bad, or because it was really, really good."

This made Aubrey laugh, eased her tension. "The latter."

"Was it?" Joanie let out a whoop of glee. Her voice all but squeaked as it lilted up in the question at the end.

"Yes."

"Well, come on, girl. Give me details."

"His parents are really nice. Asa looks so much like his father, it's crazy. His mom is like Suzy Homemaker, but so sweet and friendly."

"Is there a 'but' coming at the end of all this? Because that's what I'm feeling."

Aubrey blew out a long breath. "But I'm kind of freaked. I found out from his mother that Asa had been engaged. His fiancée, his *pregnant fiancée,* was killed in a car accident four years ago. And, according to his mother, Asa has stayed far, far away from any involvement with a woman ever since."

"Wow."

"Yeah. Wow."

"He hasn't told you about it?"

"Nope. Nada. It scares me because, well, you know, I'm starting to like him. Really like him."

"I saw that coming. Just saying." Joanie was great at lightening the mood, but this attempt didn't dispel the clench in Aubrey's chest. "I'm sensing there's more between you two than séances and doggie interviews."

"You could say that, yes. Things have, um, happened."

"Horizontal things?"

Aubrey laughed despite her nervousness. "Really, really good horizontal things."

"Sounds real as real." Joanie's voice brimmed with affection.

"But you know me, Joanie. Don't I always do this, despite my renewed vows to never again throw myself in the path of disappointment? I mean, I'm like a walking billboard for how not to pick a man."

"Hold up." Joanie's voice was firm. "Just because this guy's stayed away from romance for a while doesn't mean he isn't ready now."

"Yeah, right. That's not how it goes."

"Asa Kavanaugh hasn't had *you* cross his path before. This is different. You're irresistible."

Aubrey grinned against the phone. "Asa's Dad said that to me tonight, regarding Scout. Scout, apparently, loves me."

"The big scary shepherd with all the—how did you put it?—razor-like teeth?"

"That would be him. Turns out he's a big softie. I'm kind of fond of him. I even fed him from my hand."

"Who'd have seen that coming?"

"It's funny. It's like just what I needed to get past my issues was put right in my face."

"Hmm," Joanie mused. "You mean just like your winding up right smack in front of Asa?"

"No, it's not the same, Joanie. Asa's not phobic about relationships. He just might be totally done with them."

"So, what does that mean for you, then?"

"Good question."

Chapter Thirty-Four

"This is it," Asa whispered. He was crouched in front of the truck, the cold November night biting his face. The vapor of Scout's breath misted the frigid air.

Scout was alert, charged, aware that this indeed was the moment they'd prepared for even if he hadn't technically understood the words Asa had spoken. They didn't need words.

The team members were assembled in their designated places, ready. The empty factory stood solemn in the night, lit by a lone streetlight casting an anemic beam over the unassuming facade.

They'd confirmed the key players were now in the condemned factory, despite a rumor earlier in the week that the drug dealers might either switch locations or call off the drop.

"Kavanaugh," Michael rasped from behind the truck. He motioned his head with the confirmation signal.

It was time. A surge of anticipation flooded his veins. He tugged on Scout's ear, their sign that this was business, this was serious. Scout met his gaze with bright black acknowledgement.

Asa and Scout advanced toward the building where four officers waited in the shadows of a rusted Dumpster.

On cue they charged through the door, breaking the

lock with their adrenaline-infused might. Scout noiselessly ran ahead, lightning-like, up a metal staircase. At the top, a dark closed metal door flashed a thin line of light from the crack beneath it.

The officers navigated the stairs with trained silence. A vacuous moment of quiet shrouded the team. What followed happened in a kind of suspended animation, a cacophony of rebellion, supplanted by apprehension.

The officers cuffed all three drug dealers, confiscating a suitcase of illegal narcotics and a gym bag filled with stacks of cash. Dylan wound up with a gash on his jaw when one of the culprits clocked him with an empty bottle.

Asa had a nasty bruise on his cheek from a punk's windmill punch, but he could tell the bone hadn't broken. There'd be a nice black and blue formation on his skin come daylight. All in all, they'd avoided major injury.

Scout had held one of the thugs with a clamp of his big jaw on the guy's lower leg while an officer applied handcuffs. That guy was going to need stitches, but that would be the least of his problems.

The suspects had been loaded into the wagon. Asa and two of his fellow officers stood beside his truck with Scout obediently at his master's feet.

Out of nowhere a black cargo van barreled down the desolate street, startling the peaceful aftermath. One of the guys being held in the wagon started to scream what sounded like a warning to *get out*. The van stopped short at the scene of police activity, then maneuvered in a jerky K-turn.

Asa went into the street and commanded the driver

of the van to exit the vehicle. Scout made a beeline to Asa's side. The big dog took two steps forward and released a string of harsh warning barks.

The engine gunned and the big machine charged forward then swung in a wide, screeching circle. The back tire knocked Scout down and rolled its big treads over his body. The dog's yowl rang out like a clap of thunder, halting everything like a judge's gavel.

The van took off on two wheels. Scout lay in a pool of blood in the middle of the road.

Chapter Thirty-Five

At the station, Melanie Robertson sat in a chair beside Dean, the two murmuring while Melanie leafed through a stack of papers.

Aubrey's nerves were taut. Everything rode on this one show today. *Why,* Aubrey lamented, *did it have to be about creepy crawling things with the Ocean County bug lady?* Why couldn't it be another episode with Asa and Scout? She'd gotten so far beyond aloof with regard to the big shepherd and his handsome handler.

"Hey, you," Dean greeted when he saw her walk in. "Grab some coffee."

Aubrey poured herself a cup of fresh brew from the carafe on the counter and pulled a chair over to where they sat.

"Good morning," Melanie said, with an elastic smile. Her eyes were sharp and unreadable, her face unlined, a poker player's countenance. "Are you ready for today's show?" Another slingshot-type snap of a smile.

"More than ready." Aubrey furnished a wide smile, fully aware that Dean's gaze was fixed on her. "Anxious even."

"Good." Melanie turned back to her paperwork. "Let's hope so."

Dean winked an eye, which did nothing to stop Aubrey's whole body from trembling.

****

Asa sat in the veterinary hospital waiting room. The medicinal smell burned his eyes and nearly made them tear. His commanding officer had been with him when they'd arrived. But, now, over an hour later, Asa was alone.

The way Scout looked at him on the ride over, his eyes fixed on his master's, his mouth slack, was etched in Asa's brain. He closed his eyes to banish the image, dispel the helplessness he felt.

His mouth was dry, his throat scratchy. Sleep-deprived and thirsty, his head ached. His eyes found the blue metal door behind which a vet was working to save Scout. He needed to see his dog.

X-rays had determined that Scout had a shattered bone in his left back leg. There were some internal injuries, but miraculously his vital organs were not seriously damaged.

Scout had lost a lot of blood. Asa scanned the dried dark splotches on his fatigues and on the front of his shirt. He'd taken his jacket off, at the scene, and had wrapped it around his dog for the ride to the veterinary hospital. It now lay in the garbage.

A technician came out from the blue door wearing a pale green set of scrubs. Her feet were covered in voluminous silly-looking paper booties. "Mr. Kavanaugh," she said.

He shot up from the chair.

She motioned her hand for him to sit back down. Her mouth was turned in a sympathetic slant. "We're not out of the woods yet," she said. "But Dr. Landing wanted to you know that they saved Scout's leg. It's going to be a while, though, before the doctor comes out to talk with you."

"Thank you." The words croaked out of his arid throat. "Is he, uh, going to be okay?"

She tilted her head. "I can't say for sure, but I will tell you that that dog of yours is a fighter. He's not giving up, I can tell you that much. For now, it's going well, but there will be infection to concern ourselves with."

"Thank you," he managed.

"There's a donut shop down the road. Why don't you go get yourself something? We're not going anywhere."

"In a while maybe." Asa watched as she went back in through that blue door. His eyes were heavy, they fought to close. *They saved Scout's leg. That dog of yours is a fighter.*

Asa swallowed what felt like a bunch of nails. There was much he didn't know yet, but there was one thing that was certain—Scout was through with active duty. His partner, his loyal companion, the most impressive, talented dog in the program, would be put out to pasture, stripped of his purpose.

It was the kind of injustice that cut to the core and should have invoked anger. But all Asa could do was thank a God he'd shunned for years that Scout was still alive.

He'd fallen asleep in the chair, his big body slouched low, his head braced against the wall. A shove startled him awake. Dylan stood before him holding a cardboard carrier with foam cups poked into the corners.

"Any news?" Dylan plopped down next to him. "You look like shit, by the way."

Asa slid his body upright. His neck was killing him, and he gave it a quick knead with one hand. "Thanks, buddy." He grabbed one of the cups out of its holder. "They saved his leg."

"Hey, that's good news."

"Yes." Asa took a sip of the hot beverage. "But, it's not over. Something about having to keep him from getting an infection."

"There's hope, though. So, that's a good thing."

Asa nodded and sipped his coffee.

A little while later Dr. Landing came out from the back room and walked over to Asa and Dylan.

Before the man had a chance to open his mouth, Asa asked, "How is he?"

"He made it through surgery."

"He's a champ, huh?" Dylan said to Asa, and patted him on the back.

"He's got a couple of crucial days ahead of him," the doctor said. His face told Asa not to get his hopes up too high. "We'll be monitoring him thoroughly. He'll be asleep for a good while. Why don't you go home and get some rest? We'll call you if there's any change."

"Good idea, bro," Dylan said.

"Can I see him first?"

The doctor thought a moment. The way his mouth pursed Asa was afraid he was going to say no, but Dr. Landing nodded. "For just a minute, and just you. He's still under anesthesia."

Asa followed the vet down the hallway and through the blue door. Crates housed various recouping cats and dogs, and a beagle wearing one of those crazy cone things around his neck. A smaller room held one large crate set up on a table. Inside, on a white cushion, Scout lay sleeping on his side.

"Just visit for one minute," Dr. Landing said. "He needs the strength sleep will provide."

Asa nodded, so overcome by the lifelessness of his dog that he could not speak. Dr. Landing took a discreet step out of the room, but kept the door ajar.

Asa cautiously stepped up to the crate, curled a hand around the cold stainless steel bars. "Hey boy," he whispered. He choked down a raggedy swallow. "Don't you dare die on me." He pulled his lips in on themselves when they began to tremble. "Don't. Just don't."

For the first time in four years, Asa cried.

Chapter Thirty-Six

Judith Barbaras, owner and operator of Southern Shore's Bug Museum arrived with an assistant who helped carry cages and glass receptacles of crawling, scaly, multi-legged specimens into the studio. Judith was a middle-aged woman who clearly loved her business. She was a walking bug aficionado.

It gave Aubrey the willies, which didn't help in psyching herself up for the interview. Normally, just thinking about such a variety of insects and such would steal Aubrey's sleep at night. But, thanks to her dead grandfather, that had already been accomplished.

She felt Melanie Robertson's steely gaze glued to her every move.

Aubrey shook hands with the bug lady and her assistant, a tall gawky young man named Doug which, unfortunately for Aubrey, rhymed with bug, making her nervous giggle park itself in her throat.

Cameras rolling, Judith and Doug standing beside her at a display table, the segment began.

First up was a display of dragonflies, Eastern Pondhawks, in a mesh-covered aquarium. Aubrey, although squeamish as hell, had to admit that the wide-winged things were colorful.

"We've grown these beauties from the larvae stage, or nymphs," Judith said with pride.

"Beautiful," Aubrey said, with what she hoped was

obvious appreciation. Inside, though, she prayed that loose mesh lid stayed put. "And, all of these are indigenous to the New Jersey Pine Barrens?"

Judith took the reins, her enthusiasm like too much soup boiling over the rim of a pot on the stove. She detailed how to raise dragonflies as pets. This baffled Aubrey, or maybe appalled her, but she continued to smile and appear engaged.

"Do they have the same life expectancy as pets as they do in the wild?" Aubrey already knew the answer was "no," thanks to her prep reading, but she knew it was a good question. There was no way she could cast a glance to Melanie, but she could almost feel approval emanating from the off-camera scrutinizer.

By the end of the segment, Aubrey's thoughts hovered around her head as if a slew of the Eastern Pondhawks had escaped their confines. She was a fraud. She didn't care about any of this.

Despite her dire need for the funding the job would provide, she didn't think she could do it. Maybe she'd tell Dean thanks, but no thanks. But, then what? Sell the house? Her muscles ached from her full-body clench.

Just as she was saying her on-camera goodbye to Judith and her sidekick Doug-as-in-bug, a producer waved a sheet of paper at her from the sidelines. He held up a cue card that read, *We have a special announcement.*

Aubrey accepted the paper into her grasp. Her mind reeled with thoughts of Melanie Robertson watching and waiting to see how she handled an unscripted task. Grounding herself, Aubrey looked into the camera and told the viewing audience with assuredness that there was a message she'd been asked to share.

Aubrey froze as the text on the page blurred and waved, like a hand telling her goodbye. She blinked once, twice. She read again the words she was expected to say. Lifting her gaze she met Dean's imploring stare.

Trembling, she began to read.

Ladies and Gentlemen, I am sorry to report that the K-9 dog, Scout, that we've all gotten to know through Pet Parade*'s series on Monmouth County's Police K-9 Program, has been critically injured in the line of duty. His handler, Asa Kavanaugh, is at his side while veterinarians work to save the dog. We will keep you apprised of any updates. Meanwhile, our thoughts go to Mr. Kavanaugh and Scout.*

A clip of Asa and Scout at the K-9 training field appeared on the screen behind Aubrey. Tears ran down her cheeks as she cast her gaze to the handsome duo. She blindly looked into the camera. "Oh, Scout," she said thickly.

A sob escaped from her throat. "Dear God, Scout, you poor sweet dog." The paper she held fluttered to the floor as they went to commercial.

Chapter Thirty-Seven

Asa sat at the workbench in his garage. Aubrey's ripped-up rocking chair sat on the wooden surface awaiting attention. Pops had yet to take a look at the chair, but Asa had no head to talk about it to his dad.

He wanted to be alone. He was so better off that way. Exhausted, and yet he couldn't sleep. Tormented by the events of the night before, his mind was a rattletrap.

He picked up his hammer and idly tapped a piece of broken porcelain too big for the pattern he had laid out on his work surface. He'd taken the bucket of broken teacups from Aubrey's garage, with her permission, determined that the pieces should not be discarded. Now, all he knew was that it felt good to tap a hammer and listen to the sound of cracking.

It would be time again soon to pair him with a new dog. Like he'd done five years before, Asa would go through the trials of finding the right match of man and dog. It had been exhilarating five years ago. Now just thinking about it made him more tired, more frustrated, more convinced he was better off without a partner at all.

He let his gaze filter to Aubrey's rocker, and the woman came to mind. She was a beautiful person, he'd decided. That was just the fact. And he had been nuts to think he could be involved with her or anyone else for that matter. He just didn't have it in him.

Aubrey Donner would be better off, anyway. To be in Asa's life was a distinct detriment to anybody's wellbeing. It was a public service, really, to just steer clear of connectedness. Want be damned—he would stay the hell away from her.

His cell phone rang, and he fished it from his pocket, fumbling with haste. He hoped it was the veterinary hospital with news about Scout.

The display flashed Aubrey's phone number. He stared at it, put the phone on the tabletop, and just let it ring until it stopped.

****

Aubrey had called Asa several times and left messages. He hadn't called back. Each time she'd attempted contact, with no avail, she was reminded by Asa's Mom's words about his pattern of walking away. It was a growing niggle in her gut that asked if this was what he was doing now.

She was worried about Scout. Not knowing anything was driving her mad. Finally, she called Asa's house phone hoping that one of his parents would answer and maybe give her some information.

No answer there either. She knew the name of the animal hospital where Scout was being cared for from the information given to her at the station.

She couldn't even think about the foolish way she'd handled the announcement while taping the show. Whatever came of it was out of her control. Right now all she could think about was a big dog that might die and his partner—who most probably wouldn't share his grief.

After all, he hadn't even told her about Cheryl.

Dear God, what was she thinking involving herself with this man? Didn't matter. She was already wrapped up in it, in him. *Crap. I suck at this.*

She dialed the number to the vet's office and a woman answered in an airy, jolly tone. Aubrey identified herself as the host of *Pet Parade*, which for the moment she assumed was still true, and asked about Scout's status.

Still with that high-pitched sound of good nature, the woman said, "Well, I think that information should come from Scout's handler, Officer Kavanaugh, or maybe the police department."

Her demeanor flicked at Aubrey's already taut nerves, making them all but ping. "I understand. Is Officer Kavanaugh there with Scout now?"

"No, but I can give you the telephone number to the police department."

"Thanks anyway. I have it. I'll give them a call."

Instead, Aubrey headed over to the police administrative building.

****

An officer that Aubrey recognized from the day of taping at the K-9 training facility greeted her. "Hello," she said. "Mid Shore Live, right?"

"Yes, hi. Regina, wasn't it? I'm inquiring about the K-9 dog that was injured, Scout."

"Have you talked with Asa?"

"Uh, no. Not yet."

Regina nodded her blonde ponytailed head. "Well, all we know right now is that Scout made it out of surgery and they're waiting it out, making sure he gets through the next few days okay."

Aubrey felt a rush of relief. "That's encouraging,

isn't it?"

"We're all trying to be optimistic, but it's still a tragedy around here. Scout was the best of the best."

"He still could be, couldn't he?"

"Once a dog has an injury that severe, we retire them. It's for everyone's safety, including the dog's."

Aubrey's heart clenched. "But what will happen to Scout?"

"He'll be adopted out."

"Can't Asa keep him as, you know, a pet?"

Regina shook her head. "Asa's job will be to bond with a new K-9 partner. Having Scout around would be a deterrent to the new partnership and what they'll need to accomplish. The circumstance is far from ideal, but comes with the territory."

Something heavy sat in the bottom of Aubrey's stomach, an anvil of sadness.

"Can I go to see Scout? Do I need permission?"

"I was heading over myself to check on him and, if he's there, Asa, too. We sent him home for a few days to decompress."

"Can I tag along? Unofficially, just as an interested friend?"

"Let me get my keys."

****

The connecting door from the kitchen opened and Asa's father stepped out into the dimly-lit garage. His son sat at the work bench playing with chips of china.

"What are you tinkering with?" He had a slow saunter that didn't fool Asa. Pops was checking on him.

Tinkering was something Louie had taught Asa to enjoy ever since he'd been a little kid. Back when his parents lived nearby, before they retired to Florida, Asa and Pops had *tinkered* away many an hour and plenty of worries.

Asa had learned, over the years, that busy hands soothed a troubled mind. "Nothing really. Just kind of hanging out here."

"That's a sorry-looking chair, huh?" Pop touched a hand to the shredded upholstery of Aubrey's rocker. "Did she get a chance to pick new fabric? I can get this back in good order in no time."

Louie's reupholstering and refinishing old furniture hobby had become a kind of post-career livelihood. Down in Bonita Springs he had a steady flow of customers that needed old pieces restored. Pops said it kept him young. The joke between Asa and his mom was her claim that Louie's pastime kept *her* sane.

"I, uh, haven't talked with her. You know, about the chair." Asa shrugged tired shoulders. "I have no idea when I will."

Louie pulled up a metal stool that had been against a cinderblock wall. He parked himself beside his son, looking over the rim of his glasses. "Let's see, the wood's still in decent shape. The seat bottom needs reinforcement. See this?" Pops held up a wad of what looked like a ratty old sheep that had gotten caught in the rain.

Asa nodded dully.

"This is not original. Back when this chair was made, the guts would have been horsehair. This is synthetic."

"Really? Huh," Asa said. "I think Aubrey was under the impression that this was a valuable antique."

"It's still valuable, but not as valuable as it would be if everything were original."

Pops stood from the stool and spun the chair a quarter turn. He ran his finger down the backing and moved his head closer to examine the piece. "Well, I'll be," he said.

"What?"

"First off, whoever worked on this piece did a pretty lousy job."

A weary smile threatened Asa's mouth. His old man loved this stuff. He was a perfectionist, particularly when it came to scrutinizing workmanship that had been performed by someone else.

His dad slid a finger into an opening in the backing. "See this? The stitches have been sliced. They're not disintegrated from rot, or popped from the damage done by the dog's attack." He put his hand into the back of the chair and tugged the fabric away from the frame. He leaned close.

When he withdrew his hand he extended it toward Asa. Lying across his palm was what looked like pointed strip of paper.

"What's that?" Asa asked.

Louie turned the slip of paper over. A brown crust ran along the pointed edge. "See that?"

"It looks like glue. An envelope flap?"

"Appears so," Louie said. "I think something was stuffed inside this old rocker." He spread the fabric wider. "There's an indentation right here where something could have been tucked."

Asa leaned closer, scrutinized the guts of the chair. He stuck his hand in and withdrew a long sliver of what looked like dried out tape.

"What'd I tell you?" Louie clapped Asa on the back. "Somebody had secured something inside this chair."

"What was it? And where is it now?" Asa sparked alive for the first time since the drug bust.

"Good question, officer," Louie said, his own eyes flashing.

"Yeah, well, I'm getting the answer."

****

Aubrey stood in front of the grate of Scout's cage. He was awake, but unmoving.

Regina went to talk with the lady at the front desk. Aubrey stood with her heart pounding, staring at the still mound of fur that was Scout.

Dogs in cages aligned around the perimeter of the room barked when she'd entered the room, but she was unfazed. Her eyes were fixed on the big shepherd whose black eyes stared at her, but showed no sign of recognition.

"How you doing, pretty man?" she whispered.

Scout continued to stare at her but did not move.

Tears filled her eyes, and she blinked them free to cascade down her cheeks. "Such a good, faithful Scout," she whispered to him with the bulky warmth of affection. "Please get well."

Scout's tail whapped one quick thump. It jarred her. "Hey," she said with a flicker of hope. "You know me, don't you Scout? You big flirt. That's what you are, you big doggie. You're a flirt."

Scout whimpered softly.

Without thinking, Aubrey reached a finger into the cage and scratched a soft spot in his fur that she could reach.

His tail thumped again, then again.

"You sweet thing." Her throat, filled with

affection, relief, and hope, nearly swelled shut.

"Hey, is he awake?"

The voice startled her and she swung around with an audible sucked-in breath. Regina and a technician had come into the room.

"Yes," Aubrey said. "He knows me."

The technician, a redhead with freckles, went to the cage and checked the IV tube attached to his foreleg. A patch of fur had been shaved bare to the pinkish skin. Scout's eyes, dark and wary, watched her.

"Look at you," the tech said appreciatively. She turned to Regina. "He's lucid. His eyes are clear. Both good signs. The doctor will examine him later this afternoon."

"Will you call Officer Kavanaugh with news of the improvement?" Regina asked.

"After the doctor performs his exam, yes. We'll give him a call." She had a toothy smile, a chirpy sound. She glanced again at Scout. "One step at a time. Huh, boy?"

After the tech left the room, Regina gave Aubrey a reassuring smile. "I'm going to update Asa. Let's hope he answers his phone this time." She shook her ponytail.

Aubrey thought of the numerous times she'd tried to reach him, to no avail. "He's avoiding you, too?"

"Don't take offense. This is the man's M.O. He retreats. He'll be okay, though. I'll let him know you came by to see the dog."

The word all but exploded from her. "No!" She settled her nerves. "Why add to his stress? Don't mention my coming here."

Regina shrugged. "Will do."

****

"Dad, don't touch the chair anymore for now, okay?" Asa stood up from the stool he'd been parked on for God knew how long. He pulled his cell phone from his pocket and punched in digits.

"Who you calling?" his father asked.

"The precinct."

When the call connected, he asked to speak with Michael, but was told he was on his way to the veterinary hospital to get any updates on Scout.

Just hearing that information slapped Asa back to the reality of the moment. His reality. A cool trickle dripped through him.

It was there again in the front of his mind, the blood in the street, the smell of mercury churning his gut, the heft of his limp animal in his arms.

And the loss was there, too, pounding its truth, threatening to knock Asa on his ass. Even if Scout recovered, their partnership was over.

What Asa wanted right now was to dull his mind again, sit and stare at nothing, desensitize his brain and the heart that knew better than to invest so deeply, but had anyway.

He cast a glance to the chair that sat on the tabletop, its backing gaped open. He held the envelope flap in his free hand along with the sliver of tape. This was no time to be numb. There was something he had to do.

He dialed Dylan's number and waited. When his friend answered, he asked the burning question. "Did you get the results from that sample I gave you?"

"Sure did," Dylan said. "You were right."

"What was it?"

"Benzodiazepine."
"Son of a bitch."

Chapter Thirty-Eight

Asa and two fellow officers stood on the front stoop of the downtown apartment building and waited for response to their knock.

"Ira Tobias?" Asa rapped his knuckles on the wooden door. "Police."

The door opened a crack. Ira stood on the other side, his eyes narrowed, his mouth a thin line surrounded by the gray fluffy beard. "Asa?" His voice was craggy.

He opened the door a bit wider. Ira was naked from the waist up with a burgundy towel wrapped around his lower half. He cast a glance at Asa's companions. "You'll have to excuse me, gentlemen. I'm readying for a trip." He looked to Asa. "You remember. I'm going to lend my brother a hand for a little while."

"Can we come in?" Asa asked.

"What is this about?"

"We have a warrant." Asa wasn't known for small talk.

"A warrant? What the hell for?"

The gentlemanly tone in Ira's voice, that had bordered on Brit formality, had disappeared. If Asa was correct, he detected a kind of Brooklyn accent, caked with attitude.

"We're here to talk with you about some robberies around town."

"What would I know about any of that horse shit?" Definitely New York.

"If you'll allow us access, it'll be a whole lot simpler."

"Okay, you want to come in? Fine." Ira swung the door wide. "But make it quick. I've got a plane to catch. And in case you haven't noticed, I'm buck naked under here."

Asa and his fellow officers followed Ira into his small living room. It was sparsely appointed with just a television propped on what looked like a dresser and a plaid loveseat where an open suitcase sat filled to the brim with belongings.

"Let's see that warrant," Ira demanded.

Asa's companion officer, Pete Nugent, produced a copy. "It's all in order."

Ira's mouth twitched while his beady eyes scanned the text. He thrust it back in Pete's face. "Let's get this done, then."

"Would you like to go put on some clothes?" Asa asked.

"Yes, if you don't mind, but not before you people get out of my house."

Pete went over to the suitcase.

"Hey, don't go rifling through that, please. It's all ironed and folded."

Pete ignored Ira and rummaged through the suitcase. From inside the brown leather toiletries case he withdrew a washcloth bundled around something and secured with a rubber band.

"Christ," Ira spat. "Really? My family heirlooms? Come on boys, give me a break."

Asa took the package from the officer and removed

the rubber band. Asa inspected the contents—jewelry, watches, and cash. His eyes fixated on one teardrop diamond earring, and anger shot through him. The image of Aubrey's dismay came to mind when she'd discovered she'd lost her mother's prized earring.

He began flipping through Ira's neatly packed clothing, tossing the garments onto the sofa cushion.

"What the hell are you doing, man?" Ira shouted. "I want to call my lawyer."

"Put some pants on and calm down, Ira. Why don't you go have some of that elderberry wine of yours? You know, the kind with the sleeping pills in it?"

"I refuse to respond to such ridiculous bullshit. I want to speak with my attorney before I utter another word."

"There will be time for that down at the station."

"What station? I'm flying to Ohio."

"Not today you're not." Asa continued to unzip pouches and fish through pockets.

Inside the pocket of a sports jacket Asa found a plastic bag. He recognized the enclosed envelope color that matched the flap his father had found wedged inside Aubrey's rocker.

With trepidatious movement of his gloved fingers, he withdrew the envelope addressed to Caroline Donner, Aubrey's mother. An old blurry black and white photograph of a young woman holding a swaddled baby was inside. Also inside was a bottom-heavy purple felt pouch cinched by a yellowed cord.

Asa was tempted to open the pouch, but enough had been robbed from Aubrey and her mother. He replaced everything into the plastic bag. He focused his gaze onto Ira. "You seriously stole Aubrey's earring and whatever sentimental items put in that old chair that were meant for her?"

He seethed at the idea that this scrawny thief had taken advantage of Aubrey's aunt and Aubrey herself. He'd duped them into thinking he could end Aubrey's torment by a ghost. That whole business had probably been a crock of shit, as well.

Pete read Ira his rights and administered handcuffs as a quirky smile slanted Ira's petulant mouth. "You have to understand, gentlemen. This has been nothing personal. It's simply business."

The British lilt was back in Ira's voice which now served as accelerant to Asa's anger level. He stormed past the apprehension in progress. He was too tempted to slug the guy.

Chapter Thirty-Nine

Aubrey's doorbell rang. Her heart, her most foolish organ, leapt with hope.

It was Dean.

"Hi," she said. Her heart took a nosedive.

"You have a few minutes, Blitzen?"

This couldn't be good. Dean didn't deliver good news in person. And today she was thinking he was the coroner for her career. "Sure. Come on in."

Dean followed her into the living room where they positioned themselves across from each other, Dean on the wing chair, she on the sofa.

"I'll offer you something to drink in a minute. I guess what you have to say will determine whether it's tea or tequila."

"Break out the Patron, then."

"Oh, boy. Okay. Give it to me straight."

"They love you!"

"What? Who loves me?"

"Everybody that tuned in to *Pet Parade* and saw your heartfelt report on that poor pooch. Social media has been blowing up ever since. Melanie Robertson is ecstatic."

Aubrey jumped up from the sofa. "Are you serious?" Relief washed over her and came out her mouth with a laugh. "I thought you were here to lower the boom."

"Kid, you're the new Queen of Sunday Mornings in the kingdom of Mid Shore Live."

She plopped back down on the couch. "Well, holy crap."

"Yeah, and that snot running down from your nose while you were crying on camera…nice touch. I'm telling you the phones haven't stopped ringing. I think Melanie finally had an orgasm."

"I'm speechless."

"Come on. Where's the tequila?"

A little while later, after Dean had done a shot and she'd made herself a cup of tea, for which he called her a wuss, Dean gave her a bear hug. He said, "I knew you could do it," into her hair before leaving in the wake of Aubrey's string of thank yous.

It still hadn't sunk in. So much had happened in the last few days, and Aubrey felt like she was caught up in a whirlwind of change. But, holy crap, she had the job.

With diligence, and a strict budget, she could keep her house, maybe even fix it up from all the neglected repairs. Her mind flashed to Asa. Would the events of the past few days change the plan for him to perform the work around here?

Why, she thought hopelessly, *did it always come back to Asa?*

Again her doorbell rang. She fleetingly wondered if Dean was coming back to tell her he'd just been kidding.

Aubrey opened the door and stared, with air locked in her lungs, into the chocolate eyes of Asa Kavanaugh.

"Hi." She offered a tentative smile.

"Hi, Aubrey. Can I come in?"

"Sure." All hope was dashed that this visit brought

any good news. "Is Scout okay?" she asked.

"He's hanging in," Asa said, with a flicker of a smile. "He's a strong dog. We're all hopeful."

Aubrey led Asa into the living room and motioned for him to sit, which he ignored. His hands were clenched, as was her heart.

"Asa, I…" Aubrey almost chickened out, but no. There was no sense holding back now. "I went to see him."

"Did you?" His brown eyes flashed with something that spoke to her, soothed her.

She nodded. A tremulous smile played over her lips. "He likes me."

"I know."

"I'm so sorry about what happened, Asa. You must have been devastated."

He looked away, cleared his throat. "I, uh, I'm here with news. Unpleasant, police news."

"Oh?"

"We've apprehended the burglar that's been wreaking havoc all over Ronan's Harbor. And, I'm afraid to report it's Ira Tobias."

She shouted, "What?"

"Can you contact your aunt? We'd like both of you to come down to the station. We've confiscated evidence, jewelry and other things. I know that some of the items belong to you."

"I'm shocked. Blown away." Her brain buzzed with snippets of conversation with the old guy, times he'd been so reassuring about the ghost, parental almost. "So, Ira the clairvoyant is a crook? A liar and a thief?"

She began to pace. "This man came into my home

and made fools out of us? Me and everybody else that was here helping try to help banish my resident ghost." Adrenaline pumped through her veins. "That was all part of his game, too, wasn't it?"

Asa took a step in her direction then stopped. "Aubrey, there'll be time to sort this out later. First, if you will, let's go down to the station."

They locked eyes. In this new frenzy, her scrambled brain knew just one thing—trust him. "I'll call Molly."

Chapter Forty

At the police station, Aunt Molly and Aubrey sat on black chairs lining the wall of the waiting area. A water cooler was nearby, and Asa brought them filled paper cones of water.

Aubrey took a sip. Molly watered the paltry-looking ivy in a ceramic pot on the corner table.

"That miserable brute." Molly had said the same phrase over and over again, and Aubrey just let her go with it. "Miserable brute."

Aubrey craned her neck to glance through the archway that led down the hall. Asa had told her that her missing earring, Mom's prized memento, was among Ira's stash of stolen articles. She and, apparently, her aunt both sucked in the man department.

Molly busily pulled drying, dead leaves from the ivy and dropped them into the empty paper cone in her hand.

"You know something, Aubrey, I could slap that man into tomorrow. And, P.S., he wasn't even a good kisser. Too slobbery."

Aubrey smirked. At least Molly wasn't heartbroken over Ira's duplicitous lifestyle.

"What sucks the most, for me, is that all that séance stuff was probably just a bunch of crap." Aubrey put her head in her hands.

"Maybe not."

Aubrey looked up to the familiar voice.

Asa and another officer, his friend Dylan, had come into the room. "I remember the way that shelf fell off the wall and how the wooden blocks spelled out E L C. I mean, even I wondered about the coincidence of that."

Aubrey's mind flashed to one of her dreams where the nebulous ghost had given her that cryptic warning—*confuse not friend or foe.*

"You know what?" she said. "The ghost really was warning us about Ira."

"Humph," Molly said. "Wonders never do cease. Old Monty Donner actually did something good."

Dylan said, "We've registered all the confiscated items. Before we lock them up, we wanted to turn over what we're certain belongs to you." He motioned his head toward Asa. "Big guy here pulled some strings."

Dylan handed over a large manila envelope.

Aubrey unclasped the fastener and pulled out the first of two plastic bags. Her heart fluttered when she saw the familiar earring. "My God. When did he snatch this?

"We don't know for sure, but I'm thinking it had something to do with his lacing that wine of his with a sleep aid."

"You mean he could have gone up into my room while Joanie and I were sleeping?" The idea of such an intrusion was worse than a ghost appearing at the foot of her bed. Much worse.

"We'll get it out of him," Asa said. "And, as we've already stated, Molly…double check your belongings."

"I'm sure there's nothing of mine in his cache," Molly said. "What he took from me was cold hard cash.

And, because I'm particularly stupid, I gave it to him willingly." She uttered a tsk sound with her teeth. "He told me some garbage about his accounts being tied up, or something."

Aubrey pulled the second plastic bag, with the purple pouch and the envelope, from the manila sheath. "Is this what you said was in Mom's rocker?"

She studied the photograph. "It's a picture of my grandmother holding my mom. And, look"—Aubrey's eyes filled with tears—"she's sitting in the rocker."

Molly leaned in and covered her mouth with her hand. "Oh, Caroline. What a mess we've made."

"The only person at fault here is Mr. Tobias," Dylan said.

Aubrey cradled the purple bag in her palm. "What's in here?"

"Asa wanted you to open the bag first, but due to the rules, we had to log in its contents. Take a look."

Tugging open the tie's cinch, Aubrey let the contents fall into her open palm. Three pennies.

"Oh my God." Aubrey stared at the copper disks. "The three pennies. But what do they mean? Obviously my grandmother didn't go through all the trouble to hide these in the rocker for no good reason. But, why?"

Molly quirked her head. "Well, if nothing else, I'll give you ninety-seven more just like them and you can buy yourself a pack of gum.

"Lots and lots of packs of gum," Dylan said. "Apparently those pennies are quite valuable."

Aubrey looked to Asa. "What's he saying?"

"One of our officers here, Emil Harvey, happens to collect coins. He took one look at those babies and got very excited. They're from back in the '40's. He suggested you take your coins to a dealer and have him give you specifics."

Aubrey looked at the coins in her hand. Could they really be valuable? How valuable? Was there enough to buy plasterboard for her house? Pay back-dated bills? Eventually get out of the red?

She could feel Asa watching her. Aubrey searched his brown eyes for some clue as to what this meant.

"Hold up," Asa said, reading her question.

He left the room and returned a few moments later with a tall, black crew-cutted, affable-faced officer.

"Aubrey Donner," Asa said. "Emil Harvey. He's the coin guy."

"Amateur collector," Emil said. "But I do know my coins. And, those '43S copper pennies are worth in the neighborhood of thirty-five or forty grand. Each."

"Each?" Molly and Aubrey asked in unison.

"Have an expert give you authentication, but yes. The Lincoln cent series has an estimated forty coins in existence. Last I heard there were just a little more than a dozen authenticated."

"What makes them so valuable?" Molly asked.

"That's the fun part," Emil said, clearly loving his knowledge of the subject. "During the '40's copper was needed for the war, so they changed the way they made pennies. They started making them with zinc-coated steel. Just a few, forty or so, were made by accident. The copper blanks were still in the press when they started making the new pennies."

"Seriously?" Aubrey was awed by the officer's information. *Is it really possible that I'm holding in my palm the monetary value of a hundred grand? This was what Jack must have felt like when he was given the magic beans.*

"How can you be certain, though?" Aubrey asked. "I mean, what's to say these pennies are the solid copper ones?"

"Easy," Emil said with a winning grin. "I weighed each one. If they were made of steel, they'd register two point seven grams. But each one of your coins weighed in at the copper weight."

"Which is?"

"Three point eleven."

Aubrey clutched the coins to her heart and sucked in her breath.

Chapter Forty-One

Aubrey sat on her living room sofa. Molly, with Roscoe in her arms, paced back and forth in front of the fireplace.

"You know, all her life your grandmother deferred to that tyrant of a husband of hers. Edith had no power whatsoever. But somehow she had the wherewithal to swipe those three pennies from Monty's collection and hide them in the rocker."

"My brain is still trying to figure it all out," Aubrey said. "Now I know why Grandmother Edith made Mom promise to get the chair refurbished. Only my mother never did."

"Poor Caroline, poor Edith," Molly lamented. She snapped her head around. "And Montgomery. He was a mean old buzzard, but look what's happened due to his persistent spirit? Life is strange, but death is even stranger."

"I want to show you something." Aubrey went to the kitchen to get the pipe and the framed photo that had been in the attic.

Molly had put her dog down and the little terrier ran right over to the spot where the rocker had been and plopped himself down.

Aubrey handed the objects from the attic to her aunt. "Monty and his pipe." Molly harrumphed. "He was all about effect, a professorial prop used for an audience."

"Look at the engraving."

"Beaver Creek, Pa.," Molly read. "That was the park near where they lived in York County." She looked at the photograph. "Yeah, see? This was taken at the park. See in the background? It's the old gristmill. I remember it well."

"They looked like such a normal, happy family." Aubrey shook her head.

Molly turned over the broken frame. "How did it break?"

"I dropped it. Not going to lie. One look at my grandfather's face kind of freaked me."

"Did you see this?" Molly had pulled away the cracked backing to reveal the blank side of the photograph.

Written in an unfamiliar script someone had written three words. Aubrey read them out loud. *"Together in Paradise."*

"That's the name of the town where Beaver Creek Park is. Paradise, Pennsylvania."

"Holy crap, Auntie. I think Montgomery wants us to know that he and Grandma and my mom are reunited. They're *together in Paradise.*"

Tears glistened in Molly's storm-cloud eyes. "Well, doesn't that beat all?"

****

The two women grew quiet, thinking their thoughts. A few moments later Roscoe scratched at Aubrey's shins, wanting attention.

"Roscoe," Molly said. "No, honey."

"He's okay, Auntie." Aubrey leaned down and rumpled the dog's fur. "You're a good boy, aren't you,

Roscoe?"

"You're more comfortable around him now. That come from your work with Asa and Scout?"

The mention of them gave Aubrey a pang. "Yes." It was the truth. Asa's diligent efforts to help her gain more confidence around the shepherd had paid off. Her heart ached for Scout who was still recovering at the veterinary hospital.

"That poor dog. Such a magnificent animal. What do you think, Aubrey? Will he be all right?"

"He has to be."

Molly came across the room, sat beside the younger woman, and clutched a hand to Aubrey's knee, giving it a squeeze. "Is it the dog you care so much about or the man that belongs to him?"

Tears welled up in her eyes. So much had happened in the brevity of a few days. Her mind zoomed. She thought of her grandmother defying her husband, her mom not knowing that her own mother had been so bold in the name of love. And what of Montgomery Donner?

"Auntie, it all makes me sad. My grandfather's ghost has been trying to steer me toward finding the pennies. Maybe he even knew his wife hid them in the chair in the first place."

Molly shook her head. "It's pathetic, really. That old coot could have done so much to help his daughter and you, his only grandchild. But he let his stubbornness and that foolish pride rob him of the love of his family."

"It's like he figured that out too late," Aubrey said. "But I'm convinced he was warning me about Ira."

"That snake was psychic enough to know what was

in the rocker." Molly made the tsk sound with her teeth. "And he used that foul wine of his to make us all sleepy enough to rob you while we slept. I hope he rots in jail."

"It's all so strange," Aubrey said.

"So, you didn't answer me before. What's with you and Asa?"

Aubrey shrugged. "I'm confused, Molly. He was engaged, and the girl died in an accident. His mother told me the story. And, even though it was years ago, I don't think he's got it in him to get past the hurt of it, or to take another chance."

"That's too bad," Molly said. "I like him."

Aubrey reached down and rumpled Roscoe's ears. He sat at her feet basking in the attention. "You're a good doggie," she said.

"Aubrey, look at me, girl."

Aubrey lifted her gaze.

"The biggest fool that ever lived was Montgomery Donner II. You know why? Because he had the chance to love and turned away from it. Apparently the man lived and died with regret. Don't let that happen to you, my love."

A smirk curved on Molly's lips. "You think I'm dissuaded by that rat of an Elk? Nuts to him. Life's too short to let that put a roadblock up on my happiness."

Aubrey's heart swelled. For all her outlandishness, Molly McFadden's wisdom ran deep. Even at her age, the woman could face anything down.

Although none of Molly's blood ran through her veins, Aubrey hoped that somehow she'd adopted some of her aunt's courage. Because what had become crystal clear was that she would need some now. She had to go talk with Asa.

****

Aubrey knew better than to call him. Instead, she drove over to Asa's house and marched to the front door, her heart pounding like a drum.

Asa's mom opened the door, her countenance so filled with gladness to see her that Aubrey thought she might cry.

"Aubrey, hello. Come in, come in." She ushered Aubrey into the house.

"Hi, Jenny. I, uh, was just stopping by to talk with Asa. Is there any news on Scout?"

"Asa's at the vet's now. They called and asked him to come over right away."

Aubrey's heart stalled. "Oh, God."

"Louie and I are beside ourselves. Louie's got an echo cardiogram scheduled for the day after tomorrow and we just can't cancel it. We're scheduled to fly home tomorrow tonight. But how can we leave Asa like this? Aubrey, it's troubling."

Louie came into the room. "I thought I heard voices. Hi, there." He came over and touched Aubrey's shoulder. "How's it going?"

"I don't know," Aubrey said. "I'm concerned about Scout."

He nodded. "We all are."

"I was just telling her that we're flying home soon and how we're upset about leaving Asa at a time like this."

"We might have to reschedule, and the airline fees be damned," Louie said. "Let's see what news Asa comes home with."

He turned to Aubrey. "I told Asa to let you know

that we'll be back for Christmas. I'll refurbish your chair then if you'll select a fabric in the meantime. Trust me, it'll be a snap."

"Thank you so much, Louie. I'm grateful that you and Asa managed to find the evidence we needed to get to the bottom of what has been going on."

"Come on out into the garage, and I'll show you how we figured it out."

Aubrey was anxious to learn about Scout. Maybe if she lingered a while, Asa would come home with the news while she was still there.

The chair sat on top of a work bench, its outer covering removed, a sorry-looking skeleton.

"I found the flap to the envelope right about here." Louie pointed with his index finger to a hollowed place in the overall matted padding. "And there's glue residue in here as well, you know, from the tape. The police came down already and dusted for prints and took samples of the padding. It's remarkable."

"It is," Aubrey said. Her heart was heavy. Asa had done so much to help her and right now she felt so lost in how to be there for him.

He had put the wall back up between them, and she had no clue as to how to navigate beyond it. Along with Scout, added to the news of her legacy, she was an emotional mess. Her eyes filled with tears.

Louie's voice was gentle. "Aubrey, can I tell you something, just between us two?"

She didn't want him to see the emotion on her face and turned away. Her eyes scanned the area around the work bench—the tools hanging on hooks from pegboard, a glass jar of screws and nails all a jumble. And then her eyes stopped at a familiar sight that managed to zap the breath right out of her lungs.

The remnants of her mother's coffee cups, the chips of china that she'd swept into a bucket had been laid out into a wood-framed rectangle of cement, a mosaic arranged to display the number of her house—44. Asa had taken pieces of heirloom and constructed a plaque for her house.

The words he had said to her that night in her kitchen filtered to her mind. *Something new from something old.*

"He's been working on that since Scout was injured. He holes himself up in here and just works."

Louie came closer. "That's what I wanted to talk with you about, Aubrey. Don't give up on my son. He's been scared to get back into the game of life ever since Cheryl died. But I know him better than anyone and, trust me...Asa cares for you. Very much. He just needs help trusting he won't get hurt again."

All of a sudden Aubrey thought of herself as a frightened young girl, cowering under a car trying to fend off a ferocious dog. The scar on her leg was nothing compared to the crippling effects that event had caused in her life. But she was no longer enfeebled.

And that made all the difference. "Louie, if you'll excuse me, I'm going over to the animal hospital to be with Asa."

"Atta girl."

Chapter Forty-Two

Asa sat on the seat in the veterinary hospital's examination cubicle. Scout was up on the stainless steel table, and Dr. Landing was busy performing his assessment of the dog's progress.

A dichotomy of emotion coursed through Asa's bloodstream. Of course he was glad that his dog was going to be okay, would be able to walk, have all mobility, all functionality. But their partnership had died that night on the Neptune Junction street. He and Scout would no longer brave the challenges, fight the crimes.

Asa had an appointment at the training facility later that afternoon to begin the steps toward partnership with a new dog. His buddy, Dylan, told him there were a few incredible candidates that showed promise. He struggled to keep the memories of his beginning with Scout from clouding his mind.

Scout's eyes were glued to him while the vet poked and prodded parts of his body. The doctor had detached the IV's and the worst of it appeared to be the bandage on his back leg and the bald patch on his foreleg.

"He's a fine dog," the vet said. "And a strong man, aren't you, fellow?"

Scout panted, his pink tongue hanging out the side of his mouth. A pulling in Asa's chest formed into a fist that clenched his heart.

"Doctor?" A technician's head poked in through a cracked-open door. "Mr. Kavanaugh? There's a friend of yours here to see you and Scout. A Miss Donner. Can I send her back?"

"It's fine by me, if it's okay with you." The doctor deferred to Asa.

"Uh, yeah, sure. Yes." The fist in his chest tightened its grasp.

He hadn't seen Aubrey since the police station. He had been so good at compartmentalizing his feelings.

Under ordinary circumstances he'd have been able to separate from Aubrey Donner, would have been able to rationalize his connectedness with her as a momentary lapse in judgment, or even a perk of having had to endure those damned interviews at the TV station.

But—when she walked in with those whiskey eyes filled with emotion for the dog she'd once been terrified to be around, and her pretty mouth curved into a smile, relief spelled all over her irresistible face—Asa had to acknowledge the truth. He loved her.

"Hey," she said, with affection. She kept a discreet distance from the exam table. "How are you, big boy?"

Scout's tail wagged hello, making the metallic surface beat like a drum. The dog made a low whimper.

"He's fond of you," the doctor said, with a smile. "Who's that, fellow?"

"He looks so good," she said with awe. She fixed her gaze on Asa. "He really does."

Asa couldn't help but return the smile, his mouth having a mind of its own when it came to this woman. "He's a tough one, thank God."

"Is he ready to be released," Aubrey asked.

"Not yet," the vet said. "We're going to do another round of blood work and more x-rays. Then, if all's well, he should be free to go in a day or two."

"That's great," Asa said. "Thank you."

He stood up from the chair and a veil of awkwardness fell over him and Aubrey. Left without the topic of Scout, everything that was unfinished between them acted like tentacles reaching to grab at them.

"I'll walk you out," he said to Aubrey.

She gave him a nod.

Outside, in the small parking lot, Aubrey and Asa stood between their cars. He could smell her honeysuckle shampoo. Her hair, with its tendency to go wild, glinted golden in the brightness of the cold day.

"What happens now?" she asked. Her neck craned, eyes imploring.

He shrugged. "I have an appointment later with the K-9 command about placement of a new dog. Dylan says they have a few strong candidates."

"And Scout will be adopted?"

"Hurts like hell, but yeah."

"You can't keep him?"

Asa shook his head. "Regulations."

She shook her head as if thinking it was a shame, which it was.

"I have the supplies for the work at your house."

"You're still on board for that?"

"A deal's a deal." He felt the wryness of his smile. "Okay."

"My Dad wanted me to tell you that, if you're okay with it, he can redo your chair when they're back up for the holidays."

"Yes, he told me. I stopped by your house before I came here."

Their eyes locked. There was so much that was unsaid between them. He wanted to tell her he loved her, to confess that admitting it scared the bejesus out of him. Instead, he said, "I have to get going."

He saw the darkness come into her eyes, turning their whiskey color to the deep caramel of brandy.

She got in her car and started the engine. She was already out of the parking lot by the time he was settled in his truck.

Chapter Forty-Three

When she got home, Aubrey paced. She'd seen the way Asa looked at her at the veterinary hospital, his chocolate eyes so filled with goodbye it almost broke her in half.

He was still bound by his former loss. There was nothing she could do about it, but mourn what they could have been.

Her heart hadn't caught up to her head yet, and it still beat with the foolishness of hope. And there was nothing she could do about that, either.

But then, there was Scout. How could Asa stand knowing that the dog would go off to live out his life with someone else? It was too hard for her to deal with. She cared about the big animal, had come to love his obvious attachment to her.

She wondered now, with a kind of awe, *When had that happened*? When had she fallen in love with a dog—a big monster-sized beast, with a heart of gold?

She paced some more, wondered if she had it in her to act on the impulse that was beating in her heart. She thought of Asa and his self-imposed crippled life. Then she dialed the number to the training facility and asked to talk with Dylan Grant.

****

Aubrey was in the kitchen preparing an early, simple dinner of grilled cheese and tomato soup. The house was quiet and peaceful. Her grandfather's ghost hadn't interrupted her sleep the night before. She assumed he was now satisfied that his message had been received.

Her disappointment over Asa still stung. And yet she basked in the satisfaction that she had put in her application to adopt Scout. Her heart whirred. Scout could become her very own pet.

Adopting a dog was nothing that had ever been on her radar. But this was so right. It was brazen, and it felt freeing and wonderful.

She only wished Asa had it in him to be free to love her. She knew in her gut that he did. Asa Kavanaugh loved her. Aubrey was sure of it. She cursed him for keeping away, for squashing their chance at happiness.

Aubrey slowly carried a bowl of soup over to the kitchen table where her open laptop waited. She had research to do on the Seeing Eye program in Monmouth County. Luckily for her, Hannah Grayson, the daughter of the owner of the Cornelia Inn, was one of the trainers. She knew Hannah and was looking forward to the prospect of getting her program's story out to the viewers.

She had come to respect her job. There were so many aspects of how animals contributed to life in Ronan's Harbor, and everywhere else. She owed that appreciation to both *Pet Parade* and to Asa.

The doorbell rang. She put down her half-eaten grilled cheese sandwich and went to the door.

Asa stood on her front stoop. The light over her door haloed his blond head. His dark eyes shone with urgency.

"Asa." His name rode out of her mouth on a breath.
"Can I come in?"

She opened the door wide, and he entered. He towered over her. He smelled good, clean and manly, mingled with the musky scent of his leather jacket.

In his hands he had a brown paper-wrapped package tied with twine. "I, uh, made this for you."

She took the parcel into her hands. She suspected it was the mosaic, but didn't say so. "Do you want me to open it now?"

"Yes."

She rid the package of its wrapping, let the paper fall to the floor. It was the mosaic, cleaned and framed. And it was beautiful.

"I have to admit"—she avoided his eyes, keeping them fixed on the prize in her hands—"I saw this in progress in your garage, when your dad invited me in to see the chair."

"I know. He told me you saw it."

She met his gaze then. "It's lovely. Thank you."

"I figured you've been so concerned with keeping your house and having it repaired, that maybe a plaque would be, you know, a good thing to have."

"Yes," she said keeping her eyes on the mosaic. "A good thing to have."

"Aubrey, I know my mother talked with you about Cheryl."

She lifted her head to meet his eyes. "She did."

"I'm sorry that I didn't level with you on that. It was rough on me, brutal actually. I spent a lot of time, four years almost, thinking that I was better off alone rather than risk loving and losing again."

"I know."

"But, before I say anything else, I have something out in my truck."

"The, uh, plasterboard and stuff?"

"Mind if I go get it?"

She swallowed hard. "Okay."

In a moment, Asa was back. With him was Scout, limping but happy, shiny-eyed, tail wagging. Scout was on a leash. Around his neck was a blue bow.

Her eyes flooded. "Scout!" She knelt and opened her arms.

Asa unlatched the leash, the dog limped over to her, and Aubrey's arms wrapped around him. "You sweet boy."

She stood up, tears pouring down her cheeks. "What does this mean, Asa? Is he mine?"

"Well, that depends."

"What do you mean?"

"Scout and I are a team. You can't have just one of us. You have to agree to take both. That's just how it goes."

"What?"

"Turns out that old grandfather of yours convinced me that I shouldn't waste time being an idiot. And, walking away from you, from what we have, would be asinine."

Aubrey swallowed hard. Was she really hearing this? Was he telling her what her heart yearned to hear?

His eyes shone with playfulness, his smile a dimpled confirmation of love. "So, like I said. Scout and I are a package deal. If you'll have us."

"I'm pretty sure I know what to do with this one..." She rumpled Scout's ears and patted his side. "But, not so sure on what to do with you."

Asa took a step closer. "Love me. That's all I want, Aubrey. Love me like I love you."

She reached out and pulled a fistful of his leather jacket into her grasp. "Do you come with your own leash?"

Asa wrapped Aubrey into his arms, held her tight and planted a kiss filled with promise, commitment, assuredness, and love.

Scout uttered a soft bark. To Aubrey's ears, it sounded like confirmation that the three of them were an instant family, the realest of real.

A word about the author…

Born to a feisty Italian mother and a gentle blue-eyed Irishman, award-winning author M. Kate Quinn draws on her quirky sense of humor, hopelessly romantic nature, highly developed sense of family and friendship, and her love for a good story while writing her novels.

Her Perennials Series began with *Summer Iris* (The Wild Rose Press, July 2010) a Golden Quill Award finalist for Best First Book. The second book, *Moonlight and Violet* (The Wild Rose Press, June 2011) won the coveted Golden Leaf Award for Best Contemporary Novel 2011. The last in the series, *Brookside Daisy* (The Wild Rose Press, February 2012) was a Gold Leaf Award finalist.

Her next project, the Ronan's Harbor Series, is a trilogy of romances set in a quaint shore town. The first installment, *Letters and Lace*, released June 26, 2013.

M. Kate Quinn, a life-long native of New Jersey, makes her home in Central Jersey with her husband and their magnificent beta fish, Indigo.

www.mkatequinn.com

Thank you for purchasing
this publication of The Wild Rose Press, Inc.

If you enjoyed the story, we would appreciate your
letting others know by leaving a review.

For other wonderful stories,
please visit our on-line bookstore at
www.thewildrosepress.com.

For questions or more information
contact us at
info@thewildrosepress.com.

The Wild Rose Press, Inc.
www.thewildrosepress.com

Stay current with The Wild Rose Press, Inc.

Like us on Facebook

https://www.facebook.com/TheWildRosePress

And Follow us on Twitter
https://twitter.com/WildRosePress

VIRGINS and MARTYRS

A novel

Hugh Mahoney

Water
Street
Press

First Edition, September 2012

Cover Design by Sally Eckhoff
Interior Design by Typeflow

ISBN 978-1-62134-003-4

Produced in the United States of America

Published by Water Street Press, LLC
Healdsburg, California

www.waterstreetpressbooks.com